REDEMPTION ISLAND

Enjoy

Michael

REDEMPTION ISLAND

By Michael Pritzkow

Copyright 2023 by Michael Pritzkow

All rights reserved. This book or any portion thereof may not be reproduced or used in any manner whatsoever without the express written permission of the publisher except for the use of brief quotations in a book review.

ISBN: 9798861525466 (paperback)

This is a work of fiction. All incidents, dialogue, and characters, with the exception of well-known figures, are products of the author's imagination and are not to be construed as real. Where real-life local figures appear, the situation, incidents, and dialogue concerning those persons are entirely fictional and are not intended to depict actual events or to change the entirely fictional nature of the work. In all other respects, any resemblance to persons living or dead is entirely coincidental.

*To my loving family: daughter, Emily Pritzkow;
son, Matthew Pritzkow; and grandson, Miles Pritzkow.*

PROLOGUE

She rolled off him and stood up on the beach towel, naked in the moonlight.

"That was nice," Ingrid Karlsen said, looking down at him. The weather was warm, a light breeze blew across the beach, and the moon was full. Except for the two lovers, Sand Bay was deserted.

That afternoon they'd sailed to Chambers Island's Sand Bay, their favorite place to have fun together. The island was in the middle of Lake Michigan's Green Bay, just a short sail from Fish Creek.

After having a few beers in town earlier and then consuming a twelve pack of beer on the island, Ingrid wanted to continue to party. She needed to, after the argument with a former lover in the Bayside Bar parking lot. It had gotten pretty heated—enough that one of the bartenders and an owner had come out from the restaurant to see what all the commotion was about.

Luckily for her, Randy Daggett missed the whole thing. He was getting the twelve pack of beer at the nearby Deli Market. Thank God the jerk left before Randy got back with the beer. It could have gotten messy trying to explain her problem to Randy. She just needed money from the asshole to fix *their* problem before it became obvious to everyone.

Ingrid smiled as she looked down at him lying there, eyes closed. She needed to feel wanted and cared about; that's why she'd stuck with Randy over the years. Now tonight, it was just the two of them on the beach. She liked that.

"I love skinny-dipping, Randy, especially under a full moon. Are you going to join me?"

He yawned. "Just let me close my eyes for a little while, and then I'll join you. I've had too much beer, and the lovemaking tired me out."

She heard the soft sound of him snoring almost immediately. If he wasn't such a nice guy to her over the years, she'd probably be with someone else. Randy could be boring, she thought, but he made her feel appreciated for who she was; it wasn't just for the sex. She liked being with Randy. His parents too. He wasn't like most of the others she'd gravitated to when he wasn't around.

I wish I didn't feel that need to be loved and appreciated. I guess it's because I never got that from my parents, who put me up for adoption. Even then, no one wanted me, so I bounced around from one foster home to the next. No wonder I'm fucked up. That must be why I end up with just about anyone that makes me feel the slightest bit good about myself. Usually they only want me for my body. Thank God I have a good body.

Even her name meant "beautiful" in Norwegian. But after each of her relationships was over, Ingrid felt cheap. Randy had never made her feel that way. She looked at him, naked on the beach towel. *He's a good egg*, she thought.

"Randy, don't wait too long. If you hurry up, I might be ready for more fun before we head back. You were good, but I know you can do more. You know me. I like more."

She heard him grunt before she waded into the water and started washing herself. Slowly she moved away from him, down the beach.

A few minutes later, she yelled over her shoulder, "Come on!" Ingrid was further down the beach, standing in waist-deep water, facing out toward the middle of Green Bay. "You've had enough snooze time. I'm ready for you now, Randy."

She giggled when she heard water splashing behind her. She didn't turn around. Still facing out toward the bay, she said, "It's about time." Then she felt a body press against her, his hardness probing against her bottom. Two hands reached around and cupped her full breasts.

"Ahh, I guess you are ready, after all." Ingrid leaned back, wiggled her butt against him, then moved forward a little. "Just a second. I want to dip my head into the water to straighten my hair."

Keeping her back to his aroused body, she slid under the shallow water, tilting her head back. Looking up through the moonlit water, she saw the blurred figure above.

His hands moved from her breasts to her shoulders, then unexpectedly he pressed her down to the gritty sand bottom.

Why is he doing this? This is not a playful dunk, she thought.

Try as she might, twisting and turning in the shallow water,

Ingrid could not escape his iron grip. Full-blown panic overtook her. She held her breath, then, wide eyed, watched the last of her air bubbles escape from her mouth and drift up to the surface.

A muffled scream escaped from her open mouth before water rushed in, filling her empty lungs. She thrashed her feet and clawed at his hands, trying to twist out of his grip until everything turned fuzzy, then black.

Minutes later, Randy awoke from his beer slumber and called out to the deserted beach, "Ingrid, where are you?" All he could see were gentle waves lapping against the shore and the moon's reflection in the water.

He yelled out, "I've got to pee. I'll be there after I'm done." He got to his feet and moved toward the nearby shrubbery. As he got closer, he tripped on a half-buried piece of driftwood, stubbing his toe and tumbling headlong into thorny bushes.

"Ouch!" Sharp thorns scraped his naked body, leaving bloody scratches on his torso, arms, and face. Standing up, swearing, he finally relieved himself.

Randy walked the beach, calling her name.

Walking down the beach, he saw a discarded man's red swimsuit lying just out of the water line with footprints circling around it, then leading into the water. Was someone else skinny dipping out here too? He didn't see anyone.

As he continued to walk toward the point of the bay, he

spotted something at the water's edge, rolling back and forth like a large piece of driftwood. As Randy got closer, he realized it wasn't driftwood.

"Ingrid!" he screamed as he ran over to her body, but she didn't answer. He dragged her on to the shore and started blowing air into her mouth and lungs, but it was futile.

Holding her limp body in his arms, he panicked.

Did he do this?

He wasn't a violent person, was he? He looked right and left, but he was the only one around. Could his insomnia medication cause him to do this? He'd read about people doing strange things, including violent acts, when they were on the medication he was taking. He was wide awake now and shaking.

"Oh my God, what have I done?" he said out loud. Randy held Ingrid's cold body against his chest and wept.

CHAPTER ONE

Randy Daggett looked around his six-by-eight-foot cell for the last time. It had seemed so small when he had first arrived there eight years earlier. At age thirty-two, he'd spent 25 percent of his life in prison. What a waste. Randy had started growing a beard the last few weeks, but before that he'd let his hair grow long, and now he had a ponytail. It was a popular look sported by athletes like former Packers linebacker Clay Matthews.

Before getting out, Randy wanted to change his look. He didn't want to be recognized when he went home to Fish Creek.

He also decided to start using his pen name, Greg Chambers, hoping he could lead a normal life in Door County as a writer. He wasn't sure how long he could keep his past a secret, but he'd try to—at least until he was comfortable with being back. He thought about moving where no one knew him, but he loved Door County and didn't want to be anywhere else. Besides, this was where his parents lived, and who knows how long they'd be around, especially with his dad's frail health, so Randy would try to blend in.

Over eight years, he'd spent countless nights lying in his prison cell racking his brain. The medication he had been taking for insomnia had been blamed for his murder of Ingrid, but now Randy was sure he didn't do it. He had no motive. The prosecution's case against him at the trial had been circumstantial, yet he was convicted of second-degree manslaughter.

Now today, he was getting out.

Randy wondered how Door County had changed as he looked at his possessions, all contained in one cardboard box. The box had gotten bigger and been replaced several times. His fingers grazed over his favorite books, his indispensable thesaurus and dictionary. He'd almost worn out their pages writing six novels, published under the pen name Greg Chambers. Stacked against the edge of the box were a dozen yellow legal pads comprising the drafts of his seventh novel. One book reviewer had said Greg Chambers was "a modern-day O. Henry," except his works were not short stories, but novels—pulp fiction, with many of the characters generated from people Randy had lived among in prison. A wealth of stories was told and acted out every day in prison, and he'd successfully captured them in print.

He looked at his watch: eighteen minutes before he went to processing. Funny, he thought, when you're in prison, all you've got is time. Now as he waited, he knew, those eighteen minutes would take forever.

He was already thinking what he would do first when he was free. He was a good golfer when he'd played for Gibraltar High School, so maybe he'd play at the nearby Peninsula State Park

Golf Course.

He loved sailing too, with his dad in his *Flying Scot* sailboat. Did Mom and Dad even have the old boat anymore? Dad couldn't sail anymore, Randy was sure. Even before he went to prison, his dad would go and sit and just watch the sailing. The few times he did later in life, Mom would join just to be with her two boys—meaning Dad and him. She loved the three of them being together. He doubted they'd kept the boat after that terrible night. It would represent nothing but a bad memory for them, he supposed. He wouldn't blame them if they'd sold it.

He heard the guard Stewart coming. For some reason, since day one Stewart had always been kind to him. Randy couldn't say the same thing about the other guards and inmates he'd had contact with over the years.

Stewart and Randy would talk about books they liked or movies they'd seen. They'd discuss the book Randy was currently writing. Stewart liked to read, so every time one of Randy's books was published, Randy would sign a copy "To Stewart. Enjoy. Gregory Chambers." After Stewart finished reading the book, they'd discuss aspects of the story—sometimes for ten or fifteen minutes before lights-out.

Finally Stewart was at his cell door. "Daggett, you ready to get out of here?"

"Yes. There's a new world waiting for me. It will be nice to wear regular clothes, eat decent food, and see how much the world has changed." Randy stuck his hand out. "You made life somewhat tolerable while I was here. I know friendship with inmates is discouraged, but I thought of you as a friend and a fair guard. Thanks."

"You were never a problem, not like some of the others in here. Good luck, and keep writing. I enjoy your books." He looked at his watch. "Let's get going. Who's picking you up, or are you taking the bus somewhere?"

"My mom. It will be good to see her and maybe Dad. After his stroke, he can't drive. This ordeal has been hard on my parents, especially Dad. It may have been harder on them than me. They live in Fish Creek and see people every day. Everyone knows the whole awful story about their son. It's a sad story for them."

"You're probably right," Stewart said.

"When you're born, parents have such big plans. They think only the best for their kids, but if something goes wrong, it can be a nightmare for parents."

Stewart nodded. "Yeah, I see it on visitation days. I see it in their eyes."

Stewart opened the cell and escorted him to processing, passing several iron gates and station doors. Half an hour later, they walked together to the front gate.

"I'm looking forward to some real quiet nights," said Randy. "Not to mention no longer fearing for my life twenty-four-seven because someone feels an uncontrolled rage."

"Well, here we are. Good luck, Randy. Maybe we'll meet for a drink sometime on the outside."

"I'd like that, Stewart." The men shook hands.

Randy walked through the gate, a free man.

His mother stood by the same Buick he remembered from eight years ago. He walked up to her, put his arms around her, and gave her a big hug. Then he gave her tearstained cheek a kiss.

"You look great, Mom."

"I do not. I look old, but it's nice of you to say that."

Her eyes gazed at his face, then down his body. "You look thin and pale," she said.

"They don't have the best food in there. I'll never eat another baloney sandwich or oatmeal again. I worked inside at the laundry on Monday, Wednesday, and Friday. It's hot. The other days I was lucky to work at the prison library, so I didn't get much sun. The only real day I got to sit in the sun was Sunday. We didn't have a big exercise area, but there was a track and a weights area, but no trees. It's nice to be out and see some green."

"Well, I'll fatten you up. I went and bought all the foods you like."

"Good. I'm looking forward to home cooking."

He bent down and looked in the back seat of the Buick. "I was hoping to see Dad."

"He's not doing too good. You'll see. Let's go home. He's waiting for you."

He got in the passenger's side. His mom got behind the wheel.

Randy's driver's license had expired, but it was just as well. It gave him a chance to enjoy the ride home, passing Lake Michigan's

Green Bay and the scenery he'd missed in prison. He'd never enjoyed a ride more, he thought. It was a route he knew well, often driving it back and forth to college in Madison.

From Green Bay, they drove north through the Door County peninsula to the family home in Fish Creek. Freedom was underappreciated, he thought. He had never been to Cape Cod, but it was often said that Door County was the Cape Cod of the Midwest. And there was no better time to be in Door County than right then: early summer. The sky was cobalt blue, and the prairie grass was just turning a golden brown. Numerous birch trees were bright green, the sun glistening on them as they leafed out. With the car window open, he breathed in clean and fresh-smelling air. Nice to breathe deeply and not smell body odors of prison inmates, even when outside in the yard.

On the way up the peninsula, he gazed at Green Bay's waters. On the other side of the road, farms and open fields were bordered by rock walls of fieldstone, prairie grasses, and flowers. He felt like a man underwater swimming toward the surface, hungry for a gulp of air—for Randy, that gulp of air was this Door County peninsula countryside.

As they approached Sturgeon Bay, his mother asked if he was hungry.

"It's Wednesday," she said. "I think Kitty O'Reilly's Irish Pub has their hamburger special today. You always liked their hamburgers, or we could stop someplace for your favorite cherry pancakes if you like."

"It's okay, Mom. I'd just like to get home and see Dad."

"He's probably sitting in his chair looking for us."

The ride from Sturgeon Bay to Fish Creek took a little longer than usual because they detoured through the business district to see the historical steel bridge. As luck would have it, the bridge was open for some pleasure boats to pass through because of the low ten-foot clearance, but that was all right with Randy. He remembered years ago when there was only this one bridge connecting the upper part of the peninsula and the lower part, but two more bridges had been built since, so now there was always a way to get across the canal. The canal had been built back in 1920s to save navigation time around the upper tip of the Door peninsula, especially for freighters. Cutting across the peninsula at Sturgeon Bay saved sailors well over a hundred miles.

Now there were three bridges, so drivers could always get across if you timed your trip so you wouldn't get caught when they were opening for boats. The openings were staggered every fifteen minutes, except for the high-rise Bay Bridge. That was open on demand, which wasn't often because it had a forty-five-foot clearance, which the two other bridges didn't have.

Randy's mom kept up a constant chatter. He could tell she was so excited to have her boy home after so many years, even if she didn't know how much he'd changed since going to prison just after graduating from the university. Hell, he'd been just a kid—he'd hardly had a chance to legally drink before going to jail.

Even now, he really didn't feel like he wanted to drink much. He might have a beer or two now that he was out, but he had no a real craving for it. Hell, that's what got him sent to prison when

Ingrid Karlsen was killed.

He was getting excited as the old Buick rounded the sweeping turn in Egg Harbor, and then they were looking west out over the Egg Harbor Marina. In the distance he saw Chambers Island.

That's where he'd gotten his pen name, Gregory Chambers. Life was funny how it could turn into either good or evil, depending on what you wanted. He had not wanted the evil to continue while in prison, so he turned toward the good. Now he was a successful author—perhaps in part a result of Ingrid's death and his jail sentence. He probably never would have started writing if he hadn't been stuck in prison. It had become his way to escape from life there. Then he chuckled to himself how ironic that his stories were based on prison life.

Ten minutes later the Buick approached the sharp downhill curve leading into Fish Creek. He sat up straighter as he glimpsed Fish Creek's harbor and the western part of beautiful Peninsula Park. Soon they were waiting in line at the three-corner stop at the bottom of the long hill.

Nothing much had changed at this corner. Hide Side Corner Store carried leather and miscellaneous clothing along with Door County items. Then there was On the Deck, a clothing store, and next to that was the Fish Creek Market and Deli. Then there was the busy family-owned Bayside Bar, where Randy used to get pizza and hamburgers and an occasional beer or something stronger.

Soon it was their turn at the three-way stop, and his mom proceeded toward the harbor and then drove the short distance to their small white house.

He was home.

Everything looked the same as it had eight-plus years ago. As his mom pulled into the driveway, he saw the *Flying Scot* under a faded, weathered gray tarp parked next to the garage.

"You didn't sell the sailboat?"

"We talked about it, but your father said you loved it, so he'd let you decide when you got out."

"Well, I'm glad you didn't," he said with a big smile. Even with everything that happened after sailing that boat to Chambers Island, he still loved it. "It will give me something to do, getting it shipshape."

She turned the car off. He heard her let out a cleansing breath and turned to him. "Your dad will be so excited to see you, but just be aware he's still not good. He's had a hard time getting around and has a tough time talking. It takes him a while to get out what he wants to say. His mind and body are falling apart, and he knows it. So be patient with him."

"Okay, I'll be ready. It's been a year since he last visited me in prison. I'll try not to act too surprised by his appearance and speech. One thing I learned in prison was patience."

They entered the house through the kitchen, which also had not changed since he was here last. He heard a radio playing softly. When they walked into the living room, Randy's dad was asleep in his well-worn leather chair with his legs stretched out on a matching leather ottoman.

Randy felt a tear run down his face. His dad was a shadow of himself since the last time he was able to visit. While sitting in his cell, Randy had sometimes thought that the stress of seeing his only son in prison had caused this most recent stroke.

His mother moved to her husband and kissed the top of his slumped head. She whispered, "Paul, look who's here."

His dad's eyes fluttered open, and then in a slow, deliberate voice, he said, "Welcome home, son. I've missed you." His gray eyes were misty at first, but then there was the familiar twinkle from happier times.

"I've missed you so much, Dad. It's good to be home with you and Mom." He watched as his dad nodded agreement to him being home. "I was so happy to see you kept the sailboat. I'll start working on it, getting it ready so we can go sailing again, okay?"

His dad smiled and, with a wave of his hand, said. "I think my sailing days are over." He turned his head to Grace, his wife of forty years. She shook her head in agreement.

"Both our sailing days are over," she said, "but we knew you'd like to fix it up when you got out. Now, what do you want to eat? How about some cherry pancakes and maple syrup with bacon or sausage?"

"Bacon and pancakes would be great," said Randy.

―――

Mom kept fussing, making sure he was happy with her pancakes and bacon.

"This is great, Mom, but what's best is just sitting here, talking and feeling like old times. I really missed being with you both."

He saw both of their eyes mist over as he said it.

"I need to tell you something. It's important for me to let you know something that I've thought about for the last eight-plus years."

"Okay," his mother said.

"I am one hundred percent sure I did not kill Ingrid that night. I went over everything in my mind, including the insomnia drug. I took that drug through high school and college and never had a problem. Yes, I was drinking that night, but I could never kill her. Someone else did, and I promise you, I will find the killer. I know you supported me through the whole ordeal of the trial and prison, but I'm sure you always wondered if I killed her. I want you to be proud of me and not have to think about what your friends and neighbors are saying behind your back about me."

His dad cleared his throat, and his speech was laborious, "Randy, we know you. We raised you to be kind and respectful to everyone, and you always were, so we were always convinced of your innocence. We love you and will always love you. And if you find the killer, do it to clear *your* name for *yourself*. For your own self-worth, go out and find the person that killed Ingrid, and put them behind bars, like you had to suffer."

Randy got to his feet, then gave his mom and dad a hug. "I promise you, I will."

CHAPTER TWO

Randy and his mother went to Sturgeon Bay the day after he got out, and he got a new driver's license. He had been a little nervous when he found out he needed to retake the written test and driver's test, but he passed both with flying colors. He spent the next few weeks repainting the house, the traditional white favored by many residences and rental units in Fish Creek. Also, the place was in need of several repairs. His parents had let things go a bit. So now he was a carpenter and painter. But after being cooped up in prison, Randy loved being outside, and he soon had a summer tan.

Each day he went to Nelson's Hardware Store to get supplies for the house, a bit nervous that someone would recognize him. Then he realized he looked a lot different than eight years ago. Also, did anyone really care? He was putting on a little weight now, and the beard and long hair altered his appearance too.

He had graduated from the university in Madison with a degree in English and received a teaching certificate, but being in prison eliminated teaching as a possible profession for him. Parents would go nuts if they found out their kids were being taught by an ex-con convicted of murder.

Being novelist Greg Chambers was his job now. He applied and received a Visa card and checking account with his name, Randy Daggett on both. His royalties were shifted to the new checking account located in Fish Creek's bank. And while his new driver's license was issued with the name Randy Daggett on it, as far as anyone was concerned, he would be Greg Chambers, novelist.

At least he would take on this Greg Chambers identity until he felt comfortable enough to use his real name. Many writers used pen names throughout their whole writing career and didn't think anything unusual about it. His reason was different: to hide from his past.

The hardware store was between Fish Creek and Ephraim, right next to one of the last remaining old-fashioned drive-in movie theaters. Randy laughed when he thought about that theater. He remembered sneaking in beer underneath the car seat and steaming up the windows with Ingrid.

After getting the supplies he needed at Nelson's Hardware, he stopped at the Bayside Bar and had his first pizza and a Coke. Even though he lived just nine blocks from the place on Main Street in Fish Creek, no one recognized him.

After the late lunch, he went home and started working on the *Flying Scot*. First, he washed down the sailboat, getting years-old dirt and algae from the mooring ball. He started stripping flaking varnish from the handholds, the hatch boards, and the wooden tiller. The boat was mostly fiberglass, so all he needed to do was buff the boat with rubbing compound, and it was good as new. He stretched out the old sails on the front lawn. Inspecting them, he determined they needed patching and stitching. They also needed to be washed to be rid of the mildew and mold, but he could do that later. He'd take the two sails down to DorSal in Sturgeon Bay later in the week.

The next few days flew by as his mind was occupied with work on his boat. Finally, after buffing the fiberglass, bottom painting the hull, and putting a couple of coats of teak oil on the teak, he decided he'd better get the sails down and fixed.

What he really wanted was to get the boat in the water and sail it around Chambers Island, ASAP, stopping in Sand Bay just like he and Ingrid had done that night. Randy intended to revisit his horror, to stare down his demons. He would do it as soon as he got the sails fixed.

The next day he drove the thirty minutes down to Sturgeon Bay and dropped off the sails. He drove across the old steel bridge and went to Kitty O'Reilly's and had a burger and Guinness, his first beer in eight years. He sat at the long curving bar and listened to normal conversations, not like the prison talk he had become accustomed to hearing.

He enjoyed the anonymity. He wasn't worrying about someone recognizing him down here in Sturgeon Bay. Besides, he thought, it was early afternoon, and the only people here were tourists or retirees. He thought the four older, potbellied guys sitting at the bar having a shot and beer were probably retired fishermen or shipwrights. When he looked at their big rough hands and craggy faces, they appeared to be guys that had been around the water their whole life, like pieces of driftwood washed up onshore.

Since it was summer, their conversation centered on the Cubs and the Brewers. Both teams were popular in Door County, especially after the Cubs won the World Series in 2016, and the Brewers fell one game short of making the World Series in 2018. Then the retirees' conversation turned to the Bears and the Packers. No question the four were Packers fans, but they still talked about the resurgent Bears of 2018 and the Packers' losing record.

Even in prison Randy had followed the teams. Now that he was out, he'd take a more active interest. He might even go to Miller Park and watch the Cubs and Brewers play.

He looked at his watch. Time to head back to Fish Creek. He walked a couple of blocks each day with his dad, neither of them in a rush. Usually they'd sit on a bench or chair near Alibi Marina or the municipal marina. His dad loved to watch the boats come and go. After thirty minutes or so, he would regain enough strength to walk back home, where Randy and his parents would then have sweet tea or lemonade.

"Randy, could you start the grill?" his mom asked when he walked in the door. "I got some nice steaks at the market in town and some fresh corn."

"Sure, Mom. That sounds great." He got up and rolled out the black Weber grill, and thirty minutes later, he was grilling. Life seemed good.

Three days later, Randy had one of the local boat storage places with a boat forklift move his *Flying Scot* to Fish Creek's municipal marina.

Once it was in the water, he attached a small 3 hp outboard to the boat's motor mount and motored the short distance to one of the town's mooring balls his family still owned. Now all he needed to do was get the sails from the sail loft in Sturgeon Bay.

That morning Randy's mom asked if they could use his car to go to the doctor's office for his dad's medical checkup. "I noticed this morning that the Buick has a nail in the rear tire. We'll have AAA come out and fix it, but we need to go this morning."

"Sure, Mom. My car's just sitting there. I'm going sailing today. Do you want me to drive? I can go sailing tomorrow."

"No, that's fine. You go sailing today and enjoy yourself."

He got his car keys and handed them to his mother. "See you later. Love you."

"Love you too."

Randy and the boat were finally ready. The wind was from the west-southwest, which was perfect to sail out of Fish Creek Harbor and around Chambers Island. Hell, he didn't even need the motor.

It felt like Christmas to Randy as he hoisted the two sails, and they luffed in the wind before he let the mooring line go. He moved back to the cockpit, tightened the main sheet and the jib line, and felt the boat heel over as she moved past the many moored boats and toward Chambers Island.

He watched the passing of several Peninsula State Park landmarks. The Eagle Bluff Lighthouse stood high on the bluff, and a new sightseeing tower stood above the trees, no doubt offering a commanding view of Chambers Island, the four strawberry islands, horseshoe island, and finally, perhaps, a picturesque view of the village of Ephraim.

As he moved past the protection of Fish Creek harbor's southern portion, the breeze freshened, and he felt the boat heel over more—not a lot, but enough that he smiled as the boat gathered the right amount of momentum. The tiller felt good in his hand, with a strong tug until he adjusted the jib and mainsail, ensuring the boat was balanced just right. He was making good time to the southern part of Chambers Island.

The first place he needed to sail was Chambers Island, the spot of Ingrid Karlsen's death. Randy liked to think that Ingrid had just drowned on her own, but the investigation had proven that she'd had help.

As he sailed along the island's southern shore, he saw several people on the beach, playing and swimming. He turned north and sailed up the long side of the island. Eventually he got to Sand Bay, where he anchored the boat in three feet of water, close to shore. He jumped into the water and waded ashore.

After looking up and down the sweeping beach, he walked a hundred feet to the spot where he and Ingrid had made love that night—where he had fallen asleep. He turned and saw the thorny bushes, a big reason he was convicted. The photos that detectives had taken of his scratches and that had been shown to the jury sealed his fate.

There was also the matter of the medication he had been taking in high school and college. The prosecutor had claimed the drug's side effect was violence. Maybe that's why he only got eight years and a manslaughter conviction.

Three pieces of driftwood rolled back and forth in gentle waves lapping on the beach, and the image of Ingrid's lifeless naked body rolling in the moonlit water flashed in his mind.

He could hold it in no longer. Randy started sobbing.

He sat on the beach for thirty minutes longer, then slowly got up and waded back to the boat. He raised the sails, letting the sails and lines luff while he pulled up the anchor and stowed it in the cuddy cabin. He sailed north toward the towns of Ephraim and Sister Bay, then back to Fish Creek. Along the way, he felt the weight of the past ease.

It felt good to be out on the water, out on his old sailboat. Randy had been sailing for four hours. Once at Fish Creek, he sailed up to his mooring ball, grabbed the two pennants, and fastened them to the cleat as the jib and mainsails luffed in the gentle breeze. He lowered the two sails, put them in their sailing bags, and placed them in the small cuddy cabin. He got in his dingy and rowed the short distance ashore. Dragging the dingy onshore, he locked it to a tree with a bicycle chain. Kids would be kids, and if it wasn't chained, it would be an easy target.

Walking home in the late afternoon, he realized he was hungry.

Mom said they were going to have chicken tonight. She had been taking Dad to Sturgeon Bay to see his doctor this afternoon while Randy went sailing. He knew his mother and dad would like to hear all about his trip.

When he turned the corner past Alibi Marina, he saw a Door County Sheriff's patrol car parked at the curb in front of the house. A deputy was leaning against the side of the car, smoking a cigarette as Randy walked up.

Now what did he do? Randy knew he didn't break any of his probation rules, and then he noticed his car wasn't in the driveway.

"Randy Daggett?" asked the cop.

"Yes, that's me."

"I've stopped by a couple of times this afternoon."

"I was out sailing. Just got back." He watched as the officer turned his head slightly toward the marina, nodded and looked back at him.

"I bet it was nice out there today." He paused. "I'm sorry to report some bad news to you. Your mother and father were in a car accident this afternoon."

"Oh God. Are they all right?" Randy knees felt weak and his stomach queasy.

"Your mother was driving and lost control of the car just south of Egg Harbor, crossing the road and hitting a tree. They both died at the scene. We think your mother had a heart attack. Witness says she just drove straight across the road and hit a tree straight on. Your father died of external injuries at the scene. We won't know for sure until autopsies are performed."

Randy sank down on his haunches like a baseball catcher might do. He might have thrown up at hearing the news, but he had nothing in his stomach.

The officer handed him a card. "Give me a call tomorrow after you've had a chance to compose yourself, and I'll go over everything in detail. Right now they're at the hospital in Sturgeon Bay, and your car is at the police garage. Our inspectors will go over it because it was involved in a fatal accident. It looks like it's a total wreck."

"Thank you. I'll call you. Thank you for spending the time waiting to tell me in person rather than a message on the phone. I appreciate it."

"Sorry I had to tell you the bad news. It never gets easy, but it's part of the job. Thankfully, we don't have to do it very often."

He watched as the officer got in the car and slowly drove away.

Four days later, Randy woke up with the first bang of thunder, then he heard pounding rain on the roof. Why did it have to rain today of all days, the day of his parents' funeral? Now his mood was going to match the weather. His parents wouldn't mind, he knew; they were at peace. He hoped they were holding hands in a better place. He had told the funeral home he wanted them both cremated and their ashes put in the same urn. If his parents were going to go, he guessed it was better that they'd gone together. They'd be together forever. He planned to bury the urn in a small plot at the local cemetery.

He didn't ever know his mother had a heart condition. It probably was caused in part by the stress of him being in prison and also the added stress of Dad's stroke. It seemed like everything had fallen on his mother's shoulders, like moms everywhere.

Deciding he had been in bed long enough, he got up and walked to the kitchen. Entering this room, his sorrow increased. His mother's memory was overwhelming here. This was her world.

He got out the old-fashioned coffee pot he favored and measured enough coffee for three large cups. He turned on the gas stove to medium and then walked back to the single bathroom to shower and shave.

Standing in front of the mirror, he decided to shave off his beard and cut off his ponytail for them. So much for him being someone else, at least in appearance. He wondered how many people at the funeral would remember Randy Daggett, the murderer?

After cutting his beard and hair, he entered the shower. After standing under the steaming shower, he started to cry, slowly at first: a whimper, then a sigh, and then all out bawling like a little kid who stubbed his toe or pounded his finger. He remembered his parents comforting him and making him feel better. He wasn't a little boy anymore, and there was no one to comfort Randy Daggett. When he got out of prison, his mom had been there and given him the hug and kiss he needed. Prison had hurt just like banging his finger or stubbing his toe but in a different way, and Mom had been there to make him feel better. He'd never get that love again.

He had never been to a funeral before, never. The minister and the funeral home director helped guide him on what to do. He hadn't even realized that after the service, you had a short lunch. Thankfully, the churchwomen organized it. About forty people turned out for the funeral and lunch in the Fish Creek Lutheran Church. He thought it was nice, and his parents would have approved because it was simple, short, and sweet. Thankfully few people remembered Randy Daggett, and those that did, did not mention his prison time or his manslaughter conviction.

But then one of his Gibraltar High School classmates stopped by to pay his respects. Jimmy Bartlett worked as a carpenter, a sort of Mr. Fix-it type of guy. He and Randy talked for five minutes. Gossip traveled fast in a small town like Fish Creek. Randy was convinced, and soon enough everyone in town would know he was back.

That afternoon, he returned to the gravesite. The hole containing the urn was covered with fresh dirt, and withered flowers from the church were still there. Looking down, he talked to the grave as if his parents were standing in front of him. "Mom, Dad, I know I told you I didn't kill Ingrid. I don't know who did, but I'll find out. I promise you! I'll clear my name and make you proud."

CHAPTER THREE

Most days Randy wrote in the morning and sailed in the afternoon. With that schedule, he didn't see many people except when he went to the local markets in Fish Creek, Egg Harbor, and Sister Bay for food. Writing and sailing kept his mind from brooding over his parents' deaths, and for a few hours, he was able to escape. When sailing, he often stopped at Sand Bay and walked the beach or hiked around the island. Maybe it was his way of trying to find answers.

Chambers Island was large enough to have several summer homes on it, as well as a few empty lots and a short private airstrip. During the summer, several families lived there. They were free-spirited people that wanted to live on a semi remote island yet still be ten minutes away by boat from Fish Creek. Properties periodically came up for sale when either a couple or family got fed up with the inconvenience of living there, or someone died, and their family decided to sell. Without city power, water, or heat—except wood, diesel heaters, or kerosene heaters—it was like camping but on a permanent basis. Not everyone enjoyed the off-the-grid experience, so properties changed hands.

While hiking around the island, he had the idea that living there full time might help him answer his questions about Ingrid's death. Also, by living on the island, Randy would escape the summer people and tourists when Door County's populations swelled to triple or quadruple its normal population.

So when he saw a sign one day near the island's lighthouse, "House and five-acre lot for sale," he contacted the owner and made quick arrangements to buy it. If nothing else, life on the island would help his writing because of the solitude. Randy planned to live in the Fish Creek house in winter and early spring when it wasn't feasible to live on the island.

The new house was perfect for his needs. Sitting on five acres at the edge of Sand Bay, the house had a large screened in porch, one bedroom, a modest bathroom, a large kitchen, and a living room with a huge picture window facing the lake. A storage shed was off to the side of the house.

The previous owner had sold Randy the house with all the furnishings, probably because it would have been such an expensive hassle to move it all off the island. Most of it was really old, though Randy was only too happy to accept everything. He did add a long wooden kitchen table and six Amish chairs he picked up at a garage sale. The table made a great desk and dining area all rolled into one spot. He also bought solar panels from West Marine that he hooked up to power his laptop computer and incidentals. A new generator would also power his electrical items in addition to the older generator that came with the house. He really didn't need the extra generator because his needs were minimal, but it never hurt to have extra capacity. He liked the idea of scaling down everything and being off the grid.

He bought a few kerosene oil lamps, camping items, and supplies for the firepit he expanded. He actually enjoyed sailing back and forth to Fish Creek with house supplies, weekly food, and gas for the generator. After an initial outlay for a few necessary items, his expenses and living costs became minimal. He understood now why more people lived off the grid.

He'd spend a day at his parents' house in Fish Creek now and again. He'd do more remodeling when fall came and he couldn't be on the island as much. He slowly started selling his parents' things to minimize the pain of going into the house.

He kept most of the paintings and photographs in their same places on the walls and on the mantel. He loved looking at the black-and-white framed photos of his mom and dad in their younger years. There were a number of pictures of Randy, in color, as he grew up. It never failed to bring a smile to his face as he gazed at them all. Besides the photos, his parents had supported many of the local Door County artists, buying paintings of local scenery and iconic establishments. Most of the paintings were watercolors, of lighthouses, barns, piers, and boats. He did move a few photos and paintings to the Chambers Island house just to make it comfortable and remind him of his parents.

He gave their clothing to local charities. A huge garage sale sold just about everything but the books and kitchen stuff. He couldn't part with the image of his mom in the kitchen, and that included all the kitchen stuff. Books had been Dad's escape.

When Randy found something he liked, he bought it and started filling the Fish Creek house with his style of furniture—a mix of Scandinavian and modern styles.

His new novel involved rival prison gangs: a Neo-Nazi skinhead gang, a black gang, a Latino gang all trying to be the top dog while behind bars. He'd had the first draft finished while in prison and was now rewriting. In Hemingway's *A Moveable Feast*, he said the real writing was in the rewriting. Hemingway always thought he could rewrite and edit out 25 percent of the novel to make it better. Randy thought it was like making a sauce when cooking. As the sauce was reduced and liquid became more concentrated, it became more flavorful.

He had just finished another day's writing when it hit him. What about his investigation into clearing his name and finding the real killer? Didn't he promise his parents at the gravesite that?

Tomorrow, he was going to the police department to talk to the arresting detective on his case.

He drove the thirty minutes to Sturgeon Bay Police Department. "I'd like to talk to Detective Steve Jenkins if he still works here."

The receptionist said, "He does still work here. And your name?"

"Randy Daggett. He should remember me. He sent me to prison nine years ago." He noticed the startled look before she picked up the phone and called him.

"Steve, a Randy Daggett is here and wants to talk to you. He said you sent him to prison nine years ago." He watched as she nodded her head. "Okay, I'll tell him."

She turned back to him. "He asked if you could come back in forty-five minutes. He's in the middle of something and can't see you until then. He asked me to get your file so he could review your case."

"Okay." And sounding like Arnold Schwarzenegger, he said, "I'll be back." Smiling, he turned and walked out. Leaving the police station, he went down the street and had a cup of coffee, reviewing what he wanted to talk about with Detective Jenkins.

He was sure Jenkins was right now going over the Ingrid Karlsen murder case, maybe looking at the questions that had never came up in the trial, issues that Randy had become convinced might have made a difference to the jury. Over the last nine years, he had discovered things that had never come up in the investigation or the courtroom.

A waitress at the downtown café brought his coffee, and he thought more about the night of Ingrid's drowning and the events leading up to her death.

Forty minutes later he was sitting in the reception area waiting for Jenkins. This was step one on his journey to prove his innocence. He hoped it was a fruitful start.

The phone buzzed on the receptionist's desk. He watched as she picked it up, nodded her head, and looked his way.

"You can go back to room three. Detective Jenkins will meet you there."

———

He sat and waited for Jenkins. He noticed a small ball-shaped ceiling camera to record the meeting. He was sure there was a mic somewhere recording. He reminded himself this was an informal request for a meeting so he could gather facts for his rogue investigation into who killed Ingrid. For the police, their investigation regarding the murder was done. He was grateful that Jenkins would even take the time to see him, so he told himself to be nice no matter what.

A few minutes later, Jenkins walked in with a coffee cup and a large brown accordion file, and he sat down in front of Randy.

"To what do I owe the honor? I took a few minutes to look over the facts of your trial, and I think it was a solid case against you, so why are you here? I'm pretty busy, so let's get right to it. Why?"

"When you're in prison, you have lots of time to think about things. I spent close to nine years in jail. I've gone over everything, and I think some facts were overlooked that could have cleared me."

"Oh, really." Randy watched as he tapped the thick case file.

"I don't think so. We covered a lot of areas that never even came up at the trial."

"At the crime scene, you missed at least two things, which might have proved there was another person at the beach that night."

"I'm listening," Jenkins said.

"When I got up from my nap that night, I had to pee. I went to some nearby bushes, stubbed my foot on some driftwood, and fell into the bushes."

"Yes, so you said. So they weren't Ingrid Karlsen's scratches as she put up a struggle?"

"If you checked under her nails, the DNA would that have proven it wasn't me."

"There wasn't anything under her nails. She had really short nails. All that was there were grains of sand. No skin scrapings."

"But you just said marks on my body might have been caused by her struggling with me. With no scraping, I don't think it happened that way," Randy said.

"The jury thought otherwise about your scratches. The water was warm and clean, and she wasn't in the water very long. You said you dragged her up on the beach and tried to give her mouth to mouth. Besides, your sperm was inside her. No other person's sperm was inside her. It was a hundred percent match."

"Another thing that bugs me and never came up at the trial."

"What's that?" Jenkins asked. "I thought we were thorough in our investigation of the crime scene that night."

"As I was walking the beach to find her, I saw a red swimsuit lying on the sand just outside the waterline. There were footprints all around it leading into the water. Someone else was there that night. If you had searched the area, you would have found the suit and could have taken pictures of the footprints. There might have even been DNA on the suit. The footprints were bigger than mine. Also, in the trial, the bruises found on Ingrid's shoulders were bigger than my hand."

"Again, the jury didn't think that was enough." Jenkins sat quietly for a moment, then said, "Okay, maybe we could have done a better job at the crime scene, but we didn't see any suit lying around near the body. That suit could have been left by a swimmer earlier in the day and dropped as the person left to go home, and the footprints just didn't wash away. There are no tides on Lake Michigan and Green Bay, so it could have been old marks. Besides, you told us no one was around."

"Yes, I remember," he said softly.

"If that suit was so important, why didn't you mention it?"

"I was wearing a blue suit that night. And I forgot about the suit until I was in prison, and then it was too late."

"Our investigation was thorough. The closest cabin and family was the Jacobs family: Marvin and his younger brother, Simon. Simon vouched for Marvin that night and said he was home all night and didn't leave. Everything we concluded from the investigation," tapping the file folder in front of him, "led to you and only you. That's why you were convicted. I think you got off light with manslaughter charges, a lesser sentence than regular murder, because of the reasonable doubt you were under the influence of the insomnia drug, so maybe you didn't know what you did. You should be thankful for that, or you'd still be in prison."

"I am thankful, but I didn't do it. Here's what I'm asking you. If you come across or recall any information that might help me with my investigation, I'd appreciate it if you could let me know."

"I don't think that's going to happen because we found who the killer was, and it was you. If something changes that, I'll let you know. I have your phone number at your parents' house. Give me your cell phone number. It will be easier to get hold of you."

Randy handed him one of his author cards with his email and cell phone from his latest book.

Jenkins looked at. "It says on this card your name is Greg Chambers, not Randy Daggett?"

"Yeah, that's my pen name."

"I've read your books. Didn't realize it was you. Not bad books. Okay, I'll call if I come up with anything, but don't hold your breath."

"I understand." Randy stood. "Thanks for seeing me. I'd appreciate any help you can give me. After all, I'm a rookie at this, and you're the professional." He shook Jenkins's hand and walked out.

CHAPTER FOUR

Almost every day at 6:00 a.m., he put on the coffee pot, then sat and wrote for three to five hours. In prison it had been even earlier because it was quiet then, before everyone was rousted up, before the day's deafening noise with its banging and yelling. Even so, he had liked writing in prison, never realizing that someday it would be his job. While he now wrote at the kitchen table, he could write anywhere. Hell, after prison, everything was a piece of cake.

Once he sat down and was into it, he was fully immersed in the story and its characters. After putting in his time, he'd stop only when he had an idea for the next day's work. He'd jot it down, letting his mind work on it in the interim, mulling it over until the next day, then he'd start working on the idea, melding it into the story. That way he was excited to get to work the next day.

After a good writing day in his new Chambers Island digs, Randy was in a fine mood. When he was done, he decided to hike the island. Randy had not met many of his neighbors yet, despite hiking the gravel roads and trails on the island. He supposed, in part, it was his fear of being discovered. Wasn't that why he was living here, or was it the memories of his parents at the house in Fish Creek? He knew it was both to a certain degree, but he also liked his new house's solitude. He felt a similar peace when sailing. The quiet let him reflect on life.

He was walking back from the southwestern point of the island when he passed one of the island's larger homes. Two male adults about his age were working in the yard, cutting the grass and trimming bushes and low-hanging tree branches. The man cutting grass pushed the mower close to the narrow gravel road.

Most islanders had four-wheel all-terrain vehicles, but a few had old pickup trucks they'd somehow gotten over here, probably in winter when there was ice thick enough. Anyhow, they weren't like Randy. He enjoyed walking and using an old Radio Flyer red wagon from his childhood for transporting supplies from the boat. It worked for him, but maybe he'd get a used four-wheeler someday in the future. For now, the wagon was just fine.

As he walked back toward his house, the twentysomething young man stopped the mower, smiled, and walked over.

"Hi. I'm Simon. We live here." He pointed to the large brown cedar-shingled house situated with a commanding view of the bay and the couple of small islands to the south. Simon pointed to another person. "That's my brother, Marvin." He turned and yelled, "Hey Marvin, come meet our neighbor." He turned to Randy. "What's your name?"

"Gregory Chambers, but just call me Greg."

"Okay, Greg. Your last name is like the island. Do you own

the island? My mommy and daddy own this house, but then my mommy died, and daddy is in a nursing home. I don't like the nursing home. Daddy just sits there with all the other people, and he just stares. He doesn't talk or remember our names. Now Marvin and I own it. It's a nice home. I used to live here in the summer with Mommy, but now it's just on the weekends mostly, with Marvin. In the winter I work at Goodwill and Pick and Save in Green Bay. I like living here better."

It didn't take Randy long to realize that Simon had special needs.

"Where do you live?" asked Simon. "I see you walking around the island sometimes, but Marvin won't let me roam around the island unless he and Jessica are with me."

"I live in the old Erickson home near the lighthouse and Sand Bay."

"I know where that is. Marvin and I go there sometimes and swim because the water is warmer there, and it has a nice beach. I can play there and build sandcastles. I like building sandcastles a lot."

Randy looked over at Marvin and saw he had put the branch trimmer and the leaf rake in a black wheelbarrow, which he pushed to a storage shed next to the house. When he saw Randy talking to Simon, he started walking toward him.

"Simon, did you meet a new friend?" Marvin reached out his right hand to shake Randy's hand. "Hi, I'm Marvin Jacobs. You must be our new neighbor. You look kind of familiar, like I know you."

"Yes. I am your new neighbor. My name's Greg Chambers. I live in town, so maybe you've seen me there, although I've been gone for a while until just recently. My parents have a house near the two marinas."

"Ahh. That's probably it. Nice to have your own island named after you." Marvin laughed. "I'm sorry we didn't come down sooner and introduce ourselves. Simon keeps me pretty busy here and in our house in Green Bay. That's where we really live most of the year, and when we do get up here in the summer, it's mostly on the weekends. We have an insurance business, Jacobs and Jacobs. My father started it back in the seventies, and now I've taken over. Dad's retired."

"Simon told me your mother passed away, and your dad's in a nursing home," said Randy.

"Yes, she got cancer, and he's got Alzheimer's and needs twenty-four-seven care. As much as I hated to, I had to put him in a nursing home."

"I can imagine that was difficult," Randy said.

"The hardest thing for Simon is missing my mother, who doted on him here and at home. When she was alive, she carried the load with Simon. He could stay here on the island all the time, but not now. As you can tell, Simon is a little slow. When he was born, the umbilical cord wrapped around his neck and cut enough oxygen off to his brain. He's usually happy, but he's a handful. He can be very demanding now and then. I'm the only relative he has. I'm his guardian. With work and him, I'm pretty busy. You have to do what you have to do, especially when it's family."

"It sounds like Simon works too."

"Yes. That helps. It keeps him busy, and the two companies are great." Marvin motioned to their house. "Would you like to come and have a soda or beer? We could sit out on the deck. It's a pretty nice view."

"I'd love a soda."

"That's fine." He turned to Simon. "Okay, Simon, put the lawnmower away in the shed, and then we'll have a snack and soda."

"Okay, Marvin." He started pushing the lawnmower to the shed, then looked over his shoulder and asked, "Ice cream too, Marvin?"

"Maybe later. Now put the lawnmower away." He turned back to Randy. "We were getting the yard and house ready for a small birthday party for Simon on Sunday. A few of the neighbors around here and my fiancée, Jessica, are coming. Nothing fancy, the usual—hamburgers and brats—but Simon loves parties. He's got the mind of a ten-year-old. You can imagine how excited he'll get. If you are not doing anything, come over. It will give you a chance to meet some of the gang here on Chambers."

Marvin went inside the house and returned with three Cokes and some pretzels and chips. "Let's sit at the picnic table near the water."

"How long have you and your family lived here?" Randy asked.

"Mom and Dad got the house from Dad's parents, and I think they bought it in the 1930s from a doctor in Green Bay who was short of money, and this was the only asset he had that was free and clear of debt back then. Anyhow, this is a choice spot where you can see Egg Harbor, Green Island, and the lights of Marinette and Menominee cities. Nice place to spend the summers. Really, the only place Simon and I know in the summer."

"Marvin, I want to swim in the water and play in the sand," said Simon. "Can I play in the sand now?"

"Sure, it's okay with me, but stay out of the water. Jessica is coming over later this evening, and I don't want you wet," Marvin said. We met when I took Simon to a life-skills class. She works with mentally challenged people."

"It must be nice for you because she understands the challenges of taking care of Simon."

"Yes, she does. She also likes to escape from that, so coming here on the weekend and taking a few longer weekends helps her too. Only problem is that Simon is in love with her too. He craves her attention as much as I do sometimes. Sometimes he gets jealous when she kisses me and wants her to kiss him too. Funny, we have to sneak around like teenagers when we want to get affectionate." He laughed. "Jessica gives him a peck on the cheek when he gets moody about us, and that satisfies him."

Marvin's face turned serious. "Simon misses my mom doting on him. Dad was always too busy with work, so he and she stayed here on the island almost all summer taking care of him. But then she died, and Dad had a stroke too, so now it's me and soon Jessica who take care of him."

"That a big responsibility," Randy said.

"Yes, but you do what you have to do. He's a good kid—even though he's twenty-eight now." Marvin looked at Simon as he started digging on the beach with his pail and shovel. "He's a big happy kid. How about a beer while he's playing?"

"Okay. One won't hurt," Randy said. Ten minutes later, they had some canvas chairs at the shore edge, watching Simon play. Sailboats and power boats were cruising around the island and going north and south between the island and the peninsula, toward Fish Creek and Egg Harbor.

Randy walked back toward his house, feeling better than he had felt since his parents' death. He had met two new friends. Now he was looking forward to Simon's birthday party, when he'd meet other neighbors and Marvin's fiancée, Jessica.

Sunday morning: Randy set down his thermos on the picnic table and poured himself a fresh cup of coffee. He watched sailboats traveling on the bay out about one mile. The big motor yachts cruised wherever they wanted because of no wind constraints.

It was a far cry from the morning view he had in prison, where he'd either stare at gray walls or two hundred inmates. He didn't eat breakfast much now, except for an occasional scrambled eggs and toast. He never ate oatmeal because that's what they'd served just about every morning in prison.

Once he was finished with his coffee, he'd cut the grass and get the yard cleaned up in case some of the party guests decided to walk up this way. Most island visitors eventually made their way toward the lighthouse, so he wanted his property to look nice.

After finishing the lawn, he decided he needed a shower. His was an outdoor solar shower with a black-painted jerry can and a gravity-fed hose. The water sometimes became so hot that he'd put cold lake water into it so it wouldn't burn him. Coconut soap lathered up just fine with the hard lake water.

Every day he tried to get two thousand words done or five hours of writing—whichever came first. In most of his novels, the characters got into trouble and ended up in prison. His protagonists were smart but for some reason they decided to take the easy way out, and that led to crime and jail. Often they faced down dangerous villains who loved to intimidate weaker individuals. Eight years in prison, Randy figured, had given him enough characters and stories to keep him busy for several novels.

He printed a map of the island from the internet indicating the location of various houses with little squares. He hoped to put names next to the squares on the map as he met people at the party. As he walked toward the other end of the island, he started to get excited, not because it was Simon's birthday party but because he was doing something normal with normal people. He had not done anything social for a long while.

When he got to Marvin and Simon's house he saw that several people were already there in lawn chairs or on blankets. Tables of food had been set out, and a big banner—"Happy Birthday Simon"—was stretched between two trees. A few families sat on the beach with coolers, beach rafts, and noodles. Marvin had a couple of grills going with brats, chicken, and hamburgers cooking. Next to that was the picnic table set up with all the fixings and side dishes. It looked like many of the families had brought food to pass too. He saw two metal tubs covered with blankets that he surmised had soft drinks and beer.

When Simon saw Randy, he came running over. "Greg, welcome to my party. Do you have a present for me?" Simon bobbed his head from side to side, looking at the large party bag Randy had in his hand. Randy had put art supplies in a Happy Birthday paper bag.

"It's my birthday today, you know. Did you bring me a present?"

Randy couldn't help but laugh, but then he saw a striking black-haired model-like women approach and put her hand on Simon's shoulder.

"Who's this, Simon? Can you introduce me?" Seeing her smile, Randy knew it had to be Marvin's fiancée.

Simon turned to her. "This is Greg. He lives near Sand Bay and the lighthouse. Greg, this is Jessica Bradley, Marvin's girlfriend."

"Actually, I'm Marvin's fiancée," she said, smiling. "I don't think Simon understands the difference. That's okay."

"Marvin told me about you," said Randy. "You're even prettier than he described." He watched as her face blushed.

"You're too kind."

"Here you go, Simon, I hope you like to paint. I got you a watercolor paint tin, paper, and a couple of extra brushes. Maybe you can come and visit me on another day and paint the lighthouse near where I live."

Simon grabbed the bag, looked inside, and then turned toward

Jessica. "Can you and Marvin go with me, and I can visit Greg and paint? Can we do that?"

"Sure, we can do that." She reached up to pat his shoulder. Jessica seemed about five feet four, but as she stood next to Simon, he towered over her. Randy hadn't thought of Simon being big until just now because he and Marvin were about the same size.

"Simon is so excited to get all this attention," Jessica said. "He knows it's his special day. For him, though, we don't talk about how old he is because it really doesn't apply to him. All these people have known him for many years and know his history, but there are a few people who are new to the island or renting for the summer that are just getting to know Simon, so we still have a little educating to do." As she looked at him, Jessica ran her fingers through her long black hair.

Randy smiled, letting her know he understood. "I think I'll let you go and help Marvin, and I'll go introduce myself to my new neighbors who don't know me—which is everyone except you, Simon, and Marvin. I'll see you later."

"Marvin is planning on food being ready in an hour. Help yourself to the refreshments in the meantime."

"I will. I also brought a bottle of wine," Randy said, holding it up and giving it to her.

"Oh good. I'm not much of a beer drinker," she said as she took it from him. "I'll put it in the ice since it's white."

After introducing himself to the couple of families on the beach, Randy walked along the tree line near the water. Glancing back toward Marvin and Simon's house, he saw a woman sitting alone on a lawn chair, staring out at the water. She looked sad—not like the others, who were laughing or in animated conversations with family or neighbors.

Most of the partygoers were island people, but he imagined some were from Green Bay, where Marvin and Simon lived when not on the island. Maybe this sad woman was from the insurance agency Marvin owned or she was a friend of Jessica's.

It looked like she needed a friend, at least someone to talk to. He walked over to the ice cooler and grabbed a Coke, then walked back toward her, leaning against a tree close enough so she couldn't help but notice him. He looked at her but didn't say anything.

She casually turned her head and glanced at him, then turned back to the water.

He cleared his throat. "Excuse me, I'm new to the island. Just moved here a few weeks ago, but I haven't met too many people except Marvin and Simon and now Jessica. This party gives me a chance to meet my neighbors and celebrate Simon's birthday. My name is Greg Chambers."

Her head slowly turned to look at him.

"Are you related to Colonel Talbot Chambers, whom the island is named after?"

"No, I don't think so. I just thought it would be nice to live on an island, and I have the same last name as the island's name. How about you? Do you live on the island, or are you a friend of Marvin and Simon and live off island?"

"Yes. Yes, and no." She seemed put off and didn't want to talk. He watched her head turn back toward the water.

"I hope we'll see each other and become friends."

She kept her eyes looking at the water, but he heard her say in a low voice, barely audible, "I don't think so."

"Sorry, I didn't mean to bother you." He turned and walked away.

CHAPTER FIVE

He got a better reception from a family on the beach with three small boys playing in the sand. The mother, father, and grandparents sat next to a cooler, and they were drinking as they watched the kids play.

Randy introduced himself. They were very friendly. He pulled out his map showing them where he lived and found out they were located near the island's marina. After writing down their names and their location on the map, they made some small talk before he moved back to the food and refreshment area. Now that's the way people should act, he thought. He got a brat and a beer. As he was having his second brat, Jessica came over and sat next to him at a picnic table.

"Are you meeting your neighbors?" Jessica asked. "They're really good people on this island. It's like the island is the matriarch, and families living here are all members of it, you know what I mean?"

"That's a good way of describing it. I am meeting them slowly, and they all seem nice except for that one woman with the black hair sitting by herself. I think she's having a bad day."

"She seems to have a lot of bad days, but she lives on the island, so she was invited. I don't even know her name." Jessica smiled as she looked at Simon in the distance. "He loves playing in the water and sand. This is a treat for him. He loves playing with other kids, but he's starting to realize he's much bigger than the other kids. He loved your present, by the way. How did you know to get him paints?"

"Just blind luck. I liked painting when I was ten years old, so I thought he might too."

"Yes, art helps the motor skills of kids with special needs. They can also see immediate results and can focus on that. They often have short attention spans."

"I'm glad he likes it. He seems like he's a good kid." He took a bite of the brat. "Nice that you know how to work with him."

"Yes. I have Simon to thank for meeting Marvin and…" She paused. Randy watched as she held up her ring finger with the diamond sparkling in the afternoon sunlight. "But the only negative is I never really get away from work when I'm here because Simon is always here too. We have a special bond. Then again, this island"—she spread her arms wide—"and the view and people on the island make it all worthwhile."

He had to agree as he gazed at the water sparkling with afternoon sunlight.

She rose from the table. "I guess I should get up and mingle. I'm hungry too. I think I'll get a brat with lots of sauerkraut on it. It tastes better that way."

"Okay. See you later."

After the candles were lit, twenty-eight of them, and the chocolate birthday cake was cut, Randy moved away from the main center of activity and found a quiet table to eat his slice.

The dark-haired woman strode up to him, but instead of sitting down, she stood across from him, looking down at him.

"Hi again," he said. "Enjoying yourself? The cake is good. You should get some."

"I don't eat stuff with lots of sugar." She was holding a half-empty glass of beer. She had on a pair of aviator glasses, and he watched as she ran her fingers through her hair as she continued looking at him.

"Would you like to sit down?" he asked.

"No. I just wanted to come over and apologize for being jerky to you before. I just don't trust men in general anymore. Men disapprove of me, and you're a man. Besides, I found they don't want me once they discover I'm damaged merchandise. I just wanted to tell you why I was the way I was to you."

"What's your name? You can tell me that, right?"

"I guess I can. It's Trisha Whitcomb."

"My name is Greg."

"Yes, Greg Chambers—like the island. You told me. I'm leaving now. I like my privacy, Greg, so don't stop by unless I invite you." With that, she turned and walked away.

He watched her go, thinking there went someone that needed help. But he wasn't going to let her ruin his day.

"Greg! Greg!" Simon ran toward him with a picture in his hand. He stopped in front of Randy, bouncing from one foot to another, excited just like a ten-year old, except Simon was twenty-eight years of age and the size of a football linebacker. He shoved the picture toward Randy.

"I made this for you. It's a picture of my birthday cake with all the candles."

Randy took the picture and smiled. "Simon, it's very nice. Just like your real cake. And the candles you painted are even lit."

"Yes. I really liked my cake. I had two pieces. Chocolate is my favorite, so I painted it for you," he said, smiling. "Do you like it?"

"Yes, I do. I know just where I'm going to put this painting," he said as he held it up. "I'm going to put it on my refrigerator when I get home later, so you can see it when you visit me, and it will remind you of your special day. How's that?"

"I have to go back and open my presents now. Jessica says I have to thank everyone, so I better go back."

"You left your party just to give me this painting? Thank you, Simon."

But he had turned and was already running back to the group. Randy followed him to rejoin the group, not seeing Trisha. He guessed she had retreated to her house somewhere on the island. Just as well.

Three days later as Randy was working on *Prison Gangs Revolt*, Randy heard footsteps on his screened-in porch, then a familiar voice, "Greg, are you here? I came to see my birthday cake picture."

"Hi, Simon. Come in. I'm in the living room."

Simon entered the house, wide eyed. "I've never been here before, but I wanted to see my picture. Is it on the refrigerator?"

Yep." Randy pointed to the refrigerator at the far end of the open style room. "See, just as I promised." He watched as Simon ambled over to the refrigerator. A big smile appeared on his face.

"You know, I blew all the candles out and made a wish, like Marvin said I should. You want to know what I wished for?"

"I do, but don't tell me or it won't come true."

"Too late. I whispered it to Jessica that I wanted a girlfriend just like her."

"Really. What did she say?"

"Nothing. She smiled and gave me a kiss on the top of my head." Simon pointed to his forehead. "I haven't washed my head there since she kissed me. Can you see the red kiss on my forehead, Greg?"

Randy smiled as he leaned in to look at Simon's forehead. "Just barely."

"I like it when Jessica kisses me. I miss my mommy's kisses. She's dead now. I miss my mommy lots."

"I know how you feel. I miss my mother and father too." He stood up and gave him a hug. "Do you want something to drink? A soft drink or water?"

"No. I just came to say hi and see my picture. The cake is all gone, and I wanted to see it again."

"Well, I'm glad you came. Maybe we should walk back to your house, so Marvin and Jessie don't worry. Did you tell them you were coming here?"

"No. I just wanted to see the cake."

"Let's go back to your house so they don't worry, okay?"

Many paths crisscrossed the island. After they reached Simon's house, Randy was going to knock on the door when he heard some moaning from an upstairs window. He smiled.

"Simon, why don't you show me your favorite place on the island?"

"We have to walk back to the lighthouse. I like to watch the light go around and around."

"Where else do you like to go? I mean, during the day."

"I like to go to the island's marina and look at the boats. I like to go to the big beach near your house and watch the boats there and the people on the boats. I like to look at the pretty women in their swimming suits that ride on the boats."

"You do? Let's go to the marina, and I'll show you my boat."

Simon nodded his head yes.

When they got to the island's private marina, Randy was surprised to see a solitary woman sitting, facing Fish Creek, with its two marinas and, sprinkled along the shoreline, many white homes and cottages. As he got closer, he saw it was Trisha. Simon and Randy didn't say anything to her as they walked to Randy's slip.

"Here's my boat, Simon. What do you think?"

"It's small, Greg. Not like the others here."

"Yes, it is, but I'm going to get a bigger sailboat someday. I'll keep this other aluminum fishing boat for running to Fish Creek for supplies."

"Will you take me along when you go sailing?" Simon asked, excitedly hopping back and forth.

Randy noticed that Trisha had turned her head and smiled. Well, that's something: she can smile. She had a nice smile, and it changed her whole demeanor.

"If Marvin says it's all right, it's all right with me," Randy said, "but you'll have to listen to me and do what I tell you. Okay?"

"Oh, that would be so neat." He turned toward Trisha and pointed. "Maybe she'd like to go with us, if she's nice to me?"

"We'll see about that." As he said that, her smile disappeared, and her head snapped back to the view of Fish Creek. "Let's head back to your house so Marvin and Jessie don't worry."

"Okay."

Out of the corner of his eye, he saw Trisha watching them go back.

CHAPTER SIX

Two days later, Randy had just finished cutting the grass around his cabin and was inside on the screen porch having some iced tea when he heard a knock at his back door.

Getting up, he went to the back door and looked out the kitchen window. As he approached the door, he was surprised to see Trisha standing there. He opened the door and smiled. "Hello. What do I owe this unexpected visit to?"

She shuffled her feet before her eyes met his. "Can I come in? That iced tea looks good."

He looked at the condensation on his iced glass. "It's sun tea I made yesterday. Would you like some?" After she nodded yes, he said, "Besides Simon and the real estate broker who sold me the cabin, you're practically my first visitor."

"Thank you. I'm kind of thirsty, with all the heat and humidity. Do you have enough?"

"I do. Come in, and I'll get you a glass." He went to his battery-powered refrigerator and got out the big jar of sun tea and a few ice cubes. "Sugar?"

"No, plain is okay."

Handing it to her, he said. "Let's go out on the porch. It'll be cooler out there with the breeze and shade."

He watched Trisha take in the furnishings of the screened-in porch. Randy thought he knew where Trisha was going to end up sitting. Each piece of the rattan furniture had deep worn depressions in the middle of the cushions, so it was natural to sit in the comfy spots.

She seemed like an emotional time bomb ready to explode. He was also sure it wouldn't be long before she started criticizing the decorations. He was right!

"You sure won't get an award for the decorations and furniture from *House Beautiful*."

"Yeah, I know, but it's okay for me. I'm not trying to impress anyone with this stuff."

"I guess not. Everything came with the house, right?"

"Yes, you're correct. Anyway, for me it's only a summer residence. I'm an author. I need to accumulate more royalty checks to get nice furniture. Or if you want the truth, I'd rather have a bigger boat. Right now, the cottage suits me just fine." He sipped his iced tea. Finally, he asked again, "What do I owe this visit to?"

She sipped her tea, looked back at him, and sighed.

"Where do I start?"

"How about how much you like the way the house is decorated? Classic cottage furniture from the '60s and '80s."

She smiled weakly before turning toward the screened window, then adjusting herself in the seat. "I'm here for two reasons.

First, I saw how you acted with Simon at the island's marina the other day."

"Yes. I saw you sitting there."

"You were friendly, caring, patient. I think you're different than most men I've known."

"Different? Why would you say that? You hardly know me."

"It was hard for me to come here, but I saw how you looked at me when you were leaving the marina. Most men think I'm damaged merchandise."

"Why would you say that? Tell me why you think you're damaged."

"I'm not going to go into why now. Maybe later. You seem like a nice guy, that's all. Not like most people I've been around lately."

She got up and started pacing. "I knew I shouldn't have come here." She paused and stood still, looking out through the trees at the water. After about fifteen seconds, she turned. "When you said you might go boating yesterday, at that moment, I wanted to go too. It sounded like fun. That's my second reason for coming. Can I go boating with you?"

He hadn't seen that coming. "Sure, I'll take you. Next time I go I'll call you or stop by your cabin." He got up and went to his desk and got the island map. He unfolded it and brought it over to her. "Where's your cabin?"

She looked at the map and pointed to a black square. "Right here. I'd rather you called. I'm not ready to have guests. I'll meet you at the marina."

"Fine. Give me your cell phone number, and I'll call you."

He watched as she wrote it down.

"Thanks for the iced tea," she said. "I look forward to the boating."

"Okay, maybe in the next couple of days. How's that?"

"That's fine. I'll be ready. Goodbye, Greg."

He watched her leave and walk down the path to her cabin. *Weird woman who's hurting inside.*

Being a writer meant he had to write every day, but Randy found it hard to work on his novel, *Prison Revolt* that afternoon. He had finished the first draft earlier but was now in the rewriting.

His editor had set a deadline of September 15. He was plugging along, but what he wrote was junk. Damn that Trisha, he thought. Why couldn't he get her out of his mind? He had to wonder why she considered herself damaged goods. Maybe it was just her outlook on life that was damaged. Enough of this, he thought. He backed up his writing on his zip drive and turned off the computer.

As it was a nice summer day, he decided to go sailing on the *Flying Scot,* seeking peace and tranquility while hearing the waves against the hull. He slipped on his boating shoes and swim trunks and headed to the island's marina for a short sail.

When he got to his slip, he saw another boat in the visiting transit slip. It was an older Catalina 27 sailboat and had a "For Sale" sign taped to the hull with a phone number.

The boat's hatch was open, so he poked around inside. He wanted a bigger boat with an inboard engine, a large sleeping berth in the bow, and a full-sized pull-out bed in the main cabin, plus a bathroom—or head, as boaters call it—something he didn't have on his *Flying Scot*. Most important, this boat fit his marina slip. He called the number on the sign.

Three hours later, after a short demo cruise, he wrote the owner a check and bought the boat. Sitting in the cockpit of his new boat, he celebrated with a glass of iced tea. He named his new boat *Island Girl*.

A couple of days later, while Randy sat drinking coffee he heard, "Greg, Greg!"

Simon was at the door, perhaps ready to hang another watercolor painting on the refrigerator. At this rate Randy was going to have to find new places to hang more pictures. He loved that Simon was frequently coming over. Randy saw the joy on Simon's face every time he arrived with new artwork.

"What do you have for me this time?" he said.

"I painted Trisha, the lady who was sitting at the end of the pier when we went to look at boats. She was at the beach, and I painted her lying on the sand. She wasn't too happy that I was painting her, but when I showed her the picture, she smiled, so I guess it was okay. She wasn't in a swimsuit but shorts and a tee shirt."

Randy looked at the painting. It was a stick figure except for the head and face. The frown on Trisha's lips was noticeable. It must be tough to go through life pissed off at everyone.

"Simon, this is nice. Let's put it here on the porch." He went to his junk drawer and got a nail and hammer. "Should we put it here?"

"That's good, Greg."

He pounded a small nail into an exposed two-by-four on the screened-in-porch and hung the painting.

"What do you think, Simon?"

"It looks nice. Trisha will like it when she sees it."

"Why do you say that?"

"She said she was going sailing with you, so I think she'll see it when she comes back here."

Randy looked at Simon, admiring his painting.

"I'm going to paint a picture of your new boat. I'm excited to ride on it today. Are we going to take Trisha too?"

"Do you want her to come along, or should just you and I go? If you'd rather it be just us boys, that's okay. I can take her out another day."

"She can go. I like older women. Sometimes I look at women in the magazines Marvin has hidden in his closet. He doesn't know that I know where he keeps them, but I do. I like the pictures of the naked woman. I like peeking at Jessie when she's naked, getting dressed or coming out of the shower. She doesn't like that. She gets mad. I don't like it when she's mad at me. Then I get sad, so I have to be careful and hide or she yells at me. Then Marvin gets angry, and both yell at me."

Randy smiled, trying not to laugh at the inquisitive nature of Simon. "I can imagine how upsetting that is to them both," he said.

"I guess. But later they calm down and are nice again. They

tell me not to do that again, but I still do." He laughed. "I really like looking at them when they're naked and on top of each other at night. They think I'm asleep, but I get up and open their bedroom door a crack, so they don't see me. I want to touch Jessica like Marvin does, but when I touch her breast like he does, she slaps my hand." He sighed. "She says only Marvin can do that, because he's special to her."

"Yes. That's the way it works, Simon. Both people are special to each other. That doesn't mean they don't love you."

Simon nodded his head yes. "I guess so."

Randy clapped his hands. "Let go and get Trisha, and then we'll all go sailing. Just the three of us, okay? I'll call her now."

"Yes, let's go sailing."

When Randy and Simon arrived at Trisha's cabin, she was on the stoop, waiting for them. She stood up with a cooler and a small plastic bag. "The cooler's got a few beers, sodas, and bottles of water. I made some tuna sandwiches and brought a bag of chips. I know we'll get hungry later. This so nice of you to include me with you and Simon."

"Both Simon and I are looking forward to sailing. Having you join us makes it even more special."

Once at *Island Girl*, Randy slid the hatch boards out and stowed everything away. Next he took the sail cover off the boom and attached the main halyard to the mainsail. Then he started up the fourteen-horse diesel inboard engine and let it warm up. After a few minutes, he cast off the lines and slowly backed out of the slip, motoring through the breakwater opening.

Randy pointed *Island Girl* toward Fish Creek and the deeper water before turning north toward the villages of Ephraim and Sister Bay. He turned the boat into the wind and then raised the mainsail. Once that was done, he rolled out the Genoa sail. With the sails set, he turned off the engine. He turned the wheel, moving the boat so the wind caught its sails. At that point, the only thing the three of them heard was the waves lapping against the hull.

Simon squealed with delight as the boat heeled over slightly, and they started sailing along the green tree-lined Peninsula State Park shoreline toward Ephraim and Horseshoe Island.

"Oh, Greg, this is so nice. I needed this," Trisha said. "Thank you."

"It's my pleasure." As he tipped his cap, he said, "It's nice to have company. I get tired sailing by myself."

"Trisha, can I have a sandwich and a soda?" Simon asked.

"Sure. Greg? There's plenty."

"I'll have a soda if you don't mind," he said.

Trisha nimbly got up, went down below into the cabin, and brought up two sandwiches, two sodas, and a beer.

"I think I'll have a beer," she said. "I haven't had one since Simon's birthday party. I think I'm ready for one, and I'm not driving."

The three toasted with their respective cans, all of them laughing when Simon toasted a little too vigorously and spilled some of his soda. Trisha wiped up the spill with her napkin.

"Thank you," Randy said. "If you didn't wipe up the spill, the cockpit would get sticky, and the flies would descend on us later. They love sugar."

Over the next hour and a half, Randy explained how to work the boat to Simon as they sailed past Ephraim's Eagle Harbor, and then to Sister Bay and the Sister Islands, before turning around and heading back toward Chambers Island.

Thirty minutes later, Randy saw a black line of clouds moving toward them fast. At least he saw no lightning. He jumped up.

"Trisha, slide over, behind the wheel, and steer the boat straight. I'm going to drop the mainsail onto the boom, lash it down, and roll up the front sail. We'll motor until this squall passes us. Just turn the wheel like you're driving a car to keep the boat going straight into the wind." He moved fast and got everything down and secured before the rain and wind hit.

When the gust of wind and rain slammed into them, the boat heeled over in a sudden tip but then righted itself because of the heavy keel. Still, the wind kept the boat tipped at a fifteen-degree angle because Randy kept the boat motoring and on course back toward Chambers Island.

Simon started laughing and was excited by the wild ride and rain. Trisha, on the other hand, screamed as the gust hit the boat.

Seeing fear in her eyes, Randy said, "Don't worry. We're fine. Just rain and a little wind. We'll duck into the small semicircular harbor at Horseshoe Island just ahead. We'll motor around in tight circles and let the storm pass." The timing was right as they approached the opening of the horseshoe shape, which provided shelter against northern winds. Here the water was relatively calm. He put the boat's engine into neutral and angled the boat into the opening, continuing to turn in tight circles, avoiding two anchored boats until the storm passed.

But that didn't seem to do the trick for Trisha. She was still terrified.

The squall passed, the wind died, but buckets of rain continued to come down, soaking them all to the skin. It was as if they were in a shower with their clothes on. The good news was it was a warm rain.

When the rain finally stopped and Randy started motoring toward Chambers Island, Randy looked at Trisha and had to think of a wet T-shirt party back in college. Trisha wore a white T-shirt with DOOR COUNTY stenciled across the top, but soaking wet she basically looked naked. Her chest and breasts were exposed to them.

Seeming to understand, she said. "I don't wear a bra, because wearing one still hurts my breasts from my surgery. I know I should have worn a bra today, but I didn't think it was going to rain. It was perfect when we left."

Randy saw tears form, or was it from the rain? It didn't make any difference because that's when Simon saw her breasts and said, "Trisha, your boobies look funny. They have red marks on them like someone took a red crayon and colored them. They don't look like Jessica's." He poked one of them with his finger.

Trisha slapped his face and screamed, "Don't touch me there or anywhere." Then she pushed his hand and him away from her.

Randy was shocked. He never expected this today. He sat steering the boat, looking at the two. Simon wailed like a kid getting his hand caught in a car door. Trisha stood up to run but realized there was no place for her to go and sat down again, crossing her basically naked chest with her arms.

Randy put the autopilot on so the boat would motor straight and went down below into the cabin and got her a dry jacket to wear over her soaked shirt.

After five minutes, both of the passengers had stopped their crying. Each wedged as far away as possible in opposite corners of the cockpit.

Simon was the first to talk between sobs. "I'm sorry, Trisha, I didn't mean to hurt you. It's just your boobies look funny with the marks on then, different than Jessica's. I know I'm not supposed to look at hers, or yours, but I like looking at boobies, even yours, the way they look."

Trisha recognized that Simon intended no malice, and said, "I'm sorry too, Simon, for hitting you. You didn't understand what you saw."

With that apology from Trisha, Simon was good with the world. "Greg, can I have a soda and a candy bar? I'm thirsty and hungry."

Going down below, he retrieved both from the cooler and continued back toward the island's marina.

Simon was happy, eating, drinking, and singing and humming.

Trisha faced forward, deep in her own thoughts until Randy turned the boat into the marina and tied up.

"I'm sorry, Greg," she said. "Simon just caught me by surprise, and my breasts still hurt from my surgery. I didn't realize it was going to rain. It was such a nice day until it rained and stormed. It was perfect until then."

"I understand how you feel. Sorry it kind of wrecked your day."

"Life's not fair. Look at Simon." She pointed to herself. "And me, I had everything going for me. I was a model and on TV. I had a great marriage. At least I thought I did. Then I got breast cancer, and I lost everything. I'm damaged goods now."

Randy looked down at his feet and then up at her, giving her sheepish smile.

"What are you smiling at?" she asked testily.

"Trisha, you aren't damaged goods. You might have scars on your breasts, but real beauty comes from within. It's the inside, not the outside that matters," he said, tapping his chest. "If you don't change your attitude, that would be the real damage."

He could tell she was furious. It was like a slap to her face. When he tied up the boat, she jumped up and off the boat.

Standing on the dock, she screamed at him, "Fuck you. You don't know what it feels like to lose everything. Now you know why I say I'm damaged goods, asshole. It's just like you to give me that shit-ass advice." She started crying again, turned, and ran away.

CHAPTER SEVEN

A fun day on the water had turned into disaster. Randy flaked the mainsail on the boom and then put the sail cover on. Putting the cockpit cushions down below, he noticed that Trisha had left her cooler and bag of food, and he placed them in the cockpit. He put the hatch boards in and slid the cabin top closed.

He and Simon walked back to Simon's cabin. Seeing Marvin and Jessie talking on the deck, he explained about the sail, the rain, and eventually about Simon touching Trisha.

"Don't get too angry at him," said Randy. "He didn't mean anything by it. He'll probably explain it all to you. He had a good time and—outside of the commotion with Trisha—he was a joy to have sailing."

After having a beer with them, he started toward Trisha house with the cooler and food—a good excuse to try to talk to her again. He hoped she had calmed down by then and he could start a friendship. He wasn't sure why he wanted to, but something about her he liked.

He knocked on her door and waited. After three minutes

hearing nothing, he knocked again, this time louder.

"Go away," she yelled. "I don't want to see you or talk about it."

"I have your cooler and food."

"Leave it on the stoop. I'll get it later."

"I'm not leaving until we talk about what happened today."

"You're going to be waiting a long time," she yelled back.

He decided to call her bluff and sat down on an Adirondack chair a few feet from the back door. He was surprised there were two chairs facing each other. She must have company sometimes. He sat down and waited.

Forty-five minutes later, he had dozed off when he heard the back door open. Opening his eyes, he saw her standing in the doorway with a black, sleeveless shirt and red shorts. She was barefoot.

"I thought I told you I wasn't going to talk to you."

"We need to settle all this damage shit. It's a small island, and we need to work out a truce." He watched her just stand in the doorway, trying to decide what to do. Eventually she slumped her shoulders in resignation and walked toward him. She took a seat, facing him, in the other chair.

Her eyes got misty as she folded her hands in her lap. "Let me tell you how things used to be. Maybe you'll know why I feel the way I do."

Randy nodded. "I'm listening."

"Adam, my ex-husband, and I met when I was a TV reporter doing a story for the station I worked for in Chicago. It was about the paper industry in the Fox River Valley area. The companies were trying to cut down on the pollution caused by the paper-making process. It's not just in the Fox River Valley in Wisconsin, but all over the United States. Adam worked in the PR department for the company I was focusing on. I was twenty-seven, young, and a reporter who happened to have a brain to go along with the good looks. I graduated from Northwestern's Communication and Journalism school in Chicago. It's one of the best in the country, so many graduates get hired by the Chicago stations or go on to other major cities. I was from the Evanston, Illinois, area, so I wanted to stay local. Anyhow, Adam was handsome and smart and came from an influential family. His father was a vice president and from one of the founding families of the paper company. Anyhow, we started going out after the story ran, and that summer I started coming up here to the family cabin on Chambers Island.

"He lived in Green Bay, on the river, so both places were an easy drive for me from Chicago. The long and short of it all was we fell in love, got married, and were supposed to live happily ever after. I moved up to Green Bay and got a reporting job for one of the local stations and did modeling on the side.

"We were happy for six years, then our lives changed forever after I felt a lump on my right breast while taking a shower. I went in to get it checked, thinking it would be just a fatty cyst or something. Nothing major, I thought, but…" She trailed off.

He watched a tear slide down her cheek. She turned away, looking toward the water, sunlight shimmering on it through the maple trees. After a few moments, she turned back.

"The doctor told me I had cancer, and after a CAT scan, they found it was in my lymph nodes too. I couldn't look to Adam for support. He almost accused me of doing something to get the cancer. He got mean toward me when I said I was going to have surgery on my breasts and remove the lymph nodes, and then have chemo. He wouldn't even drive me to the hospital. I had to have a friend do it. He couldn't handle that I was no longer his perfect wife, someone he could be proud of and show off. Even when I told him I was going to have breast reconstruction later, so I'd be like before, he still didn't like it. Not long after, he filed for divorce.

"Not only did I have to fight for my life against the cancer, but I felt betrayed by his lack of support, so I went after what hurt him the most. It wasn't money. It was this cabin. He loved it. His parents had given it to us as a wedding present, so I took it. He cried when I was given it and alimony. I wanted to hurt him so bad, and I did. I love being in Door County and on this island."

"Yes, Door County has that effect on many people. I've lived here almost my whole life, so I know what you mean. I'm sorry about the cancer and your divorce."

"My family had been coming up from the Chicago area since I was a kid. I think most of Chicago comes up here sometime or another. This island is really special and peaceful all year—not like it can get on the peninsula when it's packed with people."

Randy nodded. "Yes. That's why I bought the place over here: to get away from the throngs of summer people. It's like a zoo with all the tourists."

"Do you see why I say I'm damaged merchandise, and I don't trust men?"

Randy cleared his throat, took a drink of a beer he grabbed

from her cooler, and said, "Not all men are like your ex, Adam. Most men would have stayed by your side. Just look at the survival stories on YouTube. A large number of husbands, boyfriends, brothers, and fathers get their hair shaved or cut off in support and go above and beyond for their loved one. Unfortunately, your ex sounds like a real asshole."

She got up and collected her cooler and the leftover food before reaching over and touching his hand. "Now you know. I want to go in now and lie down. It's been a long afternoon." She handed him back his jacket. "Here's your jacket you gave me to cover up. I appreciated it. I had a good time sailing and would love to do it again if you're willing to take a chance again with me."

"I'd love to."

Randy walked back to his cabin, his thoughts still on Trisha. He knew the best avenue for him and her was just to be friends. He wished she could realize that not all men were like her ex, Adam. She had to like herself, and right now he wasn't sure she liked anything or anyone except the island and her house. Sailing might help.

Later that night, he felt like a few beers and some time at the beach near his house. Getting three beers out of the refrigerator, he put them into his cooler and headed to the beach.

Even after what had happened here, this beach was his favorite place to sit. After finishing two beers, he realized he was at almost the same spot as he'd been that long-ago night with Ingrid.

Randy had thought Ingrid loved him. Or maybe she was just looking for something she never got growing up, someone who cared for her like a mother or father should. Too bad she never found that love. He had tried.

Was that what Trisha was doing too: trying to find answers? Escaping to a safe place, or hiding out? She didn't kill anyone, but she had a lot of anger against her husband, men, and life in general.

Maybe he was drawn to Trisha because he wanted to prove to himself he was a good, compassionate man, not a killer. Randy grabbed his last beer and brought it to his lips.

He stopped, then slowly tipped the can and its contents to the sand. Drinking too much beer that night was what had gotten him into trouble.

It was time to get back on track with his investigation and honor his vow to his parents. He needed to call Detective Jenkins. He needed to get off his ass.

He sat on the beach, looking at the red and green bow lights of passing boats before finally getting to his feet. It must have been a couple of hours because the moon had risen, and when he looked at his watch, it was eleven o'clock. He dusted the sand off his pants and turned to walk back to his cabin. It had been a long day and night, and as with his long nights of contemplation in prison, he still had no answers about Ingrid.

The next morning he called Jenkins's number, but he was unavailable. He asked if he could stop by again for some help and advise on how to continue with his investigation. When he hung up he really didn't think he'd hear anything from Detective Jenkins, but a few hours later, he got a call.

"Funny you should call. I do have a couple of leads for you."

CHAPTER EIGHT

"Don't get your hopes up," said the detective, "but I ran searches in our files to see if there was any activity for Ingrid Karlsen. I got two hits that might help you."

"I'd appreciate anything. Not sure where to start, so this will help."

"Here's what I got. Seems like she had a sexual harassment complaint against two men. One was against a Ramon Rodrigo, a short-order cook at a café in Baileys Harbor, where Ingrid and he worked for a short time. She was a waitress, and he was a cook.

"Seems Rodrigo had been harassing her often, but one day toward the end of her shift, he caught her in the pantry when no one was around and aggressively started touching her breasts and pulled her panties down and tried to enter her. When she screamed, it raised the attention of the owner's wife in the café's dining room, and she fired him on the spot. He said that day to everyone there that he'd get revenge for getting fired. He told the owner's wife that Ingrid had been a real cock tease, and she really wanted it. Ingrid said to the detective investigating that she did like him but not that way, because he tried to rape her. The owner's wife was the one that brought it to our attention. It went no further because Ingrid never pressed charges. That was fifteen years ago, and Rodrigo's in Illinois now—in prison for rape. Don't think he tried to do anything against her after being fired, but if you want, you can go visit him in Joliet."

"Thanks, I might. What about the other guy?"

"The second complaint filed by Ingrid was against a Jimmy DeLeo, a carpenter who was building an extra bath and bedroom on Chambers Island for the Jacobs family. Seems Ingrid had been involved with Marvin Jacobs, the oldest son of the cabin owner."

"Really. That's interesting."

Jenkins nodded. "They had a hot and heavy romance going on. According to Jimmy, while he was working out there he saw what was going on, approached Ingrid when Marvin wasn't there, and tried to get a piece of the action when Marvin wasn't around. Jimmy told the cops she had been agreeable, because, she said, he seemed like a good guy and was sexy and was always nice. I guess they did it a few times. Jimmy said Ingrid liked anyone who was nice to her. He said she was needy and liked to party. Eventually she could see it wasn't going to go the way she wanted it. She told the detective investigating the case she liked Marvin better with all his benefits and being out there, drinking, and the sex was good with him. Eventually Jimmy was making too many demands on her, and toward the end, Marvin caught him forcing himself on her. He waited until the cabin was finished, and then he and Marvin got into a big fight. When Jimmy left the project, he threatened Ingrid."

"Threatened her? Like how?"

"Just said she'd be sorry, and he'd make her pay big time. That's when she called our department, and we talked to him."

"The person who killed Ingrid had to get out there with a boat and use it to escape," Randy said. "Jimmy had a boat to get back and forth when bringing building supplies. That could explain how he got out there the night she died."

"Could be, but once again she didn't press charges. She did continue to go to the cabin and be with Marvin. She and Marvin must have patched things up," Jenkins said.

"I just met Marvin and his brother, Simon, plus his fiancée, Jessica. I know this all happened like ten or eleven years ago, but Marvin seems like a good guy. I will check up on this DeLeo guy. Do you know where he is now?"

"Last address we have is in Green Bay. No complaints since then." Jenkin paused. "That's all I have for you. Like I said when you were here before, you're the guy that comes up as the number-one person that did it. Until I get something else, in my opinion, you did it."

Randy jumped at his comment and just looked at his phone in disbelief. "I didn't do it! And I'll prove it." He paused, then said, "I appreciate your help." He clicked off, not wanting to hear anymore. "Fuck him."

Randy had not known Ingrid was seeing Marvin back then. But he guessed he didn't know a lot about Ingrid. One thing Randy did know: she wanted to be accepted and needed to be loved. She told him she never got that from her parents or the foster homes she had been placed in growing up.

"You were always kind and caring to me, Randy," he remembered her saying to him one night, after they'd gotten ice cream in Ephraim at Wilson's. "You and your parents treated me the same way." That's why she always came back to him when others weren't so nice.

———

Later that day, after Randy tied up the boat at the Fish Creek municipal dock, he walked to his house to get the car and drive to Sister Bay's Piggly Wiggly for his bimonthly shopping. He didn't need a lot of stuff, but he liked to get fresh vegetables; also, soda, tea for his sun tea, and beer and wine in case he had guests, which would be Simon, Marvin, Jessica, and now Trisha. He bought soup, chili, and two boxes of brats that were on special. Never can have enough brats, he thought, having grown up in Wisconsin. Then there was bottled spaghetti sauce and several boxes of paste, plus two bags of apples, and he was done. Loading up the car, he headed back to Fish Creek.

Feeling like a burger, he decided to stop at Bayside Bar for a hamburger special and maybe a Bloody Mary for a change. He remembered the Bayside made good Bloody Marys. He knew none of the stuff in the back seat needed refrigeration, at least not for a few hours. After finding a parking spot in back, he walked in and sat at the bar. It was a little early for the lunch crowd, so he had his choice of stools.

After ordering he sipped his Bloody Mary, enjoying the semiquiet, unusual for this bar in Fish Creek, and especially for Door County this time of the year.

A big construction-worker type wearing a dirty, bright-yellow-green T-shirt took the stool next to him. The man looked hot and dirty and had a scruffy beard, sweat-stained Green Bay Packers hat, big work boots, and dirt-stained blue jean shorts. Working construction, or whatever field he was evidently in, gets you dirty, Randy thought. Randy didn't think much of it.

After a minute or two, the guy tried to strike up a conversation. "You from Illinois or from Wisconsin?"

Randy looked over. "Wisconsin."

"Where in Wisconsin?"

"I live on Chambers Island in the summer, and here in Fish Creek in the nonisland months."

"Must be nice on the island. Never been back on the island since about ten years ago. Used to go there a lot in an old aluminum fishing boat I had. Partied a lot at Sandy Bay. Nice spot. We'd get beer, hot dogs, et cetera and party all day. It was never hard to get some women that like to drink and have fun."

"Yeah. That hasn't changed much over the years. Seems like the boats are bigger, but it's still popular."

The guy drained his first beer and ordered a second as he waited for his lunch. "I just had an old aluminum fishing boat with a fifteen-horse outboard on it, but it worked. We'd get three couples, squeezed into that small boat, and party at night with a campfire. We really had a good time of it. Sometimes we'd have sex if it weren't too crowded. I remember this one girl who hung around with our group. She was a wild one. She'd do it with anyone she happened to be with. I had her a few times, and she was great. She loved to be on top. Liked to control everything. Turned out she must have fooled around one too many times, because she ended up being killed. Drowned by some guy. Too bad, I would have loved to have sex with her a few more times."

Randy looked at the guy. He couldn't believe what he was hearing. "You said nine or ten years ago. Just curious, do you know what her name was?"

"Some Norwegian name. Ingrid. That's it."

Randy stared at him. "Ingrid?"

"Yeah. I quit going out there because I knocked up my girlfriend, plus the group fell apart a short time after the drowning, and I sold my boat. I remember some guy got convicted. Too bad, she was a great fuck. But then I had to get married around that time. It was the honorable thing to do back then. Not like now. We'd just live together. Hell, I got two more boys after the first one. We got married after the second one was born, so I guess things turned out okay."

They both ate their hamburgers in silence.

Finally, the guy wiped his greasy hands on his pants, wiped his beard with a napkin, and stood up.

"I miss my little fishing boat. I haven't been back since. Someday I'll have to rent one of those pontoon boats in town here and go back to Chambers with my wife and kids. But I'll tell you what, I remember those nights, having a good time. Especially with that one that died."

Randy sat quietly.

"Nice talking to you. Got to go. Maybe see you out there on the island?"

"Sure. Have a good rest of your afternoon." He watched as the guy walked out into the bright sunlight. He looked at his half-finished burger, his appetite lost. Did this guy just confirm what he thought about Ingrid being needy for any kind of relationship that made her feel wanted?

Randy had known Ingrid was popular in high school. Now he realized why. If what this guy said was true, maybe one of her lovers got jealous, had seen Randy and her sailing out to Chambers Island that afternoon, and had followed.

After he got back to the island and had put away his food, Randy walked to Sand Bay. No beer as a companion, just a bottle of water. He sat in damp sand near the water's edge, close to the spot he remembered dozing off after making love to Ingrid. He had missed signs that she was fooling around on him, and he hadn't known what she did and who she saw when he was away at the university in Madison. Maybe he'd even been unaware when he'd been up here in the summers, working construction to help pay for school. It seemed he was always exhausted.

It was a warm, sunny afternoon, with little wind. The island's bay was occupied with about six powerboats and people playing in the water. The youngest beachgoers were with their parents, building castles and digging with the bright plastic shovels.

Summertime in Door County could be great, Randy thought.

Then he remembered that night, a lifeless naked body rolling gently back and forth at the waterline, right where the kids were now playing.

Ingrid was just like a piece of driftwood he saw today, just a few feet from the same spot.

He sat there for another half an hour. Ingrid might have been unfaithful to him and an easy fuck, like the guy said, but that didn't explain who had killed her while Randy slept off his beer stupor that night.

At least, thanks to Detective Jenkins, he had two prospects now.

It was almost a six-hour drive, just shy of three hundred miles from Fish Creek to the new prison called Stateville Correctional Center near Joliet, Illinois. It took Randy over a week to get approval to visit Ramon Rodrigo. Being a convicted felon had created problems. Randy had to get the warden's approval. He enlisted the help of Detective Jenkins to get that approval and speed up the process.

Once at the prison, Randy had to take everything out of his pockets, placing his keys, wallet, watch, and cell phone into a small locker. Then he was checked off the approved visitor's list and directed to a numbered table in a large room.

As he waited to see Rodrigo, he thought of his mother and dad. He realized now how taxing it was just to visit someone in prison.

An hour later, Rodrigo was led in. If a prisoner didn't want to see a visitor, they could refuse the visit, but Randy was hoping he'd meet with him.

Rodrigo didn't know who he was. Even so, the convict was either curious or just happy to get a break in his daily routine.

Rodrigo walked to his table, confusion etched on his face. With a mild Spanish accent, he asked, "Do I know you? Why am I seeing you?"

"Sit down, and I'll explain."

He pulled the chair back and sat down, shaking his head.

"I'm Randy Daggett from Fish Creek. Does the name ring a bell?"

"Fish Creek does, but I haven't been back there in ten or eleven years. Your name doesn't mean anything to me. Why, should I know you?"

"Does the name Ingrid Karlsen ring a bell with you?"

"That bitch got me fired from my job. I didn't do anything that she didn't want. She was a horny bitch. She liked to tease me, and she was good at it. I was nice to her, made her favorite sandwich, and gave her desserts. She knew I didn't do that for anyone but her. She liked that and me, she said."

"But you got fired for going too far."

"Yeah. I used to keep tequila stashed behind pickles in the cupboard and would take a shot when things were slow. One day

I guess I took too many. Because it was slow for everyone, Ingrid was spending more time than usual with me. She was wearing a short, short tennis type of skirt and a thong. One thing led to another, I lifted up the skirt, slid the thong to the side…That's when the owner came in, saw what was happening. Ingrid started yelling, I think to protect her fucking job. But she had wanted it, man. The owner fired me and called the cops. The cops tracked me down and were going to arrest me, but Ingrid didn't press charges. She told them it was all a misunderstanding."

"You got pretty angry at the time, said you'd make her pay—or something like that?"

"Yeah, I was pretty mad about the whole thing. I like living and working in Door County. It was like being on vacation."

"Did you see Ingrid again?"

"I would have liked to. She was a screwed-up girl, looking for somebody to take care of her. I wasn't the guy she was looking for. I'm not sure if she ever found that guy. I would have stayed up there, but this local detective strongly suggested I leave the county, or they'd bring some charges against me. I should have called their bluff because I went to Chicago and got into trouble there. The one-eyed monster has no conscience."

Randy watched as he laughed at his joke.

"Now I'm in this fucking prison for fifteen years for rape. I didn't rape anyone. Just like with Ingrid, it was a misunderstanding. Of course the fucking jury didn't believe me."

"Where were you on July 14 that summer?" Randy asked.

"Probably in Chicago. I was working at some hotel cooking.

That's what I did. I worked just about every night. It was an shitty job, but the pay was good. Why are you so interested in that date? Hell, that's over ten years ago. Where were you that day?"

"I was with Ingrid that night, the night she died."

"What! You think I killed her? Man, I didn't kill her. I didn't kill anyone. If you were with her, you probably know who killed her. Hell, it might have been you!"

Randy moved his chair closer to Ramon. "I got convicted for killing her, but I didn't do it. I think you did."

Randy watched as his eyes got big for a second, then Rodrigo started laughing. He pointed his finger at Randy, speaking loudly so everyone in the room could hear: "This guy got convicted for killing someone, and now he's here trying to say I did it! What a sorry fucker. I ain't talking to you anymore."

He stood up. "Guard, I'm done here. Take me back to my cell. I don't want to talk anymore to this motherfucker."

Randy didn't know what to say, but he knew he wasn't going to get any more out of Ramon Rodrigo.

It was a long drive back to Fish Creek. He didn't have much to show for his efforts. Ramon was in Chicago working at the time of her death it appeared, though he had one less suspect in Ingrid's death.

CHAPTER NINE

The next day, walking back to his cabin after checking on his boat, he was surprised to see Trisha walking toward him with a smile on her face.

"Hello. I stopped by your cabin just now, but you weren't there, so then I thought you might be at the beach or the marina."

"You were looking for me?" he asked. "What did I do?"

"I appreciated our little talk the other day, and I was wondering if you'd like to come over for dinner tonight. I know it's short notice."

"For dinner?" he said, looking at her and noticing a change. Maybe she'd done something with her hair. She'd even put on mascara. He noticed how green her eyes were—almost the color of emeralds, like the earrings his mother had worn when she and Dad went out for a special dinner. He couldn't help but notice how pretty Trisha looked.

"I'd love to. I get tired of eating alone and my own cooking. You know, chili, hot dogs, or spaghetti. Can I bring something?'

"Oh, you mean bachelor food?" she said and laughed. "I have

everything I need, but if you like you can bring some of that sun tea you make. I'll have wine with the fish I'm going to cook. Do you like fish?"

"Sure. I haven't had any for a while. Is it salmon?"

"No, smallmouth bass. I caught them at the island's marina this morning. When I was little, my dad and mom would go to a cabin in northern Wisconsin and then come here for a week. The sunfish and blue gills would hang under the pier and around the docks on the lake. Back then I got to be pretty good at catching them, even cleaning them. The fish do the same thing here with the finger piers that separate the boats and around the base of the retaining wall."

"You're right. I see them in those spots when I go to my boat."

"Sometimes there's even trout there in the spring, but the waters are too warm now, so it's just bass and pan fish. I caught a couple of bass."

"Bass is good. I'll make sun tea. What time would you like me to come over?"

"How about six? Should still be light but cooler."

"Okay. I'll see you tonight." He watched as she turned and headed back to her cabin. He noticed the little sashay of her hips as she walked away. Was he imagining that? He didn't know, but he liked the look.

———

He had just set out the jar of water and tea bags when he heard a familiar voice.

"Greg, I have another picture for you."

"Hi, Simon. I haven't seen you for a couple of days. Where have you been?"

"I had to go with Marvin to see a doctor in Green Bay. You know, that's where the Packers play. I saw the stadium with the big G on it. Someday Marvin said he and Jessica would take me to a game. He said it would be preseason, and they could get tickets for Family Night. I'd like to see the Packers."

"Were you sick?"

"No. It's a doctor that I see once in a while to make sure I'm good. I need to take medicine from him to stay healthy, Marvin says." He held out a piece of paper. "I painted a picture of your boat, *Island Girl*. Do you like it?"

He took it from Simon and looked at it. "I sure do. Matter of fact we're going to put it in its own special spot right above my desk so I can look at it every day when I work on my writing." He went to the junk drawer, got a nail and hammer, and hung the painting up. "How's that?"

"That's great. One other thing, I'm out of paper to paint on. Can you get me more? I know it's not my birthday, but you know where to get it. Could you please? I can't paint without the paper. I love to paint pictures."

"Sure. Later this week when I go to Sturgeon Bay, I'll get you watercolor paper." He reached into a desk drawer and gave Simon some white computer paper. "Use this paper until I get you the watercolor paper, okay?"

"Oh, good. Thanks, Greg."

Randy watched as Simon went to a kitchen chair and sat down.

"Simon, I know you usually stay here, and we talk, but today I have some work to do before I go to Trisha's cabin for dinner."

"I saw you with her before. Can I come? We're friends now. She's not mad at me for touching her boobies. She was sorry she slapped me, she said, and I told her I won't touch them again, so maybe I can come for dinner too?"

"Not tonight. I'll talk to her about the three of us getting together and having dinner. She likes you, so I'm sure it won't be a problem. Or the three of us can have dinner here. But tonight is a special dinner for Trisha and me to get to know each other better." Randy led him to the door. "I'm sorry, Simon, but I need to get some work done and get ready for dinner, so you'll have to go home now, okay?"

"Okay. Thanks for the paper."

It didn't take long to walk to Trisha's house, but Randy started walking there fifteen minutes early. He had a jar of fresh sun tea he'd made earlier in the day, and along the way to her house, he decided to pick wildflowers, which grew in the woods and meadows on the path. He found mostly orange and yellow day lilies and some purple flowers whose name he wasn't sure of. It was the thought that counted, right?

As he emerged from the woods surrounding the path, Randy

saw Trisha sitting on one of the Adirondack chairs and a tablecloth on the nearby picnic table with two plates and silverware already set.

She had gone to a lot of trouble. He was glad he'd brought the flowers. They'd look nice on the table.

When she saw him coming, a big smile appeared on her face.

"Right on time. I like a punctual man that doesn't keep a woman waiting." And he heard her laugh again. After handing her the tea and flowers, he took a seat.

"You seem to have gone to a lot of trouble for this dinner. I'm a pretty simple guy."

"It's only fair. You showed a lot of patience and guts to be my friend and say what you did to me to try and help me. It worked. It was the least I could do. Plus, I like to cook, and I haven't cooked for anyone in a long, long, time. So it wasn't too much trouble, and I wanted to try a recipe I saw in *Food & Wine*. It's for sea bass, but I thought it would work for Green Bay's smallmouth bass. We'll soon find out, I guess."

"I'm drooling already."

"Would you like some wine? I have Sauvignon Blanc to go with the fish."

"I'll have some of the iced tea I made, since we're going to have wine with dinner."

"Okay, I'll get the ice. I think I'll have a glass of wine. I'm a little nervous about this all. You're the first man I've gone out with since my divorce and the cancer. It will help me relax."

You're the first woman I've gone out with since I got out of prison. Don't worry about anything. We're just having a friendly dinner.

There's nothing to worry about.

"Maybe I will have that beer after all," he said. "Just to make you feel more comfortable too."

After she went inside, he looked at the cabin and her property. It was a large cabin with a view through the trees. Across the sparkling waters, he saw Fish Creek in the distance. Like his cabin, Trisha's place had a big screened-in-porch. The second floor looked like it probably had bedrooms. It had been a family cabin, not a simple one-story affair like his.

She came out with a beer and a glass of white wine.

"*Whew*," she said as she sat down. "I've been going a hundred miles an hour once I knew you were coming. I just put the fish in the oven, so it will be about twenty minutes—just long enough for us to enjoy the evening and our drink. I hope you're hungry."

"I am. I just had Cheerios for breakfast—that was it all day."

"Good. I made a salad and new potatoes too, so we'll have more than just fish."

"Great."

"You really have a nice place here," he added. "It looks like a lot more room than my cabin. Someday maybe you can give me a tour," he said before taking a sip of beer.

There was an uncomfortable silence, then she finished her wine and got up.

"Time for dinner," she said.

A few minutes later, she came out of the house with a platter on which were two plates and two salad bowls. Setting it on the picnic table, he saw fish, new potatoes, corn, and a small salad.

After a second trip, she came out with a bottle of white wine.

"Hope you like the fish," she said. "I have to say I enjoyed cooking for someone besides myself."

"It's a treat to have something different." He watched as she opened the new bottle of wine and poured two glasses.

She raised her glass and touched his. "Bon appétit."

They both began eating. After a couple of bites, he looked up. "This is great. God bless the cook."

"That's a nice thing to say. Thank you, but I don't think God has blessed me much; otherwise I wouldn't have had gotten cancer."

"I didn't mean to upset you," he said. "That's just an old family saying we used to say to whoever fixed dinner. It was silly, but it was a family tradition to start a dinner. It actually felt good to say it to someone. My parents are gone now. I really don't get out much and have a chance to say it. This is actually the first time since the accident."

"The accident?"

"Yes. I thought I told you. My parents were both killed in a car accident. I miss them. It's the small little things they used to do or say that I really miss."

"Oh, I'm so sorry."

"It's getting better. That's why I moved out to the island. Their house—I mean my house now—is in Fish Creek. It's still painful to be there. The memories flood back. Out on the island, I'm making new memories."

Should I tell her about being in prison, and eight years for murder? It's the real reason I moved here. To hide.

"Living on the island is good for my writing. Not many distractions. I can focus."

"I understand how that could help your work." She took a forkful of fish, licked her lips, and smiled.

"This fish is great, along with the potatoes," he said. "I love the corn too, so it's perfect."

She got up from the table and grabbed the two empty plates and the silverware.

"Actually, I saved the best for last. I made a cherry pie. I used to help my mother bake pies, but they were usually strawberry rhubarb. Anyway, I think I got the recipe right for cherry. I hope you like it as much as you liked the fish."

"I'm sure I will."

"I'm really glad we did this. Being busy helps me improve my mood so thank you for giving me that talking-to the other day. You're right about what's on the inside that counts, not the outside. As you could tell from the boat incident, my reconstructive surgery hasn't healed completely yet, but it will. The original surgery hurt so much, I don't want to go through any more pain, plus the pain of divorce. I didn't feel I had anyone in my life that it might matter how I looked. You were spot on: living with a black cloud over me every day made everything worse. I need to get on with my life and start new."

Randy raised his glass. "Let's toast to the new you."

After another bottle of wine, Randy could tell Trisha was getting tipsy. She started giggling as she recalled her younger days before being married and being on the island with Adam. "Like most young people, I didn't think my parents knew anything, but like Mark Twain said, 'When I moved away from home at a young age, and then returned years later, I was amazed at how much they'd learned while I was gone.' That was me."

"Yes, funny how that works," he said. "Didn't happen with me. But I was gone for a while and really couldn't get back for eight years to home and Fish Creek. They'd come and visit me when they could."

"Really. Where were you?"

"I was around but just couldn't make it home."

This would be a great time to tell her the truth.

"I was working on location with my new novel series at the time," he said.

"Oh. What kind of novels do you write?"

"Crime, prison life, and the interplay of gangs, prisoners, and prisons. I spent a lot of time in prisons."

She poured them more wine, emptying the bottle. "Can't believe we finished another bottle." Then she turned back to him. "Where can I get a copy?"

"I got one. I'll let you read it, but you have to give it back when you're done. I need it sometimes to refresh my memory about some gangs and prison life for my new books."

"Sure. I'll stop by and get it. I'm a fast reader because of my television days, so I'll give it back to you in a couple of days. It's not like I have a lot to do here on the island." She raised her hand to her mouth and yawned. "I think it's time for me to go to bed."

"It was a wonderful dinner."

"I'm pleased with myself," she said.

"I think we've turned the corner on our relationship, for the better," he said. He watched her nod, yawn again, and rise from the table. She walked around the table and stood in front of him. He thought she was going to give him a goodbye hug but instead she wrapped her arms around him and gave him a kiss.

It wasn't a simple good-night peck but a real kiss that lasted seconds. He hadn't kissed a woman in over nine years, and it felt good. His body hadn't reacted like that for a long time.

When she stepped back from the kiss, she had a smile on her face.

"Tonight—with dinner and the wine—I guess I wanted to kiss you. I hope you don't mind."

"It felt good. I haven't kissed a woman for a long time either."

"Well, good. I'd call tonight a success. Now I think I'm going inside and going to bed. I'm suddenly very tired. I'll stop by tomorrow and get your book. There's a full moon tonight, so you shouldn't have any problem finding your way home."

"I'll see you tomorrow. Thanks again for the great dinner."

CHAPTER TEN

Trisha was right. With the moonlight, he had no problem seeing the path to his cabin. Being located in the middle of Green Bay, the island was really quite dark at night. If you had lights, they were either powered by a generator or batteries or they were candles or gas lanterns. As he walked past a house, he heard the telltale sounds of the generator.

"Greg."

"Who's there?" he asked, startled.

"It's me, Simon."

"What are you doing out at this hour?"

"I like to explore at night. If I'm quiet and don't move much, I hear animals. I like the night animals and birds. Owls are my favorite. There's one near Trisha's house in a dead tree, with a big hole in the side. I like to hear the owl say 'Who, who.'"

"Were you spying on Trisha?"

"I was just walking. You had dinner with her, didn't you? I saw you. Then you were kissing. Not like Marvin and Jessie, but still, you were kissing."

He smiled at Simon. "I'm tired, Simon. I need to go home and get some sleep."

"I'll see you tomorrow. Good night. You're almost home."

"Yes, I'm almost home. Good night."

Randy turned and walked home, but he wondered if Simon was going to spy on Trisha. He said he looked at Marvin's girl magazines. He hoped Trisha had her drapes closed.

He was up early the next morning. After crossing the bay to Fish Creek, he quickly got on the road to Green Bay and a visit with his parole officer. That went fine, and then he went to get office supplies and a few things to spruce up his house.

He took to heart the comments Trisha had made about his house. It was kind of dumpy and needed some accents to liven it up a bit. He stopped in Sturgeon Bay at Bliss and got some throw rugs and pillows and a couple of landscape prints, including frames. He also bought Simon more watercolor paper, as promised.

He felt so good about everything that he decided to stop at Kitty's for lunch. As he entered the stone and wood building, he noticed the place's owners had done a good job upgrading the outside and inside. He remembered when they'd bought it. The inside bar was the same as when it was called The Stein, but since then there had been huge changes, especially to the outside garden area and a new garage dining bar building. He took a spot at the bar to eat.

Just then Randy saw the owners, Buster and his wife, Amy, come in with their young son, Jamison. They were a nice friendly couple, as were all their employees.

"You haven't been here for a while," Buster said.

"You're right. I recently came back to Fish Creek after nine years. I missed Door County and places like Kitty's. You're looking fit. Life must be good."

"It is. This place keeps us busy, and spending time with Jamison is good too. I've been working out, trying to stay in shape. I saw the movie *Thor* and wanted to get my body to look like him. I'm getting there." Then Randy heard laughing coming from Amy. "Yeah he looks just like Thor...*not!*" Then Buster laughed. "Well it's nice to see you. Thanks for coming."

Carla came to get his order.

"I'll have a Guinness and Irish stew."

"Gotcha," she said.

It was cool out, so he ate inside. It didn't take him long to finish off his stew and Guinness. As he was walking to his car parked on the street, he passed the guy who'd talked to him about Ingrid at the Bayside Bar a few weeks before.

Randy nodded and kept on walking, but the guy called back to him. He started walking toward Randy, moving fast.

"I know who you are. I couldn't get you out of my head after we talked about Ingrid at the Bayside that day. You seemed overly interested in that girl's story, especially about her fooling around. It kept bugging me. It seemed like I knew you, so I started going back, and there you were. We don't get many murders in Door

County, so you were big news. Front page. You killed her. I'm surprised you only got eight years for manslaughter. You should have gotten life."

"You've got the wrong guy, buddy. I'm Greg Chambers."

"Don't give me that shit. You're Randy Daggett, and you killed her, asshole. Granted, Ingrid liked to fool around. A party girl. She did with me and others. When you found out about it, you took her out to Chambers and killed her. Now you're out of prison, and she's still dead. You're probably looking for your next victim. I've read about your type." He stepped closer to Randy. "This is for Ingrid."

The guy punched him in the face, followed by a blow to his stomach.

Randy doubled over and fell to the ground. The guy kicked him a couple of times with his steel-toed boot. Randy felt a rib crack. He slid under his car, trying to get away from the guy.

"I wish I could do more to you than that," the guy yelled, "but then I'd get thrown into prison like you did."

With blurry vision and throbbing pain with each breath, Randy watched the guy's shoes walk away. His stomach hurt, his ribs hurt, and he could tell that his right eye was swelling. He slid from underneath his car. He'd probably have a black eye. He had seen fights like this in prison, but they had never been directed at him.

A good day had taken a painful turn. Even if he lived on an island, Randy couldn't hide from his past.

Though in excruciating pain, he somehow got everything he'd bought loaded into the boat. He motored back to the island and his cabin with the groceries and other goods. Once packed away, he tried to clean his face as best he could. Next, he started walking toward Trisha's cabin with one of his books.

If he was going to be honest about his past, he would start with her. After all, she had been honest with him about her breast cancer and ex-husband.

As he walked the path, he decided he was going to come clean and start being his real self. No Greg Chambers except for his reading public. From now on he was Randy Daggett, for better or worse. He was going to have to live with his past.

Approaching her cabin, Randy saw Trisha on her knees, planting flowers around the steps to the porch. His stomach felt queasy as he neared her, but it wasn't from the punch or cracked ribs. Instead, it was about telling the truth.

When his shadow crossed the plot where she was planting, she jumped in alarm. He saw she had earbuds in her ears.

A smile appeared on her face, and then he heard her gasp.

"What happened to you? You look like you got in a fight or something."

"Yeah, something like that. I can explain it to you later. I wanted to give you my book and invite you to my place for dinner."

She got up, dusted her hands off, and stood close to him.

"That eye looks painful, and it's starting to blacken. Stay here for a second, and I'll get something for it."

"No, that's okay."

But she turned and walked into the cabin. A minute later she came out with a bag of frozen peas.

"Yes, I'd love to come for dinner," she said, "but are you sure you're up to it?"

"I'm all right."

"Put these peas on your eye, but don't press too hard. I've read where this is good to use instead of ice. Besides, you can cook these for dinner later." She smiled as she gently placed the cold veggies on his eye area.

He put his hand on hers. It felt smooth and nice even with the small amount of dirt on the skin.

"As for dinner, I guess I don't need to bring anything else since I already contributed the vegetables." She smiled.

He hoped she would still be smiling after he told her everything about himself at dinner. Not here. Not now.

"How about six thirty? Do you like chicken? I'll grill it. I bought some potato salad and, for dessert, Door County cherry pie."

"Great. I'll be really hungry by then." She gently cupped his face and gave him a gentle kiss. "See you then."

As he walked away, he thought that kiss would probably be the last one he'd ever get from her.

After they ate, sitting at the kitchen table inside his cabin, she said, "Your chicken was great. Even the frozen peas—or, should I say, the thawed veggies I provided. You're quite the cook, grilling. The corn on the cob was wonderful too, almost southwestern with the blackened kernels. I've never had it that way. I've always just boiled it. And the potato salad was good. You said you got cherry pie? Yum. Let's wait for a while so my stomach settles."

I wish my stomach would settle.

She got down to the matter at hand sooner than he did. "How did you get beat up?" she asked. "You don't strike me as a violent person."

"I'm not!" he said forcefully.

"Geez, I didn't mean it that way." She slid her hand across the table and touched his hand.

"I'm sorry. I just mean I'm not a violent person." He reached for his glass of wine and drained it, then filled it again. "Would you like more wine?"

"Sure. Why do I think you're going to tell me something?"

"You're perceptive."

"Remember, I was a TV reporter."

"Oh, that's right." He took a smaller sip of wine this time. "I want to tell you a story about something that happened nine years ago. It's related to why I was attacked today. I want you to listen to the whole story before you say anything or make any judgments. Okay?"

Her eyes widened, then she nodded. "I'm sure it can't be that bad, but I'm listening."

"First of all, my real name isn't Greg Chambers. It's Randy Daggett. In the winter, I live in Fish Creek. I lived there my whole life with my parents. I think you know they died this spring."

"I knew that. But your name is Randy, not Greg? Why?"

"Greg is my pen name. I've been gone for over eight years and wanted to drop out of sight, change my appearance and identity. You'll understand when you hear the rest of the story."

She reached for her glass of wine and took a big gulp.

"I guess authors have pen names. I get that, but changing your identity. Why?"

"Eight years ago I was sent to prison for something I'm convinced I didn't do."

"Prison? I don't understand. I know people get sent to jail who are later proven innocent. Is that why you are out now?"

"No. I served my full term, eight years."

"Full term. But you're *not sure* you did what you were convicted for? What was it?"

He drained his glass of wine. "I was convicted of manslaughter," he said in a soft voice.

"Manslaughter! You mean you killed someone. Like murder," she said in an almost screaming voice. "Oh my god. I don't believe it." She slid her chair back away from the table and him. He saw the fear in her eyes.

"Trisha, let me explain."

"What's to explain? You killed someone." She reached out for the wine glass, brought it to her lips but stopped. Then she stood. "I'm going home. This is too much. I always thought you were kind and good, but now…now I find out—"

"Please, Trisha, you agreed to listen to my whole story. You were a reporter. Don't you normally get all the facts before you report a story? I want to tell you the facts. Please sit and hear me out."

She stood over him, trying to decide. Then he saw a resignation in her posture, and she slowly sat, her eyes never leaving his face.

"Okay, tell me the rest of the story."

"Ingrid Karlsen and I had been dating off and on since high school—then even after I went to college in Madison. One night we were drinking beer—too much, it turned out for me. Ingrid was a free spirit. That's what I liked about her. Anyway, that night she said she wanted to go out to Chambers and go skinny-dipping. It was a perfect night: warm and dry with the wind from the west so it would blow the warmer top water into Sand Bay. We got a twelve pack to go, and I sailed *Flying Scot* out there. It was beautiful. We rolled a blanket out, drank a lot of beer, and when everyone finally left the beach for the night, we made love under the moon and stars. Ingrid was wild. After lovemaking, I fell asleep. She got up and went swimming. Later, I walked down the beach looking for her, and I found her dead, floating at the water's edge." He took another drink of wine. "There was enough circumstantial evidence to convict me of her murder. I did eight years in prison in Green Bay."

"I think I need some more wine," Trisha asked.

Randy went and retrieved another bottle, opened it, and poured. Trisha sat at the table, her hands folded in front of her.

He continued, watching her face, especially her eyes.

"Every night I lay in my cell, trying to remember every detail, anything to let me know if somehow it was true: I killed her. Maybe I blocked it out because it was so horrible, but I don't think so. The thing is I'm not a violent person. I never got into fights growing up. Even in prison. Granted, I wasn't a Boy Scout–type guy, but I wasn't mean. I never hit anyone. I avoided confrontations. I liked to have fun. When I got up and found Ingrid dead, I was devastated and confused by everything. Maybe it was the beer or maybe it was an insomnia drug I was taking since high school. I was confused and devastated by the whole mess."

Trisha fingered her wine glass. "Well, someone killed her, and you were the only one there, right?"

"That's what the DA said. My attorney thought this insomnia drug I was taking could have produced violence that night. With that drug, there had been several reported instances of violence, sleepwalking, even driving while asleep."

The sun was going down as they looked at the water and the sunset.

"Would you like some pie?" he asked.

"No, I don't have much of an appetite. I want to go outside and get some air if you don't mind."

"Sure. We can go out and finish our wine out there."

They got up and walked to the sandy beach and sat on a couple of chairs Randy had placed there earlier in the summer to watch the sunset over the bay.

"It's beautiful here," she said. "A different view from my place."

When the sun had dipped below the horizon, Trisha stood

and turned toward him. "Thank you for the dinner. I appreciate you telling me about your real life. I need to process all this information. It's surreal. I need to do some checking on my own, like I used to do as a reporter. Until I have everything straight in my mind, I'm going to ask you to not to contact me. You don't seem like a bad person, Randy, but—" She handed him her glass. "I can find my own way home. Good night." She turned back to him. "Is this where she died? I mean on the beach here?"

"Yes." He pointed down the shore. "Where the beach curves toward the point is where I found her."

"Strange you would come back here. Why?"

"I want to find out who killed her. I hope there is something here on the island to give me my answer."

She nodded her head, then turned and left.

Randy didn't get up but sat in the chair and looked out at the beach where Ingrid had been murdered.

CHAPTER ELEVEN

The next morning was rainy, with strong winds from the north. The stormy weather reflected his foul mood. It wasn't because of getting beat up and then coming clean with Trisha. It really boiled down to finding the real killer. Randy had one more suspect, courtesy of Detective Jenkins.

He looked up Jimmy DeLeo on Google and paid the fee to get his address, where he worked, and his phone number. He jumped in the car and headed for Green Bay. Once there, Randy phoned DeLeo, and they arranged to meet for lunch at a sports bar near Lambeau Field.

"Can I call you Jimmy?" Randy said as he pulled up a chair.

"Sure."

"Thanks for seeing me on short notice. I'm trying to get information on two people from about ten years ago. One is a Marvin Jacobs and the second is Ingrid Karlsen. I was told by a Detective Jenkins you might be able to help me."

"Yeah, I remember them. What do you want to know?"

"I write crime novels, and I thought I would do a cold case

follow up on the death of Ms. Karlsen. Jenkins said you could fill me in on her and Jacobs."

"That was a long time ago. Ingrid was a hot number. She and Jacobs had a thing going. She was out on the big island several times a week and stayed out there when she wasn't waitressing or bartending. I was doing carpentry work, electrical and plumbing, adding an extra bedroom and bath. It was nice work. Ingrid provided the fringe benefits, if you know what I mean."

"No, tell me."

"If you were nice to her, she could get very friendly. She got bored easily. When Marvin wasn't around, she and I would hook up. Everything was fine until Marvin caught us fucking one time. He exploded at both of us, mostly at me. We got into a fistfight. I beat him up a bit. He fired me. I got pissed at both of them."

"Jenkins said you threatened her."

"Yes, I shot off my mouth. It was really just in the heat of the moment. Working out there was a good job. The money was really good, and she was quite the sex nymph. Couldn't get enough. But after the fight and losing my summer job, I was angry. I guess I threatened her, but I didn't do anything.

"Where were you the night she died?"

"I was with another girl down here in Green Bay."

"Oh."

"Yeah. Detective Somebody checked it out. I had a strong alibi. What else do you want from me? I'm hungry, and this is my lunch hour."

"Thanks for your help. Do you think Marvin Jacobs could

have killed Ingrid?"

"Could have, but they caught the guy that did it."

Driving home, Randy was disappointed. He'd struck out again, but he still thought Marvin might be crucial to his investigation. Only thing was, he seemed like a nice guy.

It was a good day to stay inside and be a writer. He was almost done with the new novel but still behind on getting his its final edit done and emailed to his publisher.

Writing helped him forget about his life. In general, he had been trying to hide who he was since he got out of prison. After the beating, he realized he should end the charade, let people out there embrace the real Randy Daggett.

Last night with Trisha had been a start. He'd just have to wait and see how it panned out with her down the road.

Even though he wasn't going to hide who he was any more, he was probably going to isolate on the island for a while, keeping a low profile. He'd let his face get back to normal and let his ribs heal.

And just as that thought entered his mind, he heard a voice at the door.

"Hello, Greg. I have another painting for you." The screen door opened and slammed shut, and there was Simon—as usual, smiling and holding out a piece of watercolor paper, this one with two sailboats.

Simon's painting was improving.

"It's the best painting I ever did," said Simon. "I wanted to give it to you because you like my paintings and you like Trisha. I saw you two kissing a few nights ago."

"Simon, she and I are just friends."

"Well, it looked like how Marvin and Jessie kiss. Then they go upstairs, close the door, and have sex. That's when I go outside and explore. That's how I saw you and Trisha."

Simon handed another watercolor painting to Randy. "It's a picture of Trisha."

Randy could tell it was a picture of a woman, but it was more like an outline of a woman with circles where her breasts would be, and she had long black hair. There was no way you could tell it was Trisha, but to Simon, and his ten year old mind, it was a painting of Trisha. Randy knew he was proud of his painting.

"You know, Simon, I really appreciate you painting this picture of Trisha for me. Did she model for you to paint this for me?"

"No, I just saw her lying on her lawn chair stretched out. She didn't know I was there. She must have gotten her boobs fixed because they looked better than they did when we were on the sailboat that day it rained. I just saw them because one morning she had her top down getting some sun when I was exploring."

"Simon, it's not right to spy on people without them knowing or saying it's okay for you to look at them like that. Do you understand?"

"Are you mad at me for painting Trisha? I thought you'd like it." Simon looked like he was going to cry.

"I like when you paint me pictures but not pictures of women like this without their knowledge. Paint their faces or them swimming but not naked. That's not right. Do you understand what I'm telling you?"

Simon wiped away tears.

"I won't do that anymore. I promise. I don't like it when people get mad at me. It makes me sad."

"I'm not angry at you, Simon. I'm glad you like to paint things but not of people this way, okay?" He looked at him, waiting until Simon got a big smile.

"Okay, Greg. I won't do it any more of people. How about dogs? I love dogs."

Randy laughed. "Dogs? Dogs are great to paint. Cats too. Now I have a surprise for you."

"What's that, Greg? Do you have a present for me?"

"Not a present but information. My real name is Randy, not Greg. That's my writing name. You can start calling me Randy from now on."

"Okay…Randy." He laughed.

"Now let's head over to your cabin so I can tell Marvin and Jessie too. But first, are you hungry?"

"Yes. I didn't have breakfast. I wanted to give you this picture first."

"How about some Cheerios?"

"I like Cheerios. Can I have some orange juice too?"

Michael Pritzkow

The walk to Simon's house after their short breakfast gave Randy time to think about how he was going to tell Marvin about his real past life. He wasn't sure how Marvin and Jessie would take the revelation of him being a convicted murderer living on the island. He had no idea how the others on the island would feel when they found out.

But this was something he had to do, even if the thought of it made his stomach queasy.

The cabin came into view. Randy grew more anxious when he spotted Marvin raking leaves and pine needles into the fire pit.

"Hi, Greg." Marvin looked over at his smiling little brother. "I was wondering where Simon went so early this morning. Jessie and I slept in. It was so quiet this morning, and now I know why. Are you hungry, Simon?"

"No. Greg—I mean, Randy—gave me Cheerios." Simon turned toward Randy and smiled. "See, I remembered your real name."

"Randy?" Marvin looked at him with a quizzical look.

"Let's sit down at the picnic table, and I'll tell you a story about me."

Randy heard the screen door slam and then saw Jessica carrying two cups of coffee. He'd get both of them out of the way at the same time and get it out in the open.

"Hi, Greg. I haven't seen you for a while. I'm sorry I didn't bring you a cup of coffee, but I didn't know you were here. Looks like you have a black eye. Hope you weren't in a fight."

Marvin turned to her. "Greg has a story he wants to tell us, and his name isn't Greg. It's Randy."

Jessica's eyebrows arched up.

"My pen name is Greg Chambers, but my real name is Randy Daggett."

"It sounds like there's more to the story you wanted to tell us than just that," Marvin said.

"There is. Hear me out before you say anything, and then I'll answer any questions you have because your friendship and understanding is important to me." He looked into their eyes and saw uncertainty.

"Geez, Greg—I mean, Randy—it can't be that bad," Marvin said, and he saw Jessica nod her head in agreement. He watched Simon walk down to the beach.

"I hope you feel that way after you hear what I have to say." And he told the whole story just like he did to Trisha the day before.

They both sat there dumbfounded.

Then Marvin jumped to his feet and screamed, "You're telling us you're a convicted murderer, and the crime happened right here on the island?"

Jessica moved behind Marvin for protection. "How could you deceive us like that?' she said.

"You don't understand. I know I was convicted, but that was based on circumstantial evidence. I didn't kill her."

"Well, they just don't convict someone of a crime like that

unless they have enough evidence," said Marvin. "Twelve jurors thought you did it. That means something to me."

"You deceived us right from the start when you came here," Jessica said.

"I don't think we can trust you," said Marvin, "so I want you to stay away from us while Jessica and I discuss this and think it over. We don't want you around Simon either, until we've made our decision about you."

"I would never hurt Simon, or anyone for that matter!" Randy said.

"So you say, but we don't want to take any chances. We'll talk to Simon and tell him you're sick or something. If you see him, please tell him the same thing. He'll understand being sick, but he's not mature enough to understand what all this means. You were convicted for the crime, Randy," said Marvin. "I think it's time for you to leave and not to come by unless we change our mind and invite you back. Understand?"

Randy got up and started walking back to his cabin.

From somewhere behind him, he heard Simon yell, "Bye Randy. See you tomorrow."

But that wasn't going to happen tomorrow—maybe never.

He needed to get off the island for a few days and stay at his place in Fish Creek. Besides, it was September. It was getting cooler at night, and the cabin didn't have a proper heating system, just an old pot belly stove that barely created enough heat to take the chill out in the morning. The stove was not efficient enough to heat the cabin in the late fall and winter months.

He wondered when Marvin, Jessica, and Simon would be closing for the winter and heading back to their other full-time residences. Marvin and Simon lived in Green Bay, and he assumed Jessica did too, since she had worked with Simon there. That's how she'd met Marvin.

And would Trisha leave soon? She was originally from the Chicago area. He thought her parents still lived in Evanston. With Trisha having breast cancer, maybe she would go live with them. They could help while she recovered from reconstructive surgery and her divorce.

She was in physical pain. She had said her breasts were still tender to the touch. That's why she hadn't worn a bra that day. Even Simon had noticed the scars.

Everyone has scars as they grow older. Some were on the outside, and some on the inside.

With little food in the house, he needed to get groceries from Piggly Wiggly in Sister Bay.

But first he looked in a mirror on the living room wall and decided he needed to shave, shower, and cut his hair. The last time he had cleaned up his act was for his parents' funeral. If he was serious about stopping his charade, he'd start today. If things got worse, so be it. He wasn't hiding who he was anymore.

An hour later he had shaved off his beard and trimmed his long hair. It wasn't a perfect haircut, but as he looked in the bathroom mirror, he smiled. He looked younger. Even so, he leaned closer to the foggy bathroom mirror and noticed small lines around his eyes and the start of gray around his temples. He smiled at the thought of his mother scrutinizing her face and hair in this same mirror, just like he was doing now.

Eventually he'd meet someone that remembered him. They'd remember he and Ingrid had gone together and what had happened to her. And would they remember why he had gone away?

He'd find out in about an hour when he went to one of the main gathering spots in the area: the Piggly Wiggly in Sister Bay.

CHAPTER TWELVE

The meat department and deli at Piggly Wiggly were busy as he walked to the counter to order honey ham and sliced cheese. Then he bought chicken, hamburger, and a couple of steaks for grilling. Randy shopped, smiled, and made small talk with those around him.

Maybe he was enjoying himself because he didn't recognize anyone there that he knew. People were friendly up here. Door County was a great place to visit and live. It seemed like half of Chicago came up here every summer. While the locals didn't always appreciate the congestion of summer—and even more in the fall during the color season—everyone mostly got along. The happiest group were the merchants and restaurants that needed the seasonal business to make it through the long winter and spring.

His shopping done, Randy headed to the checkout line. As he piled his groceries on the checkout conveyer belt and waited his turn, he noticed the check-out person staring at him.

When it was his turn, she wasted no time asking questions. Her nametag said Janet, and she looked kind of familiar, though not enough for him to recall who she was. As she scanned the items, she stopped suddenly. He watched her look at him closer, then she said, "I think I know you from a while ago. Are you back visiting family, because I haven't seen you around the area for a long time?"

He smiled at her as he watched her resume scanning.

"My name's Randy Daggett. I grew up in Fish Creek."

"You were one grade ahead of me at Gibraltar High School. Nice to have you back. I'll probably see you a lot more now that you're living here. Working here at the Pig, I see and know everyone—we all have to eat."

"Good to see you," he said.

"You might see me at Husby's Bar," she volunteered. "I like to go there and unwind after doing this all day and standing on my feet."

"I'll look for you when I stop in. I like their pizza, but at sixteen inches they might be too big. I need to share it with someone. If I see you there, we'll do that, and we can catch up on old times."

"That would be fun." She froze for a second after she said that.

Randy noticed the funny look she got on her face.

"I just remembered something about you from way back. Didn't you used to go with Ingrid Karlsen?"

Here it comes, he thought. "Yeah, I did."

"You must have moved away, but I'm sure you know she died. Some guy was convicted for killing her in a jealous rage. She was a wild one. This all probably happened after you moved away."

"Geez, that's too bad she died."

"Yeah. I feel sorry for you if you didn't know that. Still, it's too bad she died. Nobody deserves that."

He watched as the packer put everything into plastic bags and then loaded it back into his shopping cart.

"Thanks for shopping with us."

As she turned to the next customer, Randy said, "It was nice talking to you, Janet. Let's see if we can meet at Husby's. I'd like to catch up."

"Sure, that be great. I usually go there on Thursdays and listen to the band playing in the garage area. Maybe I'll see you then."

"Sounds good."

Once he loaded the groceries in the back seat and got back to his car, he just sat in the parking lot.

It was hard for him to hear that gossipy talk about Ingrid again. Randy didn't know how many jealous lovers she'd had. But it only took one to kill her.

As he turned the key and started home, he thought he was making progress in a weird sort of way, even if it was coming too slowly.

After unpacking his groceries at the house, he decided to head back to the island and start readying the cabin for closing up in a few weeks. He decided to take a long sail to the island instead of just kicking in the diesel engine and motoring straight back to the island's marina. It was a warm fall day, and in Peninsula State

Park, the trees were turning yellow, orange, and red. A moderate wind blew straight into him, so he turned northwest until his sails filled out. He decided to head up to Ephraim and back for a nice feel-good afternoon sail.

As he pulled the boat into the Chambers Island marina, Randy saw Trisha talking to Marvin. Both of them had boxes and duffel bags next to their boats. Neither seemed happy to see Randy, but he couldn't really blame them. He'd lied to them all summer about who he was.

He expertly piloted *Island Girl* into his slip. Then he tied it up and went over to them. He thought, the best defense is a good offence.

"Hi, looks like you're packed up and heading home."

Marvin spoke first. "This is just some of our stuff. We accumulated a lot over the summer, and we're leaving a lot here over the winter, nothing that can't be left. All of this needs to go back to the house in Green Bay."

Trisha nodded. "I'm leaving a lot at the cabin too. I have a lot of winter and fall clothing at the apartment in Green Bay, and in Chicago at my parents'. I plan to spend more time with my parents while I'm recovering."

"I understand. I'm staying at the house in Fish Creek all winter, so if either of you need something, call me on my cell, and I can get it. At least until the ice starts coming in."

"Thanks, but I think we're all right," said Marvin. "Besides, the house is locked."

He still seemed put off with Randy, but he sensed that Trisha was mellowing toward him.

She said, "Yeah, my cabin is locked too—although there's nothing there anyone would want to steal. Thanks, Randy. I think I'm okay."

Randy smiled. He reached for his wallet and pulled out two business cards with his pen name on the card. "Here is my card with my cell phone and email address on it if you need to get ahold of me. All the info is correct."

Marvin looked at it and gave it back. "I won't need it. I don't want to have anything to do with you."

Both Randy and Trisha looked at Marvin in disbelief.

She took the card. "Thanks, Randy. We'll talk. If I don't see you again, have a nice winter."

"You too." At least she smiled at him, but Marvin wore a big scowl on his face.

Randy was surprised how much he'd missed Simon's visits. He was sure Simon didn't know why he couldn't see Randy, but that was out of his control, and he'd respect Marvin's wishes.

Trisha and Marvin got into their respective boats and headed out of the harbor for the last time that season.

Randy stood on the dock and watched them leave the island, motoring in tandem: Marvin in a large powerboat leading the way, and Trisha's small aluminum fishing boat following closely in his wake.

Michael Pritzkow

He headed back to his cabin, wondering about the two and how he might regain their friendship after the long winter.

On numerous days, he walked the deserted island's length, enjoying the fall colors and crisp air.

Finally it was time for him to pack up his boat and make the final trip back to Fish Creek and home. There were always many local events in the fall to keep it interesting. All the towns and villages had their own special events, like Fish Creek's fall festival, with pumpkins and corn mazes. Good old family events. He missed his parents as he thought about the good times he had with them on these outings.

He closed up his cabin for the winter, draining water from the pipes, then hauling food and writing stuff he'd need over the coming winter to his house in Fish Creek. He took his time, savoring his last moments on the island this year.

Two weeks before Christmas, he got out his big puffy down jacket, stocking cap, and winter gloves. He remembered how excited he got as a kid when it had snowed for the first time. His mother would bundle him up in a snowsuit like the boy in *The Christmas Story*. He hated wearing that bulky snowsuit, but it kept him warm.

Randy looked out the window at the short driveway and

decided he'd better shovel before he packed down the snow with his tires. He was just about to head out when his cell phone rang.

"Who'd be calling me?" he said out loud to the empty house.

"Randy, it's Trisha. Is this a good time to call?"

"Sure. I was just going out to shovel. Nice to hear your voice. I wasn't sure I was ever going to hear from you again."

"Well, it took me a while to process what you told me. And then I was still recovering from my cancer and surgery."

"I get it. When I decided to come clean with my story, you were the first one I needed to tell. To be honest, I wasn't surprised by your reaction."

"I wish I could have been more supportive, but it was such a shock, and I've had enough surprises. I wasn't ready for any more."

"So you just calling to wish me an early Merry Christmas?"

He heard her laugh. "No. It's more important than that."

"Oh?"

"You know, I was a TV reporter for a station in Chicago. I'm pretty good at digging up facts. In your case, about Ingrid Karlsen, I decided to do some investigative work double-checking your story, checking facts about you and your trial, about the people involved that knew you and Ingrid back then. I'd like to come up and talk to you about what I found. I think it will surprise you. It sure surprised me. Besides, I'd like to see you again. We were just getting comfortable with each other and then *wham*—we left on not the best of terms."

"It would be great to see you again, and you're welcome to

stay here. I have a guest room at my house. I guess you can call it that. It's my old room. I've decluttered my stuff from it."

"That would be great."

"When were you thinking of coming up?" he asked.

"How about tomorrow about two? Is that too soon?"

"No. It's great. Call when you get to Egg Harbor, and I'll give you directions. It's pretty easy to find."

"Sounds good. See you tomorrow."

After she hung up, he looked at his cell phone and smiled. He was curious to hear what news she had. It had to be important for her to want to travel all this way.

He hoped their relationship could be salvaged. Maybe this was a step in that direction.

―――

The next morning, he was up early. It was pleasant to be busily getting ready for her. He shoveled the driveway again. Then got the vacuum cleaner out and gave the living room, his room, and the extra bedroom the once over. He dusted lamps, tables, even the cocktail table. As he stood back and examined his handiwork, he thought the house looked presentable.

He took a shower and shaved, then dressed in old jeans, a long-sleeved flannel shirt, and an Irish Fishermen's knit wool sweater. Next he made coffee, chilled wine, and sliced up sausage, cheese, and apples, putting them on a serving plate with grapes and crackers.

He was ready. He sat nervously on the living room couch, awaiting her call.

At two o'clock, a white Chevy SUV pulled into his drive.

When she got out, he saw that she was dressed for the weather but otherwise looked the same. She had on red lipstick, which looked great against her white skin and dark black hair. She opened the car's back door and took out a backpack, slung it over her shoulder, and walked to his front door.

"Welcome to my other house," he said. As she stepped past him, he inhaled her perfume. Just that small female touch sent a stirring in his body—the same feelings he'd felt during their kiss last summer.

Relax, boy. She's not here for romance.

After setting down her backpack, she gave him a friendly peck on the cheek. "It's nice to be back here in Fish Creek, even if it is winter and everything is white. It looks so different with the Christmas decorations. I was glad to get out of Chicago and my parents' place. They mean well. They've been good to me during my recovery, like when I had to have some follow-up stuff. They preferred to have me there with them instead of on Chambers Island. They didn't think it was good for me to be there all alone."

"So you're still there, or are you back in Green Bay?"

"I'm in Chicago until January. I'll go back to Green Bay after the holidays. I've rented a small condo downtown. I'm going to try to get back into TV, maybe do modeling again. My body is back to the way I looked before the cancer. The scars you saw are now just light pinkish marks, barely visible. The reconstructive surgery was successful, and in part thanks to your pep talk, I'm mentally back too. Thanks again."

"Glad to help, but you're the one that did it."

"How did your investigation go after I left here?" she asked. "Did you find anything?"

"It's okay, I guess. I'm sorry to say that while Ingrid was basically a good person, she had some abandonment issues. She had an overpowering need to be loved by someone, anyone, and that meant she fooled around a lot. I don't have anything outside of two suspects Detective Jenkins told me about, but they didn't really pan out. So far I've yet to pinpoint anyone who might have been at the scene and angry enough to kill her."

He looked at Trisha, still not believing she was here in his house. "I have some wine and other drinks, if you'd care for some refreshment after your drive."

CHAPTER THIRTEEN

She sat on the sofa in the living room. He brought out a bottle of Pinot Noir and poured her a glass.

"If someone else drowned Ingrid that night, they'd have to be on the island watching, hiding, waiting for their chance to kill her," he said, shaking his head. "It seems so unlikely."

Trisha sipped her wine, then ate an apple slice. Neither said anything for a while, picking at the tray of food.

Finally, Randy asked. "It seems like you must have had better luck than me. Isn't that why you called?"

"Yes." She smiled at him. "But I also missed seeing you and wanted to catch up."

He reached over and squeezed her hand. "That's nice to hear. Tell me about what you've found."

"Well, as you said, Ingrid got around. She was in sexual relationships with both men and women, seeking self-gratification or to feel wanted. In the process, she pissed off lots of people. I questioned a few of her ex-partners over the phone; when she got tired or bored, she'd drop them. It was like the old saying: love 'em and leave 'em. I'm surprised she lasted as long as she did with you. You two dated in high school and college, right?"

"Yes. In high school, then off and on in college, but I only saw her during the summer because I was at school in Madison and not up here. My family and I always treated her like she wanted to be treated."

"That's probably why it worked well for her," Trisha said.

"Seems she got a few people that she had relationships with very upset, and maybe someone went so far as to seek the ultimate revenge." She finished her glass of wine. "May I have another glass? I might need it after I tell you what else I found. It might shock you."

"Here you go. What did you find?"

"Ingrid Karlsen had three restraining orders protecting her; one was against a woman, Shelly Furano, and then there were two men. One of them was a guy named Cliff Jones. The other man will really surprise you when I tell you who it is. Restraining orders are civil actions of the court, so the information is available to the public."

"Would one of these three be mad enough to kill Ingrid?" Randy asked.

"Well, obviously someone killed her, and it wasn't you, right? And these people threatened Ingrid in ways that made her concerned for her safety. She took the trouble to go to court to protect herself from them. I spoke to Shelly Furano. Having lived with Ingrid, she had the most background info about her. Even now she is still mad at Ingrid—ten years after she died. The way she told it, they had moved in together for the fall, after you went back to school. They were going to split the rent. Several times Ingrid had expressed her love for Shelly. She moved in with her and paid a few months' rent, but Ingrid never got around to signing a lease. They worked together at a restaurant in Baileys Harbor. Then suddenly Ingrid moved out and moved in with a guy she met in Sturgeon Bay at some Irish pub. This guy told Ingrid she didn't need to pay him rent as long as they were together and she kept him satisfied. Shelly Furano said she left her because she loved 'having a dick inside her.' This new guy lasted three months. It was like that over and over. Another guy actually proposed to her, with a ring and all. Surprisingly, she accepted. Again, you were away at school. She moved in for the winter with him. When summer came, Ingrid backed out of the engagement and moved out. He got upset and slapped her around when she refused to give back the engagement ring, which had been his grandmother's. She didn't file a restraining order against him. Shelley said she did give him back his grandmother's ring, which seemed to solve the problem." Trisha stopped talking long enough to finish her glass of wine.

"If someone wanted to kill her that night on the beach, they followed us there," said Randy. "We sailed over in my *Flying Scot*. If a person saw us leave Fish Creek, and they had a power boat, they could have easily cruised around the island. They could go to the island's marina or even anchor around the point, then walk to Sand Bay and wait for their chance. It had to be that way. I didn't see or hear anyone. There were no boats or people around later that night. And I didn't hear any screams or anything before I found her down the beach, a good hundred and fifty yards away, dead."

Trisha appeared to be analyzing everything he said.

"There were light winds that night," said Randy, "so the Sand Bay side was relatively calm. When I called the police to report what happened, they came out in their boat and ended up towing the *Flying Scot* back to Fish Creek because there was no wind, not that they'd let me sail back alone anyhow. They took me to the police station and interrogated me most of the night. They let me go home after collecting DNA samples and scraping my fingernails.

"Ingrid had my sperm inside her, but nothing of mine under her fingernails, even though I had several scratches on my body. I was booked the next day when the DA said there was enough evidence to charge me." Randy drained his glass of wine and looked at Trisha.

"You're smiling," he said. "Why are you smiling? What do you know?"

"Remember I said there were two men that had restraining orders filed against them by Ingrid?" she asked. "The first was Cliff Jones, the guy that beat you up. He was married, and Ingrid threatened to tell his wife if she didn't get some money or new clothes to keep her quiet. Blackmail. Jones threatened her and roughed her up a bit. He really scared her, which is why she got the restraining order."

"And the third?" he asked.

"Ready for this?"

"Yes. Who?"

"The third person Ingrid took out a restraining order against was Marvin Jacobs."

"You've got to be kidding me. That righteous asshole. Marvin. I can't believe it."

"He would have access to a boat and could park it at the marina. He could have seen you two heading out to the island. He probably knew where you were headed too."

"Ingrid liked that beach a lot. We often went there."

"Marvin and Ingrid had a torrid relationship. Even when you were dating her during the summer, Marvin had her out to the island several times."

"I found that out when I talked to Detective Jenkins," he said, looking wistful. "There was always doubt in my mind for the eight years I was in prison. Now I'm sure I didn't kill her. Your information just strengthens that." He leaned over and gave her a kiss. "Thank you," he said.

"For the record, I don't think you killed Ingrid. Instead I think the police had enough circumstantial evidence on you, so they really didn't need to do much more investigating. All the evidence pointed to you, and the jury bought it. It happens."

"Yes. I can see why they did. That being said, I didn't kill her."

She slid over closer to him and kissed him back. "I missed you, Randy."

"I missed you too. I'm glad you came up to give me the news. More wine?"

"Yes, more wine." She leaned over again and kissed him. "I forgot how much I liked kissing. It's been a long time since I let anyone touch me, and I think I'm ready for some special touching and kissing now."

They tapped glasses and toasted.

"To us," he said, and they kissed again.

The next morning he woke before her and gazed at the naked Trisha. He watched her breasts slowly rise and fall as the sun streamed in. He couldn't help but stare. Her reconstructed breast had just the faintest scar where the surgery had taken place. Last night, as they made love with tender foreplay, she asked him to touch and kiss her breasts. He had to laugh to himself when she quizzed him about what he thought of them.

"Do you like them? Are they too hard? Too small? I want to know."

To answer, he bent over and kissed and rubbed the nipples and caressed the sides. "The surgeon gets my seal of approval. They're perfect."

"I'm glad you like them. I was nervous about you seeing me, besides making love. Now I can relax."

"You were nervous? I was nervous. I haven't been with a woman since the night on the beach with Ingrid. That was ten years ago. I was afraid I was not going to get hard, or I'd come right away, but at least I waited a little while before that happened."

"Well, we both have something to celebrate."

He slipped out of the bed and went to make coffee. Soon after, he heard footsteps. When he turned around, he saw the gorgeous Trisha, hair rumpled and wearing one of his long-sleeved flannel shirts.

"Coffee should be ready momentarily. I can offer you toast and Door County cherry jam, or I can make pancakes?"

"Coffee will be just fine." She came over and wrapped her arms around him, and her warm lips kissed him on the neck.

"I could get used to this, having you around me."

"It's nice, isn't it?" she said. "Thank you for last night. You were wonderful."

"Thanks for the compliment. I hope you can stay for a while. There's enough snow to ski and walk the trails in the park, and even in the off-season there are enough restaurants open to offer a good choice of food."

"I can stay a couple of days, but I need to be with my parents for the holidays. I owe them that."

"I understand completely. This is my first Christmas without my parents. It will be lonely. Maybe you make it more festive by helping me get a Christmas tree and decorating it."

"That would be fun. I'll stay a few days longer, then go back to my parents' just before Christmas."

He watched as she raised her arm and made a circle with thumb and index finger above her.

"What are you doing?" he asked.

"You mean you can't see the mistletoe?" she asked with a coy smile.

"Now that you mention it, I do see it." After a long kiss with swirling tongues, he felt her grab his hand and lead him back to the bedroom.

"We'll need our rest if we're going tree-cutting and decorating later." He said.

He saw the twinkle in her eyes as she turned and said, "Here comes Santa Claus, here comes Santa Claus, right down Santa Claus Lane."

It was eleven o'clock before they really got going. Trisha wore another of Randy's shirts—an up north red-and-black-checked shirt—jeans, and a heavy down jacket. Randy sang "Jingle Bells" as the two piled into his car.

"Where are we going?" she asked.

"It was a family tradition for my dad and me to go to one of the many swampy areas around Ephraim and Fish Creek that no one goes to or even really knows about." In his mind, Randy pictured the old rock-strewn logging path with several overhanging tamarack trees that gave the area an almost Black Forest feel. "Almost no people go there. You'll see today: there won't be any tracks on the trail except for a few animals. Dad and I would go maybe a quarter mile to the edge of the swamp and cut down a pine tree. It's public land, so I'm not sure if it's legal, but we did it back then, and we'll do it again. It's a tradition!"

"Oh, now I understand why you have a saw and some rope.

We aren't going to a traditional Christmas tree lot?"

"No. After we cut it down, then we drag it out to the car and tie it to the roof, and then we'll celebrate."

"Good, I hope this doesn't take too long. I'm hungry. After last night and this morning, you're going to have to buy me a big lunch." She rubbed her tummy. "And a couple of beers."

"That's my girl." They both laughed. "I love the Bayside for lunch," he said. "Good burgers and chili, and it's close to home."

"Sounds like a good plan," she said as she squeezed his hand.

When he looked at her now, he noticed how happy she seemed. It had been a long time since either of them had sex with anyone. For her, not quite as long as him, but still, long enough after battling cancer and getting past her divorce. That meant trusting a male again. After last night and this morning, it meant Trisha trusted him.

It wasn't a long drive to the turnoff in the Ephraim area. The road ran behind homes, cabins, and condos. He parked the car near an old stone path. It hadn't changed much in the thirty-some years since he and his dad had started the family tradition of walking back to the swampy area. With six inches of snow, it would be easy to drag out the tree.

"Here we are," he said.

Trisha laughed. "You and your dad came to this place every year to get your Christmas tree?"

"Dad used to say, 'No one will never miss a tree from the swamp.' In all the years we came here, we never even saw a car on the road back here. We'd walk back, me dragging the tree out, and once we got back to the car, Dad would tie it to the top of the car, and we'd drive home, discussing the various trees we'd looked at. It seemed like we never cut down the best tree, but rather some second- or third-best tree we came across. When I asked Dad why that was, he just laughed and said, 'Our chosen tree would always be second or third best, but now it leaped above the other trees.' Dad thought a pine tree could never have a higher calling than a Christmas tree. After I thought about it, I had to agree with his reasoning. It really became part of the spirit of our family's Christmas."

She leaned over and kissed his cheek. "That's a nice story. Your dad sounds like a sensitive and caring person."

"He was. Both he and Mom were great people. I miss them both. This Christmas will be tough without them." He smiled as he looked over at Trisha. "Having you here helps me feel less alone, that's for sure. Come on, let's get that tree."

He grabbed the saw and rope to drag the tree out, and they headed down the snow-covered path toward the swamp. As they walked, Randy pointed out animal tracks in the snow. Besides the obvious deer and rabbit prints, they spotted cat, dog or coyote, and raccoon tracks. They even saw where a rabbit had probably lost a battle with a hawk or owl. Randy pointed out the blood splatter and wing marks in the snow.

Soon they were at the familiar Christmas tree spot, and they started the selection process.

"It should be about six or seven feet high. Remember, we have to drag it back to the car."

"What's this *we*?" she asked. "I'm here to help you pick the tree and provide moral support and Christmas spirit."

"That's how it is, is it? Okay, let's pick one from this grouping of eight trees. Which one do you like?"

He watched as she walked around, judging each tree. Finally she pointed to the smallest of them, one about six feet high.

"This one is perfect," she said, smiling.

"I can drag a bigger one. It's not that hard or far to drag it out."

"No. This one." She reached into its branches and pulled out an empty bird's nest. "It's a good luck tree. It gave life, and protection, to some bird and I think it will give your home that same life, protection, and joyous spirit."

"How nice. I like that." He lay down on the snowy ground with the saw and in a few minutes cut down the tree. Dusting the snow and pine needles off his pants and jacket, he straightened his hat and lashed the rope around the base of the tree stump. Then they started walking and dragging the tree back to the car. Thirty minutes later, they had it on top of the car.

"Are you hungry?" he asked.

"Famished. I'm ready for some chili and a hot chocolate with a shot of something in it. Is that okay?"

CHAPTER FOURTEEN

After finishing lunch, they drove the short distance to Randy's house. They dusted the snow, loose dirt, and pine needles off the tree. It took Randy a while to find where his mother stored the ornaments and boxes of tinsel. Once he found that stuff, he settled the tree in the Christmas stand. Then he added water, a traditional penny at the base of the stand, and stood a few feet back to admire the tree.

"What do you think, Trisha?" He watched as she reached for the small bird's nest she had carried back from the swamp. "You need to put the nest on this tree branch."

"You remembered where it was?"

"Yes." She got up and looked at the tree from one side, then the other. She pointed to a spot just a little right of center, halfway up the tree, and in about eight inches. "On this branch right here," she said with a big smile.

Randy took the nest and set it where her finger was touching. "There?"

"Now we can decorate it."

Michael Pritzkow

He reached over to the box of lights, ornaments, and tinsel. "I hate this tinsel crap. My mom used to make me put it on one strand at a time, and then off one strand at a time. I'm sad she's not here to tell me to do it, but I'm throwing all of it out. Bah humbug!" he said and laughed.

The next morning—three days before Christmas—was sunny but bitter cold. Randy's mother had always had an Advent calendar with little doors that opened to reveal a small piece of chocolate for him each day as the holiday approached. All he had now was a bank calendar.

Randy was up early, making coffee. As he walked into the living room to start a fire to take the chill out of the house, he looked into the living room and with pleasure saw the decorated Christmas tree. The tree lights were lit, and the ornaments and lights were haphazardly distributed. He and Trisha had made garlands of popcorn and Wisconsin cranberries, stringing three popcorns kernels and two cranberries on heavy thread, then wrapping the garlands around the tree.

Popcorn had been eaten as they strung. It went well with the beer and wine they were consuming. As he remembered the evening, he was surprised they were able to string, eat and drink. The decorations were concentrated on the front and lower part of the tree. The lights were strung close together, almost like a large belt on someone's waist. It had looked grand last night, but this morning it looked comical. He knew they'd had a jolly time doing it. Then he looked again at the three bottles of wine and six beer bottles in the sink and laughed. No wonder his mouth felt like cotton. They'd even ordered pizza from Bayside Bar after they got the munchies.

He needed caffeine this morning, and he turned on the Mr. Coffee—no old-fashioned stovetop percolator with the glass bubble.

Last night they'd talked about life on Chambers Island. Trish had spent more time there than he had. Getting married and then being introduced to the island life for a few years at the cottage had been really meaningful to her.

This past year had been hard on her, not only because of the cancer but also because of spending so much time alone at the cottage. The island was a good place to hide from people. Wasn't he proof of that? That's what he had been trying to do. But then he'd realized you can't hide your whole life.

And still, that fight in the street near Kitty O'Reilly's might lead to some answers. Thankfully, Trisha, through her investigative efforts, had given him some of those answers.

This was Trisha's last day. Last night, in a sane moment, they had decided to rise early in the morning and go to Sister Bay for a traditional breakfast of Swedish pancakes, Swedish meatballs, and lingberries at Al Johnson's. No goats to see this time of year on the roof.

Afterward she would head back to Chicago and her parents. She could even get gifts at the gift shop there for them.

Michael Pritzkow

As he thought of the last few days and how close they had become, he decided he wanted to give her a Christmas gift. He went to the old wooden desk in the study and pulled out a drawer.

He got out his mother's jewelry box. His mother had never cared for fancy jewelry. Simple, stylish things were her preference. He started thumbing through her earrings and necklaces until he found something he thought Trisha would like: an earring set of turquoise surrounded by silver. A matching necklace went with the earrings. His mother had bought them while vacationing one winter in New Mexico.

Randy had never given a present like this to any of his girlfriends, so he wasn't sure how Trisha would react.

"Good morning." He felt her hand on his back, and then a light kiss on the top of his head. "The coffee smell woke me up, and I sure need some right now. I'm a bit hung over, though I can't remember when I ever had so much fun decorating a tree." She laughed. "You were especially sweet and caring. Last night was very special."

"Most definitely."

"I wish I could stay longer, but my parents were expecting me yesterday, so I really need to go today. That coffee smells delicious."

"It's almost ready."

"What have you got there?"

"It's my mom's jewelry. I want to give you something for Christmas. I hope you don't mind if its old, but I'd like you to have these earrings and necklace."

She picked up the jewelry and walked to a mirror. She held one of the earrings to her ear, then slipped the necklace over her head.

She turned to him and smiled. "I love them. They're simple but beautiful, and I'm honored that you're giving them to me."

He felt her hands on both sides of his face, and felt her lips give him an intense kiss on his lips.

Pulling back she said, "Are you sure you really want to give me these?"

"I'm not going to wear them. Besides, you gave me a great Christmas present with the information you brought about Ingrid. I still can't believe Marvin never said anything to me about his relationship with her, although I remember he did look at me strangely when he first met me. Now I know why."

"I'm glad that gave you peace of mind." She looked at the earrings and necklace. "I'm going to wear these to breakfast and home. They're beautiful. Let's make love one last time before breakfast and my trip home."

An hour later, he said, "This house is going to seem empty without you," said Randy, pulling on a T-shirt. "I'm just getting used to you being here."

"I know. I feel the same way. It's nice to have companionship and maybe something more."

Christmas Eve was lonely. He went to the traditional church service in town, then stopped for a burger at the Bayside before they closed. He needed company. Christmas Eve should be with family. The closest he came to an old tradition was watching the old movie *It's a Wonderful Life* on Christmas Eve.

On Christmas Day, he went cross-country skiing in Peninsula Park, where he encountered several other cross-country skiers and snowshoers enjoying the holiday with loved ones. Being among them made him a bit less lonely. When he got home, he built a fire in the fireplace, made hot cocoa, and then turned on the radio station playing Christmas songs all day. That helped, but he missed Trisha. And he missed his parents even more.

He assumed she was having a good time with her family, and maybe some old friends. He wished he could call her, but he didn't want to interfere with her family time.

———

Three days later, his cell phone rang, and to his joy, it was Trisha.

"Hello. I was hoping you'd call. I missed you."

"I miss you too. I didn't get a chance to be alone so that I could talk until today. My parents and relatives have been keeping me busy. I'm wearing your mother's earrings and necklace. I've gotten lots of compliments on them. Your mother would be happy."

He smiled. "Yes, she would. How was Christmas?"

"Boring. My mother still thinks I'm a little kid. She gave me a stocking filled with candy, but my dad gave me six airline bottles of Jamison whiskey. Dad doesn't do much shopping anymore, but he always knew what I really wanted growing up." She laughed. "I would be happier being with you right now than sitting around here."

"Come on up. I'm not doing anything. We can celebrate New Year's in a couple of days."

There was a pause before she said, "I can't make it up there for New Year's. I accepted an invitation a few weeks ago from friends to their party in Green Bay. They were a couple that my ex and I did a lot with. It was nice that they invited me. I accepted their invitation. I don't want to back out. I always liked them and the people we hung out with. I hope you aren't too disappointed."

"I am disappointed, although I understand."

"I'll come up in a week. How's that?"

"Great. You made my day. I can wait a week. See you next soon."

―――

Tom Leonard, his high school buddy, texted him saying he had to cancel meeting New Year's Day and having a drink—New Year's Day family obligations, he said. So Randy spent the day like most men that day, watching football. The Wisconsin Badgers were playing in the Rose Bowl, and they won by two touchdowns. As a Badger alumnus, he was happy. It had been a long time since they won there.

Late that night, the phone rang with a call from Trisha. "Happy New Year, Randy. How was your night last night? Did you stay up and watch the ball come down at midnight in New York?"

"No watching the ball go down. Matter of fact, I didn't even have the TV on last night. Actually, the day sucked outside of the Badgers winning the Rose Bowl. Happy New Year's to you. How was the party?"

"It was nice to see old friends. One surprise, my ex was invited too, so I skirted around him and tried to avoid him as much as I could. We chatted, but it was strained. My friends were great, and outside of Adam being there, it was nice. Got home a little after midnight. I was a good girl. Ha ha."

"I bet it was a little strained with Adam, but I'm glad you enjoyed yourself. I ended up going to the Bayside for a pizza and a couple of Guinnesses early before heading home for a quiet night reading an old Hemingway novel, *For Whom the Bell Tolls*. I wanted to study Hemingway's short sentence style. I'm getting ready to start a new novel, but first I have to figure out what it's about. Maybe I'll write some short stories and see if anything develops into a longer novel. Stephen King does that."

"I have good news. I'm interviewing for jobs at a couple of TV stations in Green Bay. I approached them about doing investigative reporting for them like I did in Chicago. They were interested. And I got a modeling job in Chicago for a couple of days in mid-January. I really feel good about getting back in the swing of working like I used to. I owe it all to you, you know, for getting me off my butt and feeling sorry for myself."

"That's great. Are you still coming up in a few days?"

"That's the bad news. I'm not going to be able to come up for about three weeks. I'm really sorry, but I have all the interviews and modeling. We're both going to be busy, so hopefully it will pass fast."

Randy felt his shoulders slump in disappointment. "I hope so. I was looking forward to spending time with you again. You're right. But I really do have to start writing, and then there's the meeting with Tom Leonard. He couldn't make New Year's for drinks with the family and all. I'm happy for you and your new work."

"I'll try to call you, so it won't feel so lonely for both of us. Bye."

He clicked off and looked at the fire burning. He felt like shit: alone again.

CHAPTER FIFTEEN

Maybe other people had known about Marvin and Ingrid. He had become Randy's main suspect. How could Randy have missed that she was fooling around with Marvin? The answer was simple: he didn't know Marvin even existed until recently and lived on the island.

He made a list of people he remembered from that time, including his best friend, Tom Leonard. Tom was still working for his dad's plumbing business in Sister Bay. He always told Randy his dad expected him to take over the business. While Randy had not talked to Tom that much after he'd gone off to college in Madison, they had gone out for a few beers over the summers.

But since what happened on Chambers Island, Randy had avoided seeing any old friends. That was going to change. It should be easy to find him down at the plumbing business in Sister Bay and catch up on things over the last ten years.

The next day Randy drove to Leonard Plumbing and Heating, which was just off the main drag near the Piggly Wiggly. Entering the office, he heard the familiar bell ring as he opened and closed the front door. Sitting behind an old rolltop desk just to the right of the entrance was Tom Leonard Sr., dressed in a light-blue work shirt and dark-blue bib overalls. Nothing much seemed to have changed in the last ten years since Randy was last here.

"Hi, Mr. Leonard; Randy Daggett. Don't know if you remember me. It's been a few years since I was here last."

"Sure, I remember you. You're right: it's been a long time. You and Tommy were always in and out of here when you were younger, getting underfoot. Ha ha."

"Just trying to spend time in between the pick-up baseball games. Is Tom around? I'm back home after my parents died. I'm living in their house—my house now."

"Yes, I was really sorry to read about that. I didn't go to the funeral because I didn't read about it until after the service. I don't read the paper like I used to." He turned to the computer screen sitting on the rolltop desk. The computer looked out of place on the old desk as Senior tapped away on the keys, one finger at a time. "Just checking Tommy's schedule. He's installing a bathroom in a new house on German Road. He'll be there all day, but I'm sure he'd like to see you."

Senior grabbed a pink message pad. "Write your phone number on this, and I'll give it to him when he gets in."

"That would be great. I thought you retired."

Senior laughed. "I did, but then I got tired of playing my

rotten golf, so I just started coming here when I wanted to and getting into Tommy's hair. What goes around comes around, so I'm bugging him now. He seems to like having me here—at least he says he does. He's doing a great job running the business. Added three plumbers this year. Business is really humming."

"That's great." Randy gave him the pink message pad with his name and cell phone number. "I'll look forward to getting together with him. It was nice seeing you again."

Getting back in his car, he hoped it wouldn't be too long before he saw his old buddy.

That night at about seven thirty, his cell phone rang, and it was Tom.

"Randy, it's Tom. It's about time I heard from you. Sorry about canceling New Year's, but you know, family stuff. Dad said you stopped in today."

"Hi. It's good to hear your voice. How are you doing?"

"Busy as all heck. Lots of new building and remodeling of old cabins and condos going on up here. Then I have two kids, a boy and girl, who are just getting into sports and music. Loraine and I are busy parents and loving it. Life is good. How about you? You've been gone for a long time."

"Yeah. I was hoping we could meet and catch up."

"I'd like that. It would have to be next week, maybe Tuesday night?"

"Sure, Tuesday works. Where?" Randy asked.

"How about the AC Tap? Remember, it's just outside of Sister Bay on Highway 57. Say about seven? We can have a few beers and a burger. I don't have to clean up from work if we meet there. The food's good. I'll tell Loraine not to make dinner that night for me."

"Sounds great. I'll look forward to it."

It was longer to wait than Randy wanted, but hell, it was January. While he waited for Tuesday to arrive, he thought of the woman classmate that worked at Piggly Wiggly. Today was Wednesday. Didn't she say she went to Husby's on Thursday? He'd go there tomorrow. Even if she wasn't there, he could have a beer and a burger or pizza tomorrow. They had good pizza.

It was four o'clock and happy hour when he arrived. He ordered a Wisconsin favorite, Spotted Cow, and sat back, hoping Janet would show up. She probably worked until four thirty and then went home to change. He was enjoying himself. He always liked this place, and the people here were friendly. He nursed his beer for about an hour, then decided he'd have a burger, fries, and maybe one more beer before calling it a night.

Just at that moment, she arrived.

"Burr, it's cold," he heard her say to no one in particular. She sat across from him on the other side of the bar.

"Hi, Janet." He waved. "It's Randy Daggett. We went to Gibraltar High School together. Mind if I move across and sit next to you? I'd like to catch up. We met at the Piggly Wiggly this past summer and talked about meeting up here."

"Sure, I remember," she said, patting the empty bar stool.

"What would you like to drink? Still happy hour for another fifteen minutes."

"I'll have a Lite. Thank you."

He moved to the other side of the bar next to her. Once they had their beers in front of them, Randy asked, "So what have you been doing over these last ten years since I saw you in school?"

She laughed. "I still live with my parents, so that tells you something. Christ, I'm twenty-nine-years old and can't say I've accomplished anything of consequence."

He watched as she took a big gulp of beer.

"I tried vocational school in Sturgeon Bay, but I didn't like school anymore. I worked up here in the summers cleaning rooms at resorts, which was okay because I would be done early, so I could go to the beach and then go to a few bars I like. Once I turned twenty-one, I bartended, which I liked. I made good tips, but I drank too much and woke up with too many hangovers. Then I started working at Piggly Wiggly, first stocking and then checkout. The pay's not as good as bartending, but I like working there, meeting lots of people, and Piggly Wiggly treats me good. I've gotten nice raises because I'm very social to the customers, and some of them must say something nice about me to the owner, so I'm happy."

"That's great, Janet. Life is all about being happy."

"Yes. Now if I can find someone to share my life with, and get away from home and my parents, I'd really be happy. I'd love to have a couple of kids as long as I'm at it, but nothing yet."

"You will. You're too nice to stay alone. Mr. Right will come along."

"Are you seeing anyone?" she asked, batting her eyes.

He laughed. At least she wasn't bashful. "Yes, I just recently started going out with someone I met on the island. If it doesn't work out, maybe we can have a few more drinks and go out."

"I'm happy for you. It's easier for guys, I think. Anyhow, what have you been doing for the last ten years? I haven't seen you for a long time."

"Yeah. I've been doing research on prison life. I write prison and crime novels under my pen name, Greg Chambers."

"I wish I could write, but that will never happen. I do enjoy reading, especially romance novels. That genre fulfills my fantasy by reading about something I haven't found yet: love!"

"Let me buy this round while it's still happy hour," she added.

It was time to get down to the reason he was really here. "Janet, you said you remembered Ingrid and me dating in high school. We did date then, but also when I came back from college during the summers. What do you know about her?"

He watched her squirm on the barstool.

"Well, only because you asked. I hate gossip. When I was bartending, Ingrid would come in alone or with different guys, usually older guys—and women too. I guess you'd call her bisexual. Whatever, she fooled around with lots of different people."

Randy shook his head. "I guess I trusted her, but then I was working during the day doing construction, working on houses, pounding nails, et cetera. So we really didn't get together until the weekend."

"I think she waitressed in the mornings or did housekeeping. She did lots of different things during the year. We all did to make ends meet."

"Didn't she waitress here in Sister Bay and some bars in Egg Harbor?" he asked.

"Yeah, I think you're right."

"You said she was with older men. Do you remember any men you still see up here? Maybe they live up here all year—or was it more guys that were visiting, probably from Chicago?"

"All of the above. Like I said, I'd see her from time to time at different places. I don't think she had regular spots like most people. Me, I like Husby's, J.J.'s, and the Bowl. I didn't venture too far from Sister Bay back then, or even now.

"Of course, Ephraim was dry back then," she said with a laugh, "but there was the Bayside in Fish Creek, Shipwreck, and Casey's in Egg Harbor, plus the Blue Ox and Coyote Roadhouse near Baileys Harbor. Ingrid went to all of them. You could even throw in the AC Tap on Highway 57."

"Can you think of any specific names of her hookups?"

"Let me think about it. A lot of people come into the Pig, and when they do, it might jog my memory. It's been a while. Oh wait. I remember one. There was a short-order cook guy from one of the restaurants that had the hots for her, and he creeped out everyone at the café. He had a history of sexually harassing the waitresses that worked there. Ingrid left her job there because of him."

"Yes, I know about him."

"Why are you so interested in these people anyhow?"

Coming clean again, he said, "Someone else killed her, but I got convicted for it. I'm looking for someone who might have had a motive to kill her—besides Ramon Rodrigo. That's the cook's name."

"Wow. You went to prison for her death?" She gulped her beer and then just stared at him.

"I deeply cared about her and thought she felt the same way about me. I truly was unaware of her unfaithfulness."

"Well, unfaithful she was to you, that's for sure, but no none deserves to die for that."

"I agree, but I didn't kill her. That's all I can say. I hope you believe me."

"I can't say if I believe you not, but I'll try to think of some others who might have had a motive. Fair enough? Are you hungry? How about pizza?"

He smiled. "Love their pizza here."

CHAPTER SIXTEEN

Maybe he'd get more information from Tom Leonard. He had a few days before meeting him, which gave Randy time to focus on his new novel. He wanted it to feature a different viewpoint from his other successful crime novels, and his publisher had been open to the idea. He didn't mind being stuck writing about prison gangs because crime novels sold well. On Tuesday he paced the house, focusing not on writing but on his meeting with Tom that night. Finally it was time to go, and he made the icy trek to the AC Tap, arriving a couple minutes early.

He needed more fresh leads, though his main suspect was still Marvin Jacobs.

Walking in, he heard a booming voice say, "It's about time you got here. I just finished my first beer. I left work a little early. I always liked this place, and the food is very good. What do you want to drink?"

Ten years had made a dramatic change in Tom's appearance. He must have added forty pounds since Randy had last seen him. He had a full beard and long hair and wore soiled bib overalls.

Tom used to be pretty clean cut.

Tom got up from his bar stool and gave him a big bear hug.

"What are you drinking?" he asked again.

"I'll have the same as you."

"Okay. Give us two more," he told the bartender.

Randy smiled at his old friend. He looked happy. "Loraine must be a pretty good cook. You've put on a few pounds."

He laughed. "As the saying goes, it's all bought and paid for. Before kids, I was in good shape. Dad had me doing most of the strenuous stuff, so I stayed fit. Then the kids showed up. I gained twenty-five pounds with the first one and thirty with the second one. Loraine lost all her weight, but I've kept mine on, and then added a few more pounds for good measure. I can't complain. I'm still in love with my high school sweetheart and have two great kids. All three keep me pretty busy. Business is good, and Dad mostly stays out of my hair. He still loves coming into work, but more than anything it gives him something to do, a reason to get up every morning. He misses Mom. If he's not at the shop, he's over at the house bugging Loraine and spending time with his grandkids. He a great grandpa."

"Yeah, I know how that is. I miss my mom and dad every day. But unlike you, I'm not married or have kids. Not ready for that. Especially with what happened. I need to find the right, understanding person."

"I'm sorry about your parents' accident. I don't read the paper that much anymore, but I'm old school. I just missed seeing the obituary. By the time I did, it was too late."

"That's all right. There were no aunts or uncles or relatives, so it was just my parents' friends. I had been gone for so long, I really didn't recognize most of them. I was glad when it was over."

"I'm trying to remember things since our high school time. You were gone to Madison, at UW for college, and then the Ingrid thing…prison. Right?"

"You got it. Prison. Eight years out of my life for something I didn't do."

"The trial was big news up here." He took a drink. "Nothing like that ever happens in Door County. Not sure there was a murder in the county since then. I'm sorry I didn't visit you in prison."

"It's okay. I really didn't want anyone seeing me there. I was too embarrassed, even now. Just Mom came. Dad didn't the last few years because he wasn't feeling well enough. It's funny. Dad was the sick one. Had been for years, but it was Mom's heart attack while driving that killed them both. Doesn't make sense…life."

Tom just nodded.

"Thanks for coming out tonight," said Randy.

"Sure," Tom said with a smile. "I wanted to catch up. What are you doing now?"

"I was an English and teaching major at the university. When I was in prison, I started writing novels. Sort of pulp fiction about prison life, gangs, stuff like that. Kind of like Elmore Leonard wrote, if you've read his stuff. Same name as you too." Randy laughed. "Shit if it didn't sell, and I wrote eight novels while in there. You write what you know. I saw the stories all around me every day: the characters, the gangs, and how the prison system worked. Actually, after the first one sold and I got extra copies, I gave them to the prison library. About all you can do there is read or watch TV. TV gets old, so a lot of the guys read. I was kind of the inside celebrity. Other folks inside wanted to be included in my stories, so I got a lot of insider information on life inside. I actually did use some of them as characters in my books, although I changed the names. Inside, they all knew who I was writing about, and they liked it. When I got out, I wanted to just disappear, so I bought a cabin out on Chambers Island."

"Really?"

"That's where I live in the summer, with occasional days at Mom and Dad's."

Tom sighed. "Really? I bet it's beautiful out there. It looks so far away. I've never been there. Someday I'll have to get out there. I'm sure my kids would like it. An adventure for sure."

"This summer I'll bring you and your family out there. They can swim, and we can grill. My cabin isn't much, but it's quiet, and I like writing there."

After they both ordered a burger and another beer, Tom said, "I know you're not a violent person, but Ingrid did die, and you were the only one on that beach that night. Maybe it was the side effect of that drug I read about that you were taking. Do you take the drug still?"

"No! Nothing since prison and nothing now. I still have a hard time sleeping, but I won't touch the stuff." He took a swig of his beer. "I found out that Ingrid had some restraining orders against two guys and a woman. I was hoping you knew of some other people she might have gone out with when I was in school and wasn't around here. I met some guy at the Bayside Bar that said she liked to go out to Chambers and party, including sex."

"Who was the guy? Maybe I know him?"

"I never got his name." *But I'll never forget what he did to me later.* "He's in construction. I think he's a carpenter or, like you, a plumber. He said he did it with her out on the island before he was married, so he's probably right around our age. If I see him again, I'll try to get his name and the company he works for. When I was gone at school down in Madison, did you see her fooling around with guys or women?"

Tom stroked his beard, thinking. "The only one I remember was Ed Livingston, but he moved away to Florida years ago. Then when she'd waitress at the different restaurants up here, she'd get hit on by the guys with money."

"Yes, and then there was a guy named Ramon that got fired for fooling around with her."

He laughed. "I don't remember Ingrid going out with anyone regular-like. But then I wasn't really paying much attention to her. I was engaged to Loraine, you know, right out of high school."

"That's right. You were hot and heavy with her even then. That's nice."

"Yes, I was lucky." He reached for his beer and drained it. He looked at his watch. "I guess I can have one more, but that's it. Can't afford to get a DWI, plus it's getting late." He tapped the bar and ordered another round. "I'll talk to Loraine and see if we can come up with anything else that might help you."

Michael Pritzkow

It was the third week in January and very cold, but his body warmed up and his heart beat faster when he saw Trisha's car pull into the driveway. He had spent most of yesterday cleaning the last of the holiday stuff, which meant vacuuming the carpet over and over again to get all of the pine needles out. Then he dusted and cleaned the ashes from the fireplace and lay in several split logs. He had gone to the market for food and drink supplies. He was hoping they wouldn't leave the house except to ski or snowshoe.

He watched as she unloaded a large rolling suitcase and a small backpack. This was good. It looked like she was planning on staying longer than a couple of days.

Moving up the short drive, he swung open the front door and grabbed her suitcase, rolling it in. Trisha followed, dropped her backpack with a thud on the slate entryway, then wrapped her arms around him. They kissed hungrily for minutes, not wanting to let go until they almost toppled over as they lost their balance.

"I couldn't wait to get here and kiss you," she said, raising her hand to his face and gently brushing his hair.

"I couldn't wait either. Door County can be really quiet during the winter. Are you hungry? I can make you something, or we can go out and grab lunch."

"No. I do need to go to the bathroom right now, but after that, I just want to stay here and be with you."

"Sounds good to me." As she made her way to the bathroom, he took her suitcase and backpack to the bedroom. When he came back, he saw she was in the kitchen, looking inside his refrigerator.

"You have enough food in here for a week. I like a man that's prepared, just in case there's a blizzard. We won't starve or die of thirst. Three bottles of wine and a twelve pack of beer. The essentials, I'd say."

He walked over and wrapped his arms around her and kissed her neck. He smiled as she started pulling out lettuce, a large tomato, mayonnaise, bacon, and some twelve-grain bread.

"I love BLTs any time of the year," she said. "Doesn't that sound good? I'm glad you have the microwave bacon. It's so fast and tastes good. You just need to put more bacon on the sandwich. Is it too early for a beer?"

He looked at her wide eyed and smiled. He loved this person. "It's not too early for a beer, but we can have all this in a little while. I want to make love. I can't help myself. It's seeming like the right thing to do, to show you how much you mean to me. Am I being too horny?"

She kissed him, grabbed two bottles of beer, then reached for his hand. "The beer is for later when were done. I know I'll be thirsty after my thirst for you is quenched."

―――――

That night, Randy made a simple pot roast with carrots, onions, and russet potatoes. He opened a bottle of Cabernet with dinner, and then for dessert they had Dove ice cream bars—his favorite apart from Door County cherry pie.

Trisha sat across the table from him, holding his hands in hers. "It doesn't get any better than this, if you ask me. And you even cooked me a romantic meal. 'God bless the cook,'" she said and kissed a hand.

"I'll make a fire and spread out a blanket. We can have another bottle of wine."

"Are you trying to get me drunk and take advantage of me?"

"I hope so, but I already did that this afternoon." He paused before getting serious. "It's just nice to hold you in my arms. In December, you awakened a need I had forgotten about. That need was to care about someone and have that same person care about me. I like caring for you. Does that make sense?"

"Yes, it does. I'm glad you do. I missed being cared for. After Adam divorced me, I was worried I'd never find that again. I told you I saw him at the New Year's Eve party, didn't I?"

Randy felt his stomach clinch. "How did that go?"

"It was okay. He was cordial to me. We made small talk. Even that started to get uncomfortable, so I moved away from him for the rest of the party. It was a small group of our friends, so I didn't want to make a scene. I didn't slap him, if that's what you were hoping for." She lightly dug her nails into his hands to let him know it was a joke.

"You two were married, so it's understandable if you still have feelings for him."

"Well, if it makes you feel any better, we didn't even hug or kiss on the cheek. Green Bay is a small town, so I'm sure I'll run into him again, but we are divorced. I have the one possession he loved the most: the cabin, not me."

"Enough about him," said Randy. "Let's talk about us."

"This fire and blanket are so romantic," she said. "Since I missed it with you, let's pretend it's New Year's and together celebrate a new year."

The next morning, after having pancakes and sausage, they got the snowshoes and walking poles out and went to Peninsula State Park. Snowshoeing three and a half miles with the sun out and calm conditions made for a delightful morning of exercise. They decided to head to Egg Harbor and stock up at the Main Street Market for snacks, a couple steaks, and a frozen pizza. After that, they went to Casey's for BBQ and beer. Soon it was time for home and a nap.

"Can you believe we're actually going to take a nap?" she asked. "A real nap."

"You'll get no complaining from me. I'm tired," he said. They both lay down on the bed in their clothes and fell asleep. Three hours later, they woke up.

"I need a shower," Trisha said.

"I'll take one after you. While you're doing that, I'll put out cheese and crackers. Then I'll start a fire."

"Too bad the shower isn't bigger for two," Trisha said with raised eyebrows.

"Should we try and see if we can both fit?"

Michael Pritzkow

A half an hour later, they were having cheese and sausage, sipping Pinot Noir while sitting before the crackling fire.

"I could get used to this," he said.

"So could I, but I have to start my new job at the TV station in a couple of days."

"Yes, and I need to work on my book too. No book, no money. Otherwise, we need to win the lottery. If that happens, then we could live the life of leisure."

"Aren't we doing that now?" she said and laughed.

———

Trisha had told him that she'd be back in a few weeks, after she got in the swing of things at the TV station in Green Bay.

Actually, she could drive up any night if she wanted, he thought. He wasn't sure where she lived in Green Bay, but it was an easy drive on a four-lane road to Sturgeon Bay and about twenty minutes from there to Fish Creek. But maybe her reporting entailed odd hours. He hoped she could get up to Fish Creek more than once in a while. He already missed her, and she had just left that morning. It must be love.

Neither had come out and said those exact words, but it was almost time for a declaration.

———

Thursday night, Trisha called to tell him she was coming up for the weekend. That news felt like Christmas again. Friday morning he went out shopping for food and wine. He vacuumed the house, dusted, changed the sheets, and made sure the kitchen looked presentable. He laughed to himself as he was busy doing all the things—things guys do when there is love, and sex is involved.

He even had made progress on his new novel, writing over a hundred pages since the first of the year. He was writing it from the point of view of a prison guard, Elmore Leonard style with lots of dialogue.

Earlier in the afternoon, he kept looking at the hand of his parents' big chiming mantel clock. The hands didn't seem to move. He went over to it and listened, but he heard the steady tick-tick of the movements. He was just anxious to see Trisha.

Finally, he saw her SUV pull into his driveway. He watched as she pulled out her backpack while he opened the door.

"Did you miss me?" she asked.

"Couldn't you come up with something more imaginative than that? Aren't you one of those quick-witted television people?"

She just smiled as she melted into his outstretched arms. They kissed for a long while.

"Let's go inside," said Randy. "It's cold out here. It's been a long week." He had built a roaring fire, and they sat cross-legged on an old quilt.

Trisha explained how she got stories for her investigative reporting segment on the morning, six-thirty, and ten o'clock news. Most times people called in because they were dissatisfied with something that happened to them or they'd witnessed disturbing activities in their neighborhood or at a business where they worked or frequented.

Randy told her about his new book and how difficult it was because he wasn't adept at the guard's point of view.

In front of a roaring fire, they talked and talked.

"I'm really hungry," said Trisha. "What can we make that's easy? Mostly, I just want to lay here with you in front of this fire and talk and make love."

"How about toasted cheese and tomato soup? That's simple."

And so it went for the rest of the night into the wee hours of the morning.

"It feels so good to be in your arms," she said.

He just nodded and snuggled his face into her long black hair and said, "It does, doesn't it?"

———

The next day they were late getting started and drove the short distance to Al Johnson's for their famous pancakes and Swedish meatballs. Randy usually had ham, but today he went with tradition.

Then they headed to Gills Rock and looked out at Washington Island and Detroit Island. The car ferry had just left, and they didn't feel like waiting around, plus they figured there won't be much going on this time of year, so they headed back to Sister Bay's bowling alley.

Trisha beat Randy by fifteen pins when he got a split in the last frame, and she got two strikes. Then they had a Bloody Mary and a light lunch of French fries and a half a cheeseburger each. All and all, a relaxing morning, he thought, as they headed back to Fish Creek and a nap.

Randy built another fire, and they sat, sipping wine and eating cheese curds.

"It's funny how you don't see someone you really don't want to meet and then boom: you run into them three times in a couple of weeks," Trisha said.

"Oh. Who didn't you want to see?" Randy asked, sitting up straighter.

"My ex, Adam. I was out with some of my coworkers after the six thirty news at a local bar, and I ran into him. He came over and chatted. The first couple of times it happened, I didn't think anything of it. The third time was at different Green Bay bar, I got upset. I accused him of stalking me. Of course he denied it."

"You don't have feelings for him, do you?" Randy asked.

"I loved him at one time, but then he left me because I wasn't perfect. He couldn't handle the cancer and the operation. Hell, I had a hard time handling everything. Thank God for my parents, and later you."

"Yes, I remember you telling me."

"This time I was at the Tundra Bar with friends when he came over, Adam told me he made a big mistake and he wanted to get back together. 'You were the love of my life.' He said he was sorry that he'd acted the way he did. He admitted he was an ass. I said getting back together was never going to happen—not if he was the last man on earth. I had found someone else that I like. I told him to go to hell and quit bugging me."

"What did he do then?"

"He turned around and went back to his friends. But he kept staring at me all night. Finally, I couldn't take it anymore. When he got up to go to the bathroom, I got up and left."

"You're here now. I care deeply for you. I shouldn't say this, Trisha"—he paused—"but I love you."

He waited for her to say, "I love you too, Randy," but she didn't. She just looked at her hands, eyes downcast.

All night as she lay in his arms, he thought about why she didn't respond. He guessed she wasn't ready to make that commitment, even if he was. Randy was tired of being alone.

CHAPTER SEVENTEEN

Over the next few weeks, they frequently talked on the phone, as Trisha said she had to work or was meeting her mother or just couldn't get away. When Randy asked if he could come down, she said no, she was too busy, Spring was coming, she'd be more settled into her job by then. And she'd be coming to the Chambers Island cabin on the weekends, they'd spend more time together there. She did come up one weeknight. They made love, but it didn't seem the same.

"Is everything all right?" he asked. "You seem different, not as engaged as in the past."

"I'm sorry, Randy. It's the stress of my job. I'm constantly under the gun. It's not like you having to write your novel and meet some eventual deadline. I have a deadline every week. It will be better when I'm on the island, just wait and see."

He saw her point. With a television segment to produce, she was constantly under the gun.

Still, things were not progressing with them, and it seemed to stem from when he had said he loved her. He thought she would be happy when he announced that to her, but…maybe he'd been wrong. He was nervous. He didn't want to lose her.

It was amazing how much writing he could get done without any distractions. Sometimes he'd write three pages, five pages, and one day he even wrote ten pages. Writing from a new point of view was interesting and exciting. He talked to Stewart, his guard friend at the prison, over a couple of drinks like they talked about when he was leaving prison. He got some good feedback about the guard's point of view.

He heard his phone ring. It was Tom Leonard.

"Hello, Tom. To what do I owe this call on a bright, sunny spring morning?"

"I think I've got a line on the guy you asked me about. The guy you said beat you up. His name is Cliff Jones."

"Are you sure?" Randy asked.

"Pretty sure. I was at the AC Tap, and he came in. There was one of those crime shows on the TV, talking about some woman being killed. One of his buddies made some comment about if he had a chance to do something to the prime suspect, he beat the shit out of the guy. That's when Cliff Jones said he had done just that, but after the guy got out of prison after eight years. He said he wanted to do more to the guy, but he was afraid he might kill him or get thrown in jail. He said the girl was someone he had a fling with. He said she was a lot of fun. He said her name was

Ingrid. When they left, I went out of the bar and saw the name on his truck. I called the company and described him, said I wanted to thank him for the nice job he did for one of my clients. They were only too happy to give me his name."

"Thanks, Tom. Cliff Jones was the same guy Ingrid had a restraining order against. Now I need to talk to this guy and try not to get beat up again. Maybe I'll bring a baseball bat with me. He's bigger than me, but I do know how to swing a bat, as you might recall."

"I remember that fight that got you kicked out of that game and suspended for the next too."

"Hey, the pitcher had it coming. He threw it at my head, so I went at him. I didn't throw the bat at his head, just at his shins, and then I hit him with my fist. So I got kicked out of that game and the next. It taught me a lesson. I never did anything violent after that, and that includes killing Ingrid."

"Well, be careful. Got to go. I've got lots of work to do today. We'll meet for a couple of drinks, maybe next week."

"I'm buying."

―――

Randy reviewed his notes from December. Trisha had given him the name of the guy, Cliff Jones, and had also mentioned a woman whom Ingrid had a restraining order against. Her name was Shelly Ferano. He got on his computer. A couple of taps, and he got her cell phone number after paying a small fee to the service.

Michael Pritzkow

———

Randy staked out Shelly Furano's townhouse in Sister Bay. It was just after five, and he was hoping she was going to go out. He sat in his car for two hours and was getting ready to pack it in, figuring she was going to stay in for the night, when the house's front door opened, and out she came.

"Finally," he said out loud.

He followed her to J.J.'s at the end of town, probably meeting someone for a margarita and Mexican food. He pulled into a parking space and followed her in.

She sat on a stool next to a woman and kissed her on the lips.

Randy was in luck. An older couple sat next to Shelly and her friend, but next to them was an empty stool for him. He sat and ordered a margarita, salsa, and chips.

Soon the older couple got up and left. He moved over the two spots.

"Mind if I sit here? I'll have a better view of the basketball game on TV."

"Sure," said Shelly's friend. "Wisconsin is playing Northwestern. Should be a good game."

Shelly said, "Are you from around here? Not many people up here this time of year unless they're local."

"I live in Fish Creek and in the summer on Chambers Island."

"Wow. What's it like to live on that island?"

"It's beautiful, interesting, and quiet. I'm a writer, so it's a perfect spot to write." He dipped a chip into the salsa.

"We both live up here now." Shelly's eyes moved to her friend. "Susan moved from Chicago to be up here a couple of years ago, but I've lived here since fifth grade. Grew up in the Milwaukee area, but this is home. My name's Shelly." She stuck out her hand.

"Hello, I'm Randy Daggett, but my books are under my pen name, Greg Chambers."

"Chambers, like the island?" Shelly asked. "How convenient."

"Yes. I liked the ring of it. I grew up looking at that island my whole life living in Fish Creek. Last summer, I had a chance to buy a cabin there, and so I did. Don't regret it one bit. A lot of people go out there to swim and party. I live near Sand Bay. A lot goes on there."

"I know," said Shelly. "I lost a friend there about ten or eleven years ago."

"Yes. So, did I. My girlfriend. Her name was Ingrid Karlsen."

Shelly gasped, then stared at him, hard.

"She was your girlfriend? She used to be mine too."

"I was just her summer boyfriend. She had lots of friends, male and female, when I was gone at school."

"Ah. She used to talk about you. How nice you were. How nice your parents were to her too. She said she felt bad about fooling around behind your back, but that was Ingrid. She always thought about herself first. She fucked me over too, so I understand why maybe she got killed. Some guy was convicted for killing her. Drowning her."

Randy stared at her, waiting, but the realization didn't come to her. Was it the margaritas she was drinking? But then he saw she finally got it, and she almost shouted, "It was you. I remember now. You killed her!"

He saw several people in the bar area turn and stare at her, then at him.

"Sorry. I didn't mean to say that so loud. You're out? Out of prison?"

"I served eight years for manslaughter. But I have some questions, and I need to talk to you."

"To me? Why" She looked surprised.

"Because I didn't killed Ingrid. I'm trying to find out who might have had a motive to kill her. I'm thinking you did."

Shelly stood up and slapped him.

Now more people stared.

He didn't even rub the spot where she slapped him, although it really stung. "You've got a little anger management problem, don't you? You must have had the same thing with Ingrid when she was living with you. You were a couple. Then she walked out on you and left you with the whole rent payment. Is that why she took out a restraining order? Because you threatened her?"

Shelly's girlfriend, sitting next to her, got wide eyed and said, "You told me about Ingrid, but you never told me about a restraining order. Why did she get a restraining order against you?"

"Yes, Shelly, what did you do to her?" asked Randy. "Did you maybe follow her to the Bayside, see us leave in my sailboat, and realize where we were going? You probably knew she liked to go out there to drink and have sex. So you grabbed a boat, waited for your chance, and killed her when I slept. Revenge is sweet, right, Shelly?"

"You're nuts. I didn't do anything. I was long past having any feelings for her. She was a bitch, a user. Ingrid got killed because of what she did to people—like to you. You got convicted for killing her. Not me."

She sat and composed herself. He noticed her friend moving her stool back from her.

"The restraining order said you physically attacked her and had your hands around her neck. Ingrid took pictures of the bruises."

"Maybe I got a little rough with her, but she used me. We ran into each other at some bar in Egg Harbor and got into a big fight. Nasty scene, I admit, but I was furious. She walked out on our lease, sticking me with the rent payments I couldn't afford. Yes, I was pissed! I needed to find another job for six months to cover the cost until I could move to a smaller place I could afford." She finished her margarita and ordered another.

"She left me for some guy she met in Sturgeon Bay at some Irish bar. I heard she went there after she dumped me. I went to find out the dirt, talked to some person named Carla. She knew everyone and everything, good and juicy. She filled me in on everything Ingrid had done with this guy. She said Ingrid was a real piece of work. As soon as this guy left her to go back to Chicago and his wife, she hooked up with another guy. If you don't believe me, go down there and talk to Carla at Kitty's. She'll fill you in. Ingrid was fucking some Chicago doctor who set her up in an apartment for the summer, evidently came up every weekend, and had sex with her. He lived in Chicago is all I know. Her sugar daddy came up for the summer. He took her out to eat, bought her nice clothes. If you ask me, she was a whore, plain and simple. Even this rich guy finally got tired of her wanting more and more things, and he dumped her. How she fit you into her schedule, Randy, is a mystery to me."

"Me too. I was working construction with long days. I was exhausted most nights and went straight to bed. We met mostly on the weekends when she wasn't busy."

She finished her margarita and asked the bartender for another. Susan's friend must have

decided, at least for now, that she wasn't dangerous. She moved her stool back near her and ordered another margarita too.

Shelly was getting chatty; maybe it was the margaritas. She probably wanted to shift the blame to someone else.

Randy ordered another drink also but decided not to drink it. He wanted to stay focused. He watched as Shelly tipped her head to the ceiling as if gathering her thoughts. When she lowered her head, she was ready to tell him something important.

"You might find this interesting. She met some construction guy a few years before when she was just eighteen. She couldn't legally drink, but this guy said he had lots of beer, and if she went out there and partied with him and two other couples, she'd have a good time. Well, she must have had a good time, because she told me they drank lots of beer, and then toward night, they found a secluded part of the beach and had sex. Then, she said she hadn't seen him for a couple of years. Just before she died, he started showing up again."

It must have been Cliff Jones, he thought.

"You mean she quit going out to the island with this guy for a few years, and then started going out there again with him?"

"Yes. He went out in a small fishing boat and partied. This guy was married by the time they started fooling around the second time. He had one or two kids and another on the way. Evidently, his wife didn't want sex anymore so—"

"So he went back to Ingrid?"

"She was always willing as long as they could party and later have sex. They went south to Sturgeon Bay, where his wife wouldn't find out. They liked an Irish bar there. I think it was Kitty O'Reilly's, if I'm not mistaken. He figured drinking in Sturgeon Bay wouldn't get back to his wife up north. Fun place. I go there myself when I go south. This guy even sprung for some sexy lingerie. Ingrid kept asking for more. She was hoping he'd dump his wife for her. She didn't think the children would be a problem, but she was wrong Finally, he'd had enough."

"Recurring pattern for Ingrid," Randy thought, "Funny, she never asked me for stuff like that, but I was still a poor student. Now I know why she always looked nice."

"She figured you didn't have the money, so why ask?"

"I guess so."

"But Ingrid got nasty to this guy and said if he didn't give her some money to buy some clothes, she was going to tell his wife. Wow, he didn't like that. To prove his point, he slapped her around, grabbed her by the throat, and left bruises on her neck. She had me take pictures just to prove it. That's when she got the restraining order against him. She was really, really afraid of him."

"She had pictures, like she had pictures of what you did to her?"

Yeah, yeah, I know, but that was different. No way I'd kill her for skipping out on the rent. There was a time when I did love her, but that changed later."

"Where are these pictures?"

"I think I have them in some box with some of her lingerie. They were nice, so I kept them, hoping I could fit into them when I lost weight. Stuff like that never goes out of style. It was a long time ago."

"I guess so," he said.

"The Cliff guy is who you should talk to.

"Was his name Cliff Jones?"

"Might have been. I forget. It was a long time ago, but you can look up his name in court documents. She was scared to death about him. She said to keep the pictures in case something happened to her. I didn't think about them because you were convicted of killing her. I should have gone to the police with what I knew and the pictures, but I thought you were the killer. Sorry about that."

"You're right. You should have gone to the police. It might have helped me. I will talk to him. Do you think you could find the pictures of the bruises on her neck and arm and give them to me? I can pick them up. I know where you live."

"You do? I guess I could."

He leaned back and started to drink the margarita. Now he knew why the guy beat him up. He had something to hide.

CHAPTER EIGHTEEN

A week later, Randy's phone rang at ten thirty on a Thursday night. When he looked at the caller ID, he got a big smile.

"Hi, Randy. Sorry for calling so late."

"What a pleasant surprise. It's not too late for you. Besides I'm still up, writing. What's up?"

"I was wondering if it was all right to come up tomorrow night after I'm done with work."

"That would be great. It's been too long. I thought you forgot about me and—"

"I didn't forget about you. Just wanted to see you, and tomorrow is Friday. It's the first time I could get up there. How about seven thirty? I should be done with my segment, and then I can drive up. Let's stay in, okay?"

"Sounds good to me. I've made progress on the investigation. I'll fill you in."

"Okay. See you tomorrow night." *Click*.

He looked at the phone. She'd sounded stressed out. Didn't say anything affectionate either. He hoped everything was all right for her at work or with her parents. He'd find out tomorrow.

―――

The day crawled by. Doing normal things was difficult. He had a sick feeling about the meeting with Trisha. She didn't seem happy like she used to be when they'd talked on the phone. He reminded himself that 90 percent of the negative things people think will happen never actually happen. Still, he worried. The day crept by.

Finally, it was time, and she showed up right on schedule.

He saw her bound out of the car, grab her backpack from the back seat, and walk toward him, smiling. At least she didn't look sad, he thought.

She walked up and kissed him.

A nice kiss, he thought.

"Would you like something to drink?" he asked. "I'm making spaghetti for dinner, so we can have a few drinks and then eat."

"I'll have wine. Red if you've got it?"

He poured her a Pinot Noir and one for himself.

"So how was your week?" he asked, but he kind of knew the answer.

"It was hectic, to say the least. I always seem to be on the short end of a deadline, plus I have to come up with investigative pieces. How about you? How's the book coming?"

"It's okay. I've got a lot done this winter, but it's from a different point of view."

"What do you mean? It's about crime and prison, isn't it?

You're familiar with that, I'm sure."

"I guess so. Since December, I've made a lot of progress." He leaned over and kissed Trisha. "There are a lot of ups and downs in the prison novels, and I'm just not sure I've perfectly captured the guard's point of view yet. We'll see when I'm done with the first draft."

"Well, there are a lot of ups and downs in life, including prison life." She finished the wine in her glass, then looked at him, wiggling her wine glass.

"I think I need more wine," she said. "I need to unwind."

———

Dinner was a joint effort. Randy started browning the hamburger in the pot they were going to use to cook the premade spaghetti sauce. Once it was browned and the fat was drawn off, he dumped in the sauce. Trisha added herbs and spices, a little sugar, and salt, and they let it simmer as they finished the first bottle of wine.

Early spring in Door County was still cold enough for ice in the bay, so Randy built a fire. This is the way it was supposed to be with someone you loved, he thought. Maybe his doubts about their relationship had been wrong.

After another bottle of wine and dinner, they lingered in front of the smoldering fire until eleven o'clock. They finished the night making love and falling asleep in each other's arms.

———

Saturday morning in Fish Creek brought a perfect late-March combination of bright blue sky and warm sunshine. With steaming mugs of coffee, they headed to Peninsula State Park's Sunset Trail for a long walk.

Life seemed good to Randy as he walked hand and hand with Trisha. As they hiked, they spotted animals scurrying around the trees and spots of snow.

As they walked the sand-and-pebble beach, Randy noticed that the ice in the bay was starting to turn black, which meant it would soon break up, especially if a strong north wind came blowing in. That wind would break up the softer ice and open up the area between Fish Creek and Chambers Island.

"Everything seems right with the world this morning," he said to Trisha. "I was worried that something was wrong between us, ever since I told you I loved you in January. You seemed so distant." He squeezed her hand. "I guess I was wrong. Last night and this morning were wonderful." He waited for her to agree.

When he turned to look at her, she didn't look at him but instead looked down at the sand and pebbles. He saw a tear slide down her cheek. His stomach clinched, and he realized his initial instincts had been correct.

"I wanted last night and this morning to be perfect and loving," she said, "because I do love you Randy, but—"

"Where are you going with this?"

"I'm getting back together with Adam," she said matter-of-factly. "When he saw me at the New Year's Eve party, he made a commitment to rekindle our love. He called me every day. We went out, and as we did, I realized he had changed. You know the cabin has been in his family forever. He missed being there. It was a big part of his life. I have to admit, I missed him being there with me too. There were so many memories there of being with him, but I was so pissed at him I had kept them suppressed. Thank God you were there, Randy, and got me out of my black hole. I fell in love with you for what you did, the way you supported me."

"Do you always fall in and out of love that easily?" he asked.

"I guess I had that coming. And the answer to your question is *no*. I'll never forget what you did for me last summer, but Adam was my first real love. I realized I need to be with him. I'm really sorry, Randy. I never wanted it to end like this, otherwise I wouldn't have started our relationship in December. Last night I wanted to spend our time together the way it was in December, and we did. Now I have to move forward with my life. We'll see each other on the island, but it won't be the same because Adam will be with me. I hope you understand. I don't know if you'll forgive me." She started crying.

Seeing her cry, Randy couldn't help himself. He wrapped his arms around her, and he felt hot tears wash down his face too. Finally, after holding each other for how long he didn't know, they separated, and he knew it was over.

"You were the first one that believed I might not have killed Ingrid," said Randy. "That was important to me. Then you investigated that idea and came up here in December and gave me three possible suspects. You gave me hope. It's just not easy for me to fall in, then out of love."

As tears rolled down her cheeks again, she nodded. Her body shook.

"You're right, Randy. I'm really sorry for causing you this pain. I didn't mean to fall in love with you. All I can tell you is that it was real in December."

"I guess I'll get over it in time, but it will be hard every time I see you on the island, especially with Adam."

"I understand."

He had been following Cliff Jones for two days, waiting for the right time to confront him. It had to be in a public location, someplace where they could talk without getting into a fight. And if a fight did break out, Randy wanted there to be witnesses.

Cliff often had a beer or two after work. This day Cliff was drinking at Kitty O'Reilly's in Sturgeon Bay with some of his fellow construction workers. Kitty's was a popular spot in Door County, and especially in Sturgeon Bay—not only for the scenery the pretty waitresses provided but also for its wide selection of beer and excellent food. Randy sometimes stopped there on his way back from his parole meetings in Green Bay or if he was in the Sturgeon Bay area.

"Welcome to Kitty's," called out Carla, his favorite waitress, as he walked in. It was Thursday, so she was bartending today and not waitressing as usual.

"Hi Greg, how's the writing coming? More crime novels, or

are you doing something different?"

"Actually, no. I'm doing a different slant on crime and prison life."

"Oh, something different. Nice."

"Carla, I should tell you, Greg is my pen name."

"Your pen name. All this time I've been calling you by your pen name. Why?"

"My actual name is Randy Daggett."

"And the reason?"

"It's a long story. I'll tell you another time."

"Got it. Your usual Guinness?"

"Yes. I'll be back inside, but first I have to talk to someone who came in here a little while ago. He was wearing a chartreuse hooded sweatshirt." He looked around. "He must be outside. It's a nice day to sit out there."

"You're right. A bunch of construction guys just went outside. I guess they're used to the cold. Me, I like it in here where it's warm, even if we have heaters out there. I'll catch you on your way out, and you can settle up with me then."

He nodded. He got up and headed outside to Cliff Jones.

CHAPTER NINETEEN

Cliff Jones was seated with other guys from the same company he worked for, by the look of their sweatshirts. Randy noticed he looked to have put on a few more pounds since the fight on the street.

Randy sat at an empty table not far away, just watching, waiting for the fellow workers to leave. He sipped his Guinness because he wanted to stay sharp for questioning, and because he might have to defend himself.

After forty-five minutes, two of the four guys got up and left. A few minutes later the third guy and Cliff finished their drinks and got up. As they were walking toward the door to go back inside the bar, Randy yelled at him.

"Hey, Cliff! Remember me? I need to talk to you before I go to the police with the information I have on you." Randy expected that would get his attention.

Cliff stared at Randy for a few seconds, trying to remember him.

The other construction worker turned and looked at Cliff

with a questioning look on his face.

"Now I remember you. You're the guy that killed Ingrid Karlsen."

"And the guy you beat up. I should have pressed charges against you. If you try it again, I will. I have witnesses now." He pointed to all the people sitting at tables.

Cliff turned to his friend. "This creep killed a friend of mine years ago, so I took a little retribution on him. That's all. I'll see you tomorrow." After his friend nodded and walked out, Cliff came over to Randy's table and stood menacingly over him.

Randy smiled. "Sit. We have a few things to talk about involving you and Ingrid. Now I know why you beat me up. I did a little digging since then and found out some reasons you did it."

"Really. What's that?"

"Sit down, and we'll talk."

Cliff looked unhappily at his watch, then at the empty chair, but he took a seat.

Randy started in: "I remember you telling me the first time we met at the Bayside, you and Ingrid used to go out to Chambers and drink, and later have sex. You realized she was underage to drink at the time?"

"Yeah, but she wasn't too young to have sex," he said, "and she loved it with me. She liked to drink and party. The cops would laugh in your face if you thought they cared about something like that. I'd just get a ticket, and that would be it."

"You're right. That's not what they'd find interesting, Cliff."

"So." Looking smug, he reached over and took the drink

sitting in front of Randy and moved in front of him, and he took a swallow from it. "I'm still thirsty."

"I remember you telling me you knocked up your girlfriend," said Randy, "and that's why you quit seeing Ingrid."

"That's right. So far you haven't told me anything new. I'm leaving. My wife and kids are waiting." He drained the rest of Randy's beer and stood up to leave. "Thanks for the beer, asshole."

"Sit down, Cliff. I haven't told you what the police would find interesting, and I have proof. What you did to Ingrid could send you to prison for the murder I was convicted of."

"I didn't kill anyone."

"We'll let the police decide. After all, Ingrid had a restraining order against you."

"So what? Lots of people get restraining orders against them. That doesn't mean they kill. I just needed to stay away from her and to stay out of trouble with the police. That's what I did."

"Ingrid was after you to spend more money and time with her. She thought you might be the nice guy she was always looking for. You were good to her when she was underage. You liked to show her a good time and buy her things later. She was hoping you'd go for a younger woman that liked sex and keep buying her the nice things in life. When you said you couldn't, she threatened to tell your wife. I'd guess you'd considered that blackmail. Ingrid told her girlfriend that you went ballistic, threatened to kill her. You slapped her around, bruised her arm, and left marks on her neck when you choked her. That's when she got the restraining order. I even have pictures to prove what you did. Her girlfriend gave them to me." He reached into his back pants pocket and pulled out some pictures. He showed him a couple of the pictures he brought to prove it.

"Okay. I'll agree I got a little too rough with her, but she was going to tell my wife, and I just couldn't let that happen. So I tried to scare her, but it didn't work. Ingrid got a gun from her foster father. Evidently they used to shoot at tin cans and stuff. She got so mad at me when I dumped her, she shot out two of my truck tires. The shooting raised the idea in my wife's mind that someone was pissed off at me. She badgered me until finally I had to tell her. Ingrid didn't tell my wife; I did. She was really pissed at me. We went to therapy, and eventually we worked everything out. We're still together, happy, and that's all that mattered to me. Besides, you're the one that killed her. You were convicted for doing it."

"Here's what I think happened. You took your fishing boat out to Chambers Island after you saw us leaving Bayside Bar. You knew just what would happen out there because it happened to you with her. You followed us out, anchored the boat, and waited. Then you saw your chance and killed her. You were pissed at her for shooting your tires and maybe wrecking your marriage."

"You're nuts. The police questioned me about that night. I was at home with my wife. It was my oldest son's birthday. She vouched for me."

"Oh really? She vouched for you. I bet the cops never even questioned you or your wife thoroughly because they had me."

"Yes, they did. I've had enough of this. Go take your pictures to the police if you want, but I didn't kill Ingrid Karlsen; you did."

Cliff got up, gave Randy the finger, and walked out.

Randy went to the bar and ordered another Guinness. He decided he would take the pictures and talk to the detective that handled the case and let him figure out whether he believed Cliff. Money, loss of kids, and his marriage can make someone like Cliff do unspeakable things. He'd stop by the police department tomorrow and lay the pictures and what he knew from Shelly in front of Jenkins. He had to keep moving forward.

The next day he drove down to Sturgeon Bay and talked to Detective Jenkins. He waited in the waiting room for forty-five minutes. Just before noon, Jenkins showed up. "You here again? Now what?"

"Since I talked to you, I've talked to two people Ingrid Karlsen had restraining orders against, Shelly Furano and Cliff Jones."

"Yes. You aren't telling me anything new. We talked to them, and we cleared them. What makes you think either of them could have killed Ingrid?"

While I don't think Shelly Furano killed her, there is a good chance Cliff Jones did. He's a violent person, and Ingrid was trying to blackmail him into giving her money or she was going to tell his wife they were having a torrid affair. After that, Ingrid got the restraining order. Here, take a look at the pictures. Also, to let him know she meant business, Ingrid shot two of his truck tires. I guess she was a good shot, going out and practicing with a foster dad who loaned her one of his pistols. Cliff was really mad at her for that."

Jenkin took the pictures and studied them. "Okay, I'll say this.

We didn't know about the tire shooting. We never saw the pictures either. It might have made us think twice about him as a suspect, but we did talk to his wife to verify he was home that night. She didn't know about his affair until later, so that ruled her out as a suspect. It was one of their kids' birthdays the night Ingrid died. They were home all night celebrating. Later we checked with the county clerk, and it was their kid's birthday that day, so the alibi checked out."

"So you're positive Cliff did not kill Ingrid?"

"Ninety-five percent positive. He would have had to sneak out that evening and then to be out past midnight when you were. Not likely. Yes, he had a boat, so he could have gone out there, but we were very certain he was home."

"Okay. I guess that is a strong alibi. Thanks for your time."

"Good luck."

He headed back to Fish Creek and stopped at the Bayside Bar and Grill to get one of their big hamburgers for lunch. At just past 1:00 p.m., he sat at the bar.

"What will it be?"

"I'll have a Coke and a burger with fries."

As he sat at the bar, Randy decided he needed to talk to Marvin Jacobs. For Ingrid to take out a restraining order, he must have had a violent temper; otherwise, why would Ingrid do that? Didn't he and Jimmy DeLeo get into a big physical fight when he found out Ingrid was fooling around behind his back. Was it like Cliff did to him? What else could have happened between the two? He need to do some digging into Marvin's past.

"Here's your Coke. The burger and fries will be up shortly. Do you mind if I ask you a question?"

"Sure, go ahead."

"I'm Bob, one of the owners here. Bill over there is a bartender whose been here a long time. You're in here a lot. You live here now, but also in the past, right?"

"Yes." Randy wondered where this was going, and he wasn't sure he liked it so far. "I live near the marina. I'm Randy Daggett. My parents recently died, and I live in their house now. My house."

"Daggett. I thought I recognized you from years ago and recently. Now the last name answers a question Bill and I have been thinking about since you started coming here recently. I'm sorry to bring this up, but didn't you get into some major legal trouble a long time ago involving a girl? Didn't the girl die?"

Why did he come in here? He just wanted to have a Coke and burger. Now this.

"Yes. Ten years ago I was convicted for manslaughter for my girlfriend Ingrid Karlsen's death. But like you hear often in crime shows, I'm innocent, even if the jury didn't see it that way. Now I'm trying to prove that."

"I thought I recognized you. You were big news up here. Read about you and the trial in the *Advocate* newspaper. You used to come in here for beers and pizza a lot when you were younger. I'm glad you came in, and we have a chance to talk, because Bill

Michael Pritzkow

and I often talk about the big argument that happened in our parking lot that night."

"I don't remember any argument."

"Not with you and that girl that died. It was with her and another guy—I think he still lives on the island. We see him once come in once in a while with his younger brother and a blacked-haired woman. I think they're engaged because she has a big ring on her finger."

"Okay, tell me more about this argument."

"Bill, come over here."

Bill walked over. "This is Randy Daggett. He's the guy who got convicted for the murder of the girl that had a big argument with the guy over on the island. Remember that night?"

"How could I not? They made so much noise yelling at each other outside the Bayside, you and I went out there to break up the fight. He wasn't there when they were fighting. Where were you?" he asked Randy.

"I guess I was next door at the Deli Market getting a twelve pack of beer and a couple of sandwiches. When I came back, Ingrid was waiting for me by my sailboat. What happened that I don't know?"

Bob said, "The woman was yelling that she needed money from the guy to fix a problem they had—a problem he caused. I think she insinuated she was pregnant with his child, because she said she needed to fix the problem unless he wanted to be a father. She said she didn't want to be a mother. He screamed, 'I thought you said you were on the pill!' And she yelled back, 'Well I guess

I missed a couple pills!' She screamed, 'I need the money. You're going to pay one way or the other.' He yelled 'Fuck you,' and he stormed off. That must have been about the time you showed up with the beer and sandwiches and then went out to Chambers. When we read about her death and you being arrested for it, we thought maybe you heard them yelling and killed her in a jealous rage. It happens."

Bill spoke, "You're saying you're innocent and didn't do it?"

"Right. I didn't do it. I'm not sure the police knew about this argument."

It's got to be Marvin, he thought.

Bob said. "They did know. We talked to a detective about it after reading about the girl's murder in the paper. They interviewed us. And I think they spoke with the guy out there on the island about it."

"That's all we can tell you about that night." Bill said. "We always wondered if you did it because she was pregnant, and it wasn't your baby. Now we know a little more. Good luck with your investigation."

CHAPTER TWENTY

Before he knew it, spring had arrived, Randy launched *Island Girl*, and it was time to get ready to go to the island. He could hardly wait to get back and confront Marvin about the argument too.

That afternoon, with the ice gone from Green Bay, he went for a sail around Chambers Island that turned out to be almost twenty-two miles. With no leaves on the surrounding trees, he could see his cabin this time of the year. The trees were just starting to bud, and the spring flowers were blooming. What a great time to be living in Door County. He docked his boat in the island's marina and was surprised to see a few boats already there.

It would be tough to see Trisha on the island with Adam. Randy would just have to learn to live with it. She'd still be a special friend. It had been two weeks since he and Trisha had broken up. Eventually he would walk past her place and feel sad. It wouldn't be the same.

Ten days later, he sat in his cabin when he heard a familiar voice.

"Randy, it's Simon. Can I come in? I missed seeing you all winter."

Randy smiled at the sound and seeing him after the long winter. "Sure, come on in. I missed seeing you too. Do you want a soda or something? Chips? I just have a few things I brought over on the boat today."

"A Coke would taste good."

"I have that." Randy went to a day cooler and got two Cokes out.

"So, what have you been doing all winter, Simon? Are you still painting?"

He shook his head. "It's not as much fun to paint at home. Marvin or Jessica don't care about my paintings like you do."

"Well, I'll take down some of your paintings to make room for new ones you're going to paint this summer. Is that okay? I'll put them in a folder and save them in my filing cabinet." He walked over and opened a long drawer in a metal filing cabinet. "I'll put your old ones in a folder like this."

For the next hour Simon filled him in on his winter job working at a local supermarket, stocking shelves and sometime bagging groceries.

"I like bagging the groceries the best, because it gives me a chance to talk to people and carry their groceries out to their car. I wish I could drive a car, but Marvin says I'll have to wait. I hope I don't have to wait too long. Did I tell you Marvin got me a new bicycle with thick black tires? It's red like a fire engine. I can go fast. I don't have it here because I walk everywhere, but maybe later I'll bring it out and show it to you."

"I'd like that, Simon. How are Marvin and Jessica? Is she helping you with your schoolwork?"

"Sometimes. She and Marvin have been arguing a lot, and sometimes she cries. Marvin has not been nice to her lately. Sometimes she leaves for a couple of days, and I don't see her. I think she goes to her mommy and daddy's house after they fight. I'm afraid for her. Sometimes Marvin is not nice. I love her. She's always so good to me, like you are."

"Oh, I'm sorry to hear about Marvin being mean to her." *Like he might have been to Ingrid when she got a restraining order against him?* "I'm sure they will work out their differences, and they'll stop fighting."

"I hope so. Can I have another soda and maybe some chips?"

"Sure, help yourself."

Randy called Detective Jenkins and talked to him about the argument in the Bayside Bar's parking lot the night of the drowning. He was surprised by his response.

"You're right about the argument and possible motive for Marvin killing her. We thought that too. When we asked him what he was doing that night, he said he was at home on the island. He said he stayed in all night. He actually said he went to bed early. When we asked if anyone could support his alibi, he said his brother Simon could. When we asked him if Marvin was there all night, he verified that he was. Not much we could do or not do after that."

"Did you feel Simon was telling the truth?"

"Simon had the mind of a ten-year-old, but that made it more believable. Ten-year-olds normally don't lie about stuff like that."

"What about Ingrid being pregnant? Bob and Bill from the Bayside said Marvin was pretty mad when he was leaving."

"We do an autopsy when there is a murder or drowning to verify certain things. We did check for pregnancy. Contrary to what Ingrid said in the parking lot, she wasn't pregnant."

"So she probably was just trying to get money from Marvin… or get him to marry her?"

"That seems to be a possibility. He has a pretty nice place out there."

"Thanks for the information."

It was inevitable that sooner or later he'd meet up with Trisha and Adam on the island. He hoped it would be later in the summer. As it turned out, it was sooner.

It was a mild day for late April with temperatures in the high sixties on the island, but at this time of the year, high sixties always seemed warmer. He saw some of the other islanders on the beach, spreading out blankets and old-fashioned picnic baskets, like his mother had done when they went to the beach. That memory made him sad, but hearing people laughing made him feel a little better.

They set out food and soccer chairs, waiting for the nightly event as the sun made its slow arc toward the horizon.

He looked at his watch. "Thirty minutes to go," and then, "Shit," he said out loud, "I forgot the beer and maybe a sweater just in case." He ran back to his cabin, laughing as he did. "How could I forget the beer?" The sweater, he knew, would feel good later. He put three beers in a cooler, some ice, and threw in some cheese curds just for good measure—he liked squeaky cheese curds with his beer. Then he walked back to his spot for the sunset on the beach.

As he got back to his chair, he saw them coming his way. There was no avoiding them. Trisha was talking intently to Adam about something, then she pointed toward the horizon and the sinking sun. Adam put his arm around her, and they kissed.

It upset him so much, he almost got out of his chair and walked back to his cabin, but there was no point in trying to postpone the inevitable. He decided to get it over with. After all, the island was not that big.

As they turned, Trisha spotted him in his chair and smiled. She gave a friendly wave. He watched her mouth the words, "That's my friend, Randy."

Adam mouthed the words, "That Randy?"

"Yes, that Randy. How many Randy's do you think are on the island? Let's go over and say hi."

"Do we have to?" he saw him mouth.

"Yes. It's about time we both say hello. You'll like him. He's nice."

They slowly made their way toward Randy. He got up from his chair, trying to smile as they came over.

"Hi, Randy," Trisha said with a smile. She surprised him when she leaned over and gave him a kiss on the cheek and a big hug. "You look like the winter has been kind to you. It's going to be a beautiful sunset tonight. We thought we'd come over and enjoy it. It's nice to see you again. I don't think you've met Adam."

Randy nodded and reluctantly stuck his hand out to shake.

Adam's eyes focused on his hand, then slowly he reached out and clasped it. "Nice to meet you. Trisha told me about you."

Randy was waiting for more, but he didn't continue.

Instead, Adam just looked at Trisha with an expression on his face that said it all: "All right, I met him. Now let's leave here and watch the sunset like we planned."

That was the same feeling Randy had. He didn't like the guy. Trisha was with him and not Randy, so he felt sad and uncomfortable about the encounter. He watched her eyes as she stared at Randy, then turned back to Adam, before giving him a half smile.

"I just wanted to say hi. Have a good night, Randy."

"I'll try. Have a nice walk." After they left, he sat down on his chair, grabbed one of his beers, and slammed it down. He quickly opened another, but this time he just took a sip.

He watched them walking down the beach, his stomach churning. They weren't hand in hand now like they'd been when he first saw them. Adam was doing the talking now, and Trisha was not looking at him. Then he saw her throw her arms in the air like someone would if they were exasperated. Randy smiled at that. Maybe it would turn out to be a good night after all.

A few days later. "Hi, Randy. I have a new painting for you. It's a dog like you asked me to paint. I like dogs. Cats too."

"Let's see it." He took the paintings and smiled. Simon's painting was getting better, he had to admit. It actually looked like a dog and cat.

"I miss painting Trisha," he said, "but not with that Adam around. He's not nice."

"I like your dog and cat paintings. You've improved. I made room for your new paintings this year right here on the refrigerator, just like last year."

He walked over and smiled. "This is a good spot just like last year, Randy. I'm not sure if Trisha wants any of my paintings anymore. I don't want to go near her house for a while."

"I'm sure that Adam is nice. Otherwise Trisha wouldn't be with him."

Even if Adam abandoned her when she got her cancer. He'd always be a jerk in Randy's mind. Once a jerk, always a jerk.

"You can paint me new ones. How's that?"

"That's good. I like this spot."

The next morning was overcast and cool, with a strong wind blowing from the north. Randy thought of building a fire to take the chill out of the cabin, but instead he fired up the tea kettle for his Earl Gray tea. Sometimes he got tired of coffee, and he liked the taste of tea and honey. He laughed to himself because he was eating some oatmeal after swearing to his mother about not ever eating it again, but this oatmeal was much better than the oatmeal he got in prison. He used the extra-hot water for some steel-cut oatmeal with walnuts, raisings, and cinnamon. It was simple and would keep him full until late afternoon. It was time to focus on writing.

After last night's sunset meeting with Trisha and Adam, while his emotions were fresh, he sat down and wrote a scene describing how a character might feel when he was replaced by another romantically. While he wasn't sure if he'd use this newly written scene in any novel in the future, he felt much better after getting the failed rejection emotion off his chest. He printed it off and placed it in a folder labeled "Breaking-up scene."

After finishing his writing for the day, he decided to sail to Sister Bay and go to J.J.'s for lunch. The wind had calmed. He needed to have some fun, and the Mexican food and margaritas there were always good.

The winds were favorable. He always enjoyed the trip passing Peninsula Park, Nicolet Bay, Horseshoe Island, Ephraim's Eagle

Harbor, and then finally Sister Bay. He found an open spot at the pier, tied up, and walked into the restaurant. As usual, the place was busy, so he sat at the bar next to a blond mannequin woman located near the end of the bar.

Many tourists had their picture taken with her. He liked sitting at the bar for the quick service, but he also got a kick out of sitting on the barstools with large painted shoe feet. Next to him was a couple ending their vacation in Door County with lunch before heading back to Chicago.

"We sure hate going back home," the man said. "We love it up here. This year we spent three days on Washington Island at a quaint place called The Hotel Washington. The food was all local and excellent. I wish we could have stayed longer, but we went there with only a few days left on our vacation."

"I wish we could have spent the whole week there," his wife said, "I felt I was in France at the Fragrant Isle Lavender Farm. The owner was actually from France. It was really nice."

Her husband added, "The island is very nice for bike riding too, which we both enjoy. Then there is Nelsen's Bitter Pub. If you drink a shot of bitters, you get a certificate," he said. He fumbled around in his wallet and then proudly pulled out a card that said he drank a shot of bitters.

Randy watched as the man's body trembled as he remembered the drink. "Very bitter, but I was told if you have hiccups, a shot will stop them. Must shock the system," he said with a laugh.

"Great old fashioned too," said his wife, "with the bitter, of course. We had it with brandy, just like most Wisconsin folks do, even if we're from Illinois." She laughed.

"Yes, we like our brandy here in Wisconsin." Randy said. "Thanks for the information on the island and the hotel. I have not been there since I was five or six. Maybe I'll sail there sometime for lunch."

"Sail for lunch?" they both said, almost in unison.

"That sounds so romantic," she said. "I wish we knew how to sail." She looked at her husband and said, "Although the ferry was fun."

He looked at his watch. "It's been nice talking to you, but we've got to get going. It's a six-hour drive back home from here."

Randy shook their hand and watched them leave. Nice couple, he thought. He'd have to make that trip to Washington Island. He could always anchor out. He knew there were at least two marinas and several docks scattered around the island. Finishing his lunch, he walked to his boat. He didn't feel like going back to Chambers Island just yet. He decided to stay in Sister Bay the rest of the afternoon and night.

He called the Sister Bay Municipal Marina and got a slip for the night. It was only a few minutes' sail down to the marina from J.J.'s, but he motored because he didn't feel like going through all the work of raising and lowering the sails for that short distance. He thought it would be fun to stay there and meet other boaters. He got assigned a slip on A Dock, which was along the breakwater protecting the marina. It gave him a nice view of the sunset and an opportunity for conversation with people strolling along the dock, especially at sunset.

After he got *Island Girl* tied up and made himself a rum and Coke, what happened next was a pleasant surprise.

A couple walked down the wide breakwater dock, watching the sun sliding toward the horizon, casting its warm colors on the water. Randy sat on a picnic table along the breakwater, sipping his rum and Coke, and like the others gathered there, waiting for sunset.

"Randy Daggett?"

He turned to look at the man who'd said his name. He looked familiar, and so did the pretty woman he was holding hands with.

"Yes? You both look familiar. Do I know you?"

"I guess it's been a while. We were in the same class at Gibraltar High School. Let's see, that's been about fourteen or fifteen years ago. Holy mackerel, time flies by. We're the Ericksons: Jake and Pat. I haven't seen you since graduating from high school."

"Are you still living here or are you tourists like most of these people on the breakwater?" Randy asked.

"Yes, we're still here," said Jake. "Well, not *here* anymore. We live in Sturgeon Bay now. I work at the shipyard, and Pat teaches at a grade school there. How about you?"

"After graduation, I went to school in Madison. I've been gone for a number of years but came back to be with my parents. Now I write novels for a living. I'm back living in Fish Creek, and in the summer, I live on Chambers Island."

"Chambers Island, how romantic," Pat said.

"Yes, it could be. The island fits me, being a writer. I like the solitude. I came to Sister Bay to have lunch at J.J.'s and decided to stay at the marina on my boat—" he pointed to *Island Girl* "—to have some fun."

Randy watched as Jake leaned over and whispered something into his wife's ear. She mouthed an "Oh" and nodded her head in agreement.

Jake asked, "Excuse me, Randy. I hope I'm wrong, but I don't think I am. Didn't you get into some kind of legal trouble about ten or eleven years ago?"

Randy took a sip of his rum and Coke, set it down, and then cleared his throat. "I served eight years for manslaughter."

"If I remember correctly, it was for killing your girlfriend. Wasn't it Ingrid Karlsen?" Jake asked.

Randy gave a shrug. "Yeah. You're right." He turned toward the sun creeping toward the horizon, wishing he could walk down the finger pier and hide inside his boat. The mood of the evening seemed about to be wrecked.

"I'm sorry about bringing that up. When we read about it in the paper and saw the story on TV, we felt sorry for you," Jake said. He saw his wife shaking her head in agreement. "I know you find this hard to believe, but we could see how it could happen."

He looked at the two former classmates in disbelief. "You could see how it could happen? Ingrid was murdered"—he paused—"and not by me!"

Now it was Pat's turn to talk. "Oh, not by you." She paused for a while before she started talking again. "Well, we opened a coffee shop and art gallery in Sturgeon Bay after we graduated. I'm sure you don't remember that we got married right out of high school and wanted to go to the big city. Ha ha, like Sturgeon Bay is the big city. But it's bigger than Fish Creek and Ephraim. Anyhow, we would see Ingrid enough times around the area with lots of guys and women. Whatever trips your trigger, I say, just so you're happy. But I have to say, Ingrid pushed the envelope to the max, we thought. We knew she dated you during the summer. When we saw that you were charged with her death, we just figured you snapped and killed her in a fit of passion or something like that."

Jake said, "No one wants to condone murder, but we could understand how you could get jealous and do it. We knew you were a good person and thought you probably just got caught up in a jealous rage. You served your time. Both Pat and I are glad that you're here. What are you doing now that you've been out for a while?"

Randy had to calm down and keep his emotions in check. He had feared this confrontation with his past. He'd have to get used to it. In this case, his two classmates were sympathetic toward him, so he tried to relax.

"Thanks for being so understanding, but I have to tell you something. I didn't kill her. It wasn't jealous rage. She had issues that caused her to fool around. She was basically a good person. That being said, yes, she died, drowned, but I didn't do it."

"Really?" Jake said. "Well, you never seemed like the vengeful type. At least we never saw that when we were in high school. Good luck on your search."

"Thanks. It was nice seeing you both. I appreciate your thoughts." They shook hands, and then he watched them walk away.

Was he going to have to tell that story for the rest of his life? He hoped not.

CHAPTER TWENTY-ONE

The next morning, he got out the old coffeepot he'd found at a flea market last summer after buying *Island Girl*. Something about the aroma and sound of an old coffeepot with the blurb, blurb, went along with the morning and boating.

He needed strong coffee. He'd been restless all night after Jake and Patricia left the marina. In addition to too many rums and cokes, he could not fall asleep. After a night of unrest, he needed something to build up positive thoughts about himself.

Just the smell and sound of the coffee perking made him feel better. He got his old navy cream-colored coffee cup and poured his first cup of the day. The hot liquid tasted good, and he felt his body respond to the jolt of caffeine. It didn't take him long to pour himself a second. Then he put the rest of the hot coffee into the green thermos he kept on the boat, so he'd have a couple more cups while sailing north toward Washington Island. He wasn't sure if he'd stop for lunch at the island this time, but it seemed like a nice morning to go that way and then head back to Chambers Island.

But first he went across the street to Al Johnson's and had a big breakfast of Swedish pancakes, a couple of scrambled eggs, and a side order of ham. Then it was off to *Island Girl* and sailing.

It was a gorgeous morning, and he made the most of it. Raising the mainsail and rolling out the full Genoa, the boat heeled over to its favorable angle of twelve degrees.

Life was good. He hadn't felt that way since he was in love with Trisha last winter.

If he thought about it, he was still in love with her. Too bad that was a one-way street. Oh well, he thought, he'd just have to get over her. Easier said than done.

He loved the feel of the boat as it sliced through the small chop. The steep deep-green bluffs and rocky shore made him feel as if he were sailing along the Maine coast. With their natural harbors, the towns of Ellison Bay and Gill's Rock were so traditional looking, it was like he imagined fishing villages along the East Coast. Once he was past the tip of Gill Rock and the Door County Peninsula, he spotted the strait separating the peninsula and Washington Island.

The gap was called Death's Door. Plum Island, with its historic lighthouse, marked the entrance, and then came Detroit Island. Two islands protected the island entrance, and as he approached from the southwest, the islands looked like they were part of the larger Washington Island. It was only when he followed the Washington Island car ferry and looked to the east, he could see that there were two other islands in addition to the big island. Complicated, he thought, if it had been night.

He sailed into the island harbor, looking for the docks where the ferry tied up to load and unload the cars and visitors to the island. Then he looked for the marina just past the entrance to the immediate west, and a larger marina with its docks east. He'd come back another day and stay there, then venture to the Hotel Washington and sample their food that the couple at J.J.'s had raved about.

The harbor was so busy he decided to head home to Chambers Island, hoping the weather would stay just like it was. Five hours later, he tied up at Chambers Island and walked home. It had been a good day on the water, a good day to get his mind in better shape. Now what he needed was to grill a cheeseburger, a couple ears of corn, and a cold beer.

The next morning Randy heard the unmistakable voice of Simon.

"Randy, are you here? Can I come in? I made a new painting for you."

"Good morning, Simon. How are you? Would you like some orange juice?"

"No. I had a big breakfast. You must have been sailing yesterday. When I walked down to the marina to fish, I saw your boat was gone. Where did you go?"

"I was actually gone for two days. First I went to Sister Bay, and then the next day I went to Washington Island and sailed home from there. I didn't get home until late in the afternoon."

"That sounds like fun. Maybe I can go sailing with you again if Marvin lets me. He doesn't want me coming here, but I don't care. He's been mean to Jessica and me. They're fighting all the time."

"That's too bad. I don't want you to get in trouble by coming here." He took the painting from Simon. "Thank you for the picture," he said. "You're getting much better. I think I'll hang this on the wall instead of the refrigerator."

"Then you can look at Trisha all the time when you look at the painting. The refrigerator is getting covered over with my paintings," he said. "I liked painting Trisha. She's nice, especially when that guy isn't around."

"You mean Adam?"

"I don't like him. Good thing he's not here as much as Trisha is. She's gone a lot too this year. Not like last year."

"That's because she's at work. You work too. Doesn't that sometimes prevent you from coming up here?"

"Yeah. I suppose. I don't like it when I can't come up here to the island. I love the island, though now the only one that plays with me is Jessica. Before Jessica, Marvin would have some friends come to the island, and some of the girls would play with me. But that hasn't happened since Jessica started coming."

"I understand. I love the island too." Randy tacked Simon's painting up on the wood wall. "There. What do you think?"

Simon walked around Randy's living room, looking at the painting from different angles, and then stood next to Randy. "I like it there because it's all by itself. When I paint more pictures, you can put them up on the other walls to make it homier." He smiled at Randy.

"I'll have to get you more watercolor paper if you're going to do that."

"I don't need any more right now. Jessica gave me some paper a little while ago, so I'm all right."

"Okay. Let's go to the marina and see if the fish are biting."

Randy enjoyed his time at the docks with Simon. He was very social and well-liked by everyone on the island. Even though Simon was taller, huskier, and younger than Randy, Randy never forgot he had the mind of a ten-year-old. The beauty of his mental age is that he said what he felt, and usually those thoughts were unfiltered. So whenever Simon saw a boat arriving at the marina, he was interested to see who it was.

Simon's demeanor changed abruptly when he saw who stepped out from the boat onto the dock and tied up.

"Oh, it's Trisha's mean friend. The guy who replaced you, Randy. I don't like him because he did that. He's not friendly to anyone either. I liked it when you and Trisha where together."

"Well, Trisha and Adam are married again. Now we are just friends."

They watched as Adam finished tying up the boat and walked away without even saying hello. "But I agree with you. I don't think Adam is very nice to anyone here, and sometimes that includes Trisha, at least from what I've seen the few times they have been together. "

He watched Simon pick up the stringer of fish, holding it high in the air. "Do we have enough fish for dinner tonight? I'm hungry. Can we go now?"

"Yes, but first we have to clean the fish. It will only take a few minutes to do that here and then you can take them home with you. I'll keep the rainbow trout, and you can have the rest."

"Marvin likes bluegills. He'll have to scale them, but we'll eat them for dinner. He'll like that."

"Don't tell him we went fishing together. Just tell him I was down here working on my boat and helped you clean the fish. You know he doesn't like me being with you."

"I don't know why. You're my best friend on the island besides Jessica. She's nice to me all the time, even when I surprise them when they're having sex."

Randy had to laugh. "That's nice that she doesn't get mad, but you need to be more aware of when they are together like that and not surprise them."

"Yes, I know, but I like to look at her when she's naked. She's very beautiful."

Again, Randy had to smile. "Yes, I bet she is." Randy handed the six fish to Simon and watched him head home. He felt like Tom Sawyer and his pal Huck Finn after a day's fishing on the Mississippi.

That night, after having the trout he'd caught that day, he headed down to Sand Bay to watch the sunset, his normal ritual. He brought down a couple of cold beers to enjoy the nightly show. As he looked at the curving beach, his eyes lingered, as they always did, on the spot where he'd found Ingrid's body.

His mind shifted as other couples arrived to watch the sunset. There were just a few clouds where he thought the sun would set, so he expected it would be a great show. He might even take a picture on his phone. He had so many pictures of sunsets; he didn't even know why he did it anymore, but it made him feel good. He realized how much he loved living here, and especially this spot.

All he had to do was not remember what happened here with Ingrid.

Sunset was about twenty minutes away. He had just opened a cold beer and sat back when he saw Trisha and Adam walking onto the beach with a small cooler and blanket. He watched as they found a spot, spread out their blanket, putting four stones on the corners and settling in. Randy felt his mood changing from happiness to something else—maybe loneliness. He finished his beer and opened the other. He drank half of that beer fast, trying to numb his senses to what he knew would happen.

Five minutes later, it did. Adam opened a bottle of wine, poured two glasses, and toasted Trisha, touching their glasses together, and then he kissed her for what seemed like minutes, though Randy was sure it was only seconds.

He sat and sulked. He needed to get off his ass and find someone to share his life with. Hell, when he thought about it, he only had maybe only three relationships in his whole thirty-two years of life. There was Ginger, his freshman year at Wisconsin, but that relationship ended in the spring; then there was Ingrid in high school and summers, and recently Trisha. He had nothing to show for these three relationships except the loss of eight years of his life in prison and doubts about his moral being.

He slammed down the rest of the beer, grabbed his collapsible soccer chair, and bolted back to the cabin. When he turned on the battery-powered light in the cabin, he saw the picture of Trisha that Simon had painted. Randy just stared at it, feeling so alone.

CHAPTER TWENTY-TWO

He got up before dawn, determined to get himself out of his funk. What better way than to take a long sail for a change of scenery? He decided to sail to Washington Island and have lunch at The Hotel Washington.

He got a cooler out for snacks and a couple of Cokes and made a thermos of coffee for the four-hour-or-more sail. He checked his chart and determined it was about twenty-three miles straight-line distance, but it all depended on the wind and the course he'd take. He didn't care about the time or distance; he just wanted to escape from the island this morning and enjoy his boat and life.

He had to move on from Trisha. It was fruitless to think she would divorce Adam a second time. Randy had to start a search for someone new. Someone out there was right for him and would believe his story like Trisha did. He was getting tired of telling it. He just had to find that someone—that's all there was to it.

Michael Pritzkow

On his marine radio at home, he listened to the marine weather forecast for the day while brewing strong black coffee. They reported that the winds on the bay were going to be blowing from twelve to fifteen knots. Just about right. Randy always tried not to overstress the rigging.

One of his sailing commandments was to reef the sails when he first thought of it. Well, he was sitting in the slip was when he thought he might need to reef—so he did it before he even started his sail. It was easy to do in the slip and only took about eight minutes. It was far easier to shake out the reef if the winds dropped. All he had to do then was turn the boat into the wind and raise the sail back up to its full area. Trying to reef as the wind increased could take twenty to thirty minutes if the wind was increasing and the waves grew higher. It could get dangerous.

The winds were from the north with small whitecaps as he passed the lee of the island and set a course of forty degrees. He was rewarded with the boat moving in balance with the waves and wind on a nice reach toward Washington Island.

An hour later, he passed the two Sister Islands just northwest of the village of Sister Bay. He felt the boat heel over even more as he changed course slightly. The wind gusts heeled the boat over before settling back to twelve degrees. He smiled as the boat scooted along. He checked the anemometer and saw the wind was blowing at seventeen knots, with gusts to twenty knots. When he looked to the west, he saw low dark-gray clouds building and getting darker.

While the sky was clear and sunny overhead, it was just a matter of time before those clouds got closer and overran him. His smile turned to concern. He didn't mind rain and wind but hated lightning. He couldn't tell if there was any coming his way. He didn't see flashes, but that didn't mean there weren't any hiding in the dark clouds higher up.

He moved the cursor on his GPS instrument to determine how far away he was from Washington Island harbor and to read his compass while heading to the harbor. He figured it was at least two hours away. He hoped he could make it before the foul weather hit. He pulled up the radar on his phone's weather app and saw the storm and clouds were definitely moving his way.

The green headland and bluffs drifted past on his starboard side as *Island Girl* moved further north. The marina and town of Ellison Bay came into view. There was a fun bar there called Mink River Basin. He'd been to a wedding reception there years ago while in college.

He saw the white building and roof of the Pioneer General Store, which sold just about everything needed by the Ellison Bay residents and tourists. He had stopped there years ago, before prison, to get snacks and beer when he and Tom Leonard went to Newport State Park beach.

Carol, the owner, was always nice to everyone who came in. She was older now, well into her social security era, but she was still very active. He only hoped he could say the same thing about himself when he reached her age.

Michael Pritzkow

This morning, even with the wind blowing in the teens and the rigging whistling, sailing now was pure joy, asking nothing but a straight course and at least one hand on the tiller—or in *Island Girl*'s case, a wheel.

Steep banks and deep-green foliage hid much of what was up top on the bluffs, though he occasionally glimpsed big homes or sometimes a barn or two.

Soon he came to the fishing village of Gills Rock. Sometimes when the winds were strong from the north, the ferry loaded and unloaded at Gill Rock instead of Northport Landing. Gills Rock was where he always stopped and got smoked fish when he drove up, but today he was just sailing by. Once past the town's harbor, he knew he would soon see the Death's Door Passage. Most people thought it got its name because of the many shipwrecks in the narrow passage between the tip of the Door County Peninsula and Washington Island, Detroit Island, and Plum Island.

True, there had been a lot of shipwrecks there, but the name really came from another story. A band of Indian warriors had been canoeing across the passage to attack another group of Indians living on Washington Island when a fierce storm came up, swamping the canoes of the attacking Indians. All were drowned, hence the name Death's Door Passage.

Still, the currents in the passage between the Green Bay Waters and Lake Michigan could be fierce. Boats sailing with no motors were at the mercy of the wind or lack of it, which had caused lots of wrecks during the heyday of the schooner.

What had started as a nice leisurely sail was turning into

something more alarming. The passage gap increased the wind strength to twenty knots, but *Island Girl* was on a reach, and the wind was coming over his left shoulder, so the boat was surfing down the three-to-four-foot waves. Not too high, but not the sail he'd envisioned when he'd left this morning.

The good news was he was making great time. He called the marina near The Hotel Washington to see about a slip, and luckily they had one. As he got further into the passage, he saw one of the car ferries leaving Northport Pier, going to the island and loaded with tourists.

He followed them in, trailing a quarter of a mile behind, dumping wind out of his mainsail by letting out the boom. Not only did it slow the boat down, but also it made it easier to steer. About fifteen minutes later, he decided to drop the mainsail and rolled up the jib. He did this all the time, but not usually in weather this windy.

He turned the engine on, then steered *Island Girl* slightly off the wind. He rolled the flapping jib around the head stay. After that, he lowered the mainsail and quickly tied the sail down on the boom. Once that was done, his world got quiet, and he motored into the basin, following the car ferry. Once in the basin, he turned east and followed the red and green channel markers to the Ship Yard Marina.

Once again, he called the marina on the marine radio and asked for the slip number and some help with the lines just in case the wind blew him the wrong way. Approaching, he reversed the engine to slow the boat down. As it turned out, the wind direction blew him gently against the dock and his slip. Then he and a guy from the marina tied the bow and stern lines to the pier. Next he set a couple of spring lines, so the boat stayed in its position in the slip. He placed boat bumpers so the hull wouldn't rub against the dock.

Total time: twenty minutes to get everything in shipshape.

After giving his helper a tip, he listened to the weather report one last time. He realized he wasn't going anyplace for a couple of days. Luckily, he was told he could stay in the slip and enjoy the island.

His stomach grumbled. He was very hungry. Isn't that why he'd sailed all this way? He looked forward to eating at The Hotel Washington and trying their excellent cuisine. He checked the hotel's location on his phone's GPS and saw it was only a short distance away.

This trip had started as whim last night as he sat near the lighthouse drinking a couple of beers on Chambers. He'd long wanted to visit Washington Island and then sail home. Now it looked like he wouldn't be sailing home that night, or maybe not even the next day.

He looked at his phone to make sure he was going the right way, but then there was no other business here except for the hotel and the marina's restaurant, but that one didn't open until late afternoon. He could always go there for dinner if the hotel didn't pan out.

Twenty minutes later he walked across the hotel's large lawn. Trees were scattered about, along with picnic tables and Adirondack chairs. The white, wooden, old-fashioned building had a large deck, and a flight of steps at the end of the building led up, he assumed, to second-floor rooms.

The hotel was just as he'd hoped it would be. It exuded Door County charm—something he felt Chambers Island lacked. It's not that the houses on his island were bad. It's just that the look and feel of The Hotel Washington was perfect. He looked forward to sitting out on the hotel's deck at sunset and having a cocktail or a glass of wine, sharing a conversation with other guests before heading back to his boat for the night.

When Randy stepped into the lobby and smelled food cooking, he knew he was in for a treat. He laughed to himself as his stomach rumbled again.

"Hello, can I help you? Are you checking in?"

He turned to the voice. "Actually, I'm here to have lunch."

"That's fine. Are you alone, or will there be more?"

He looked at the nametag. Jeanette. "No, just me. I actually sailed up here just to have lunch. Some people told me how good the food was, and I decided to find out for myself."

"Sailed up? Where from?"

"I have a cabin on Chambers Island, but I needed a little diversion and some adventure today. I didn't realize the weather would turn against me. Probably will have dinner here too tonight."

"We're honored that you thought of us. You'll find the food excellent. We try to use local providers here on the island, and what we can't get on the island, we get from others located in Door County. Usually, it's the meats that we get off island."

"Sounds healthy and delicious."

She reached for a menu. "Would you like to sit inside or out on the deck?"

"I think I'll sit inside. I've had enough wind and sun so far today. In case you haven't noticed, it's very windy." Just then a small twig or something hit the window next to the entrance door. "Don't need to fight that wind anymore," he said with a smile.

"I'll find a table for you. The hotel is full, but most of the guests are away enjoying the island. I'll seat you at a table with a nice view of the lawn. Karen will be your server. Enjoy your lunch."

"Thank you."

A minute later, a slim sandy-haired woman appeared at his table. She asked if he wanted something to drink.

"I'll have some water and a beer. I'm not going anywhere. I walked here from the marina."

"The marina? You sailed here? How exciting."

"Yes. It got more exciting when the wind picked up. Had I known it was going to get like this, I would have stayed on Chambers Island."

"Oh, you're an island resident too. So am I. I used to live in Madison, but I moved back here when my mother died five years ago. I decided I'd keep my dad company. He's lost without my mother. I love being here with him, the water, and everything. This island offers less distractions, and that's okay with me."

"I understand that. I feel the same way on Chambers. I lost both my parents last year. I inherited their place in Fish Creek, so I'm a full-time Door County resident like you."

He watched her smile and nod in agreement. Nice smile, he thought.

"Sorry for your loss. What kind of beer would you like?'

"Oh, something dark?"

"Okay."

He watched her walk away. *She's cute*, he thought.

She returned with a local dark ale. "Here's a menu. Sorry I forgot to give you it when you sat down. Would you like some bread? It just came out of the oven."

"Great. I'd like that very much."

She smiled at him. "I'll be right back with the bread. Our special today is salmon. Just caught this morning and brought here just a little while ago. The vegetables, soups, and salads are all locally grown right here on the island. Very fresh. I went to the fields this morning to gather some of the greens just down the road from here."

"That salmon sounds great. I need to eat more fish and get that Omega-3. I'll have that and maybe a nice chilled glass of white wine when you bring the fish. Sauvignon Blanc if you have it."

"Oh, that's my favorite white wine too. That will go nice with the salmon. I'll be right back with the bread."

He watched her go and smiled. She's pleasant. Not like the nasty "Karens" he read about on the internet. Funny how the internet can change the way a name and person are perceived in the world.

As he looked out the window at the large lawn, he saw tree limbs swaying, and the leaves on the trees were moving violently.

A hammock was twisting in the wind on its green steel frame. The porch's Adirondack chairs wobbled. He figured it had to be blowing twenty to twenty-five miles per hour. It was probably going to storm tonight or this afternoon. He was glad again that *Island Girl* was securely tied up at the marina.

Karen brought his bread and lots of butter. In addition, she brought a small garden salad with raspberry vinaigrette.

"Hope you enjoy the bread and salad. I'll bring your wine and the salmon shortly."

"Thank you; I'm starved." And he broke the bread and slathered on the creamy butter.

The salmon and fresh vegetables of carrots and green beans were perfect. He ended up adding a slice of Door County apple pie and a scoop of vanilla ice cream to top off the lunch.

When Karen came back and cleared off the dishes from the table, she said, "I'd say you were hungry! I hope that satisfies you for a while. We don't serve dinner until five, so you have about three and a half hours until then. Can I get you anything else?"

"If you have a chance, I might have another beer in an hour or two, if you're still here? I think I'll go out and sit in one of those Adirondack chairs."

"I'll be here. I'm just leaving to bring Dad his lunch. I spend a little time with him, then come back and get ready for the dinner crowd. It will be more crowded then because the guests will be back.

If you're going to have dinner, should I reserve this table for you?"

"Sure, that will be great. Will you wait on me again?"

"If you like. Just being one person, you won't take me away from the others. I can fit you in."

"Yes, I'd like that if it's not too much trouble."

"No trouble at all. We try to please everyone here at The Hotel Washington."

"Great, maybe I'll try taking a nap in a hammock if I don't blow away. Another beer might help me to relax and take a nap. I'm still keyed up from the sail here."

"Good luck with that hammock. Do you want the same beer?"

"Yes. Why don't you bring me a beer now, and another when you come back before dinner? I'll go out to the chair or hammock now, and you can bring it to me there when you bring your dad his lunch. It's a long time until dinner, and that beer will taste good and help me take a nap."

She laughed at his comment about needing the beer to fall asleep. She turned and walked away, taking her apron off as she did.

He smiled as he watched her walk away, then he walked outside.

Sitting in the white Adirondack chair, looking at his phone to see what was around the Hotel Washington, he found there was nothing besides Sand Dunes Park, the marina, and The Sailors Pub, located at the marina. He'd visit the Sailors Pub before he left the island. If nothing else, he thought he'd need to stock up with a bottle of wine or a couple of beers and watch the sunset that night. That was, if it didn't storm.

He looked at the hammock and decided to give it a try. Why was he drinking so much today? Was it to try to forget Trisha?

He got up from the chair and moved to the white hammock. It had been a long time since he'd stretched out in one. He grabbed the edge and gingerly sat down, making sure it didn't move up behind his back, and then he would slide off and land on the ground. He slowly moved into the center, then lifted one leg over the far side while keeping one leg on the ground. Once he was centered, he leaned back, holding on to the sides. He lifted his feet, and the hammock gently started rocking in the wind.

"Ahh, this is good," he said out loud.

A voice came from behind him. "You made it. Congratulations. I was watching to see if you'd tip out onto the ground." She laughed. "But you didn't."

As she came around the side of the hammock, Karen extended her arm with his sweating bottle of beer wrapped in a paper napkin.

"Here you go."

He saw her holding a brown paper bag, which she held up for him to see.

"Dad's lunch: salmon sandwich and a small garden salad. I better be going. He's waiting. See you later."

"Thanks for the beer."

"Sure, I'll just put it on your bill."

He brought the beer to his lips and closed his eyes to the sun, wind, and negative thoughts that had crept into his mind about Trisha and Ingrid. The wind gently rocked the hammock back and forth as he drank his beer. He settled back and closed his eyes for a little snooze.

CHAPTER TWENTY-THREE

As it turned out, he finished the beer, and then it didn't take long to fall asleep.

In a dream, he looked up into Ingrid's face, which was moving in an undulating motion, her voice filled with excitement as they had sex. She sped up her motions until she collapsed on him as they both came. A few seconds passed before she rose from her position.

"That was nice, Randy, but I'm going to go in the water and wash your love off of me. Come and join me."

"I'm just going to take a little nap. I've had too much to drink. I'll meet you in a few minutes."

"Aw, come on; I want some more of what you got. If you can't do it, I'll just walk around the point and find my friend and old love interest, Marvin, who lives on the island. He was always up to doing it a few times."

"Who the fuck is Marvin?" Randy said. "You never told me

about him."

"Well, when you weren't around, I'd meet him out here, and we'd have sex and drink—both things I like to do, as you know. So if you can't get it up or want to sleep, I'll just walk over and see if he's around to satisfy me." Randy watched as she started wading in the water to her waist, heading toward the point.

He watched her go, closed his eyes, and tried to rest, but instead he got furious. The fucking two-timing bitch. I'll teach her, he thought.

She was halfway down the beach, toward the point. Randy assumed that around that point was Marvin's place. He got up to take a pee, tripped on something, fell into some bushes, and scratched himself, then started walking fast toward her. "The bitch."

In a few minutes, he was even with her. He was breathing hard. He was frustrated and incensed by her. She had her back to him. He stomped into the water, making sure the water sounds were loud enough to let her know he was behind her. He snuggled up behind her. When he did, he couldn't help himself and got aroused, at the same time cupping her breasts and pulling her close to him.

"Ahh, that's better. I can tell you're ready for me. Just let me dip down into the water to straighten my hair, and let's see what we can do."

She slid down his body into the water. He watched as she went under and tilted her head back. He saw her face looking up toward him in the moonlight. Her hair fanned out as she straightened her hair, and that's when he snapped.

The bitch. He grabbed her shoulders and pushed her down

hard, keeping her on the bottom as she struggled in the shallow water. He saw her eyes bug out wide in terror, her hands reaching for his to release his grip, but he was in a fury. He saw the release of bubbles from her mouth, and in a few moments, she was limp. He released her shoulders and watched as she drifted right and left with the gentle wave action.

Satisfied, Randy turned around and walked back to the beach to lay down. And that's when it hit him. What had he done? He threw up. He had killed her. Exhausted and still drunk, he went back to the towel and slept. It was so unlike him, but then, his last thoughts before he drifted off to sleep were of this guy Marvin, who lived on the island. Someone he didn't even know, but right now, he knew one thing: Marvin wasn't going to fuck Ingrid Karlsen anymore. No one was.

He jumped when someone tapped his shoulder.

He snapped out of his dreaming slumber. When he opened his eyes, it took him a moment to realize where he was. It wasn't the scene he was just dreaming about. He looked up into the kind face of Karen.

"I'm sorry if I woke you. It's just that you said when I came back from Dad's to bring you a beer. Here it is. You seemed restless, like you were having a bad dream. Are you all right?"

"I guess so. You're right. I was having a bad dream. Under the circumstances, I could use a beer to calm down."

Wow. What a dream, he thought. The realization smacked him. Did he really kill Ingrid after all? Had he blacked out killing her all these years.

"Thank you for remembering the beer," he said.

"That's what I'm here for. We start dinner in forty-five minutes. You'll be at the same table as before. See you then."

"I'm looking forward to it." He watched her walk away.

His mind flashed back to the dream, and the bottle of beer shook in his hand as he brought it to his lips. Please Lord, don't let it be true.

He got up from the hammock and started walking around the hotel grounds, trying to get the dream off his mind, but it was no use.

A fun day of sailing had turned into a nightmare.

―――

An hour later, he returned to the hotel dining room and sat at the same table where he'd had lunch. Karen approached with the evening menu and a smile. "Did you have a nice walk around our grounds? It's quite lovely with all the flowers and trees, isn't it? I love working here. Besides, the food is good."

"Yes, I agree. It's lovely. If dinner is anything like lunch, I'll be happy."

"Would you like something to drink?"

"I'll stick with water for now. I think I had too much alcohol this afternoon. When I took my nap in the hammock, I ended up having a horrible nightmare, as you surmised. That dream is upsetting me."

"Oh, really? That's too bad. Are you okay now?"

"No, not really. Have you ever had a nasty nightmare that you can't shake off?"

She squinted, then closed her eyes in thought. "I did. It haunted me for several years. When I was younger, I dreamt I got caught in a rip current while I was swimming at Little School Beach. Since that dream, I have never liked swimming there. In the dream, I was sucked out and couldn't get back in. Eventually I became exhausted and started slipping under the water—then I'd wake up, screaming. I don't know why I had the dream because I've never ever been caught in a rip current, and that beach is one of the best on the island. It's a favorite beach for those that live here or visit. I must have seen someone on TV or a movie like when the girl in the movie *Jaws* gets attacked by the great white shark when she's swimming at night. I haven't had that dream for years, thank goodness. I'm sure your dream was frightening to you, but it was just a dream, like mine."

"Yeah, you're probably right." *If she only knew.*

"I'll bring you some water. Our special tonight is a Door County pork chop or freshly caught whitefish, both from a local provider. I'll be back with some bread and a garden salad. Anything else to drink?"

"Water's fine for now. Maybe later," he said, although he could use a whisky right now to calm his nerves. The beers and the hammock must have relaxed him so that his suppressed thoughts about that night with Ingrid had escaped from his subconscious to create the dream. He hoped he never had to relive the frightening thought that he killed Ingrid. When he came out of his thoughts about the dream, sitting at his table, Karen had already gone to the kitchen.

He had nothing to do but look out the window and at the people sitting or standing in small groups, having cocktails. He waited for Karen to return with his dinner. If he really thought about it, it wasn't dinner he craved, but her company. She was attractive for sure, but there was that gentle kindness about her he liked. He thought she would be easy to be with.

Dinner came and went. Like his lunch, it was delicious, and the portions were just the right size, so he wasn't stuffed but not hungry either. He even had a slice of apple pie. The apples were from a local orchard, the salad from the hotel's own garden, and the White Fish from the waters of Green Bay. It was a way for everyone to support one another.

He watched as Karen came back with his bill.

"Is there anything else you'd like? Otherwise, here is your bill for the day. That's your lunch, drinks, and tonight's dinner." She placed the bill down on a plate on the table.

"I might want a bottle of your favorite wine."

"My favorite wine? Why mine? You're the one that's going to drink it." She looked at him with big blue eyes, eyebrows arched.

"I was wondering if you'd like to join me and have a drink on my boat after you're done working tonight. That is, if it's not against the rules or you must get home to your father."

He watched for a reaction from her, and he was encouraged when she smiled.

"I could drink Sauvignon Blanc, but I need to go home and bring Dad his dinner. He'll be waiting."

"What about after you do that? I'm at the marina for the evening, and it's still a couple of hours until sunset. We'll have the wine and chat."

He watched as she mulled over his offer, then smiled. "You seem like a nice guy. Not some killer type! I don't go down to the marina very often, and we don't have any rule about fraternizing with guests because most people that come here are either couples or groups for yoga, painting, or something. Yeah, I can meet you, but it will be after I get done with Dad."

"Great. I'm in slip twelve. See you when you get there."

"I'll add the wine to your bill. I'll give you the employee discount on the wine." She picked up the check. "I'll bring a new bill when I come back with the wine."

He handed her his credit card. As she walked away, he thought maybe tonight would end up on a positive note. He wasn't envisioning anything more than some good conversation with someone he found attractive and nice.

When Karen came back with his receipt for dinner and the wine, she mentioned she'd bring a couple of actual wine glasses from home. "Wine tastes so much better when sipped from a proper wine glass. I'll see you in a couple of hours. I need to change into something warmer for being on the water."

"Sounds good, although I have extra fleece pullovers on the boat. They probably aren't as stylish as yours."

She laughed at that. "If you want to call a Washington Island zippered fleece stylish, then I have it. It's a light gray, so it goes with everything. I'll see you in little over an hour."

He grabbed the wine bottle and headed to his boat to tidy it up a bit for Karen's visit.

It must have taken a little more time with her father and getting ready. It was close to two hours later when he saw Karen peddling down the road with what looked like an old-fashioned fat tire bike with a wicker picnic basket attached to the handlebars. He wondered what was in the basket besides the wine glasses.

"Hi, Captain. Permission to come aboard?" she called out. Reaching for his hand, she stepped lightly onto the boat.

"What's in the basket? I hope not more wine?"

She laughed. "Our chef made a few cherry pies for tomorrow. He knew Dad likes pie, so he gave me one. Working there has its benefits. I thought we could have a piece with the wine. Dad won't miss two pieces."

"That was nice of you. Make my piece small. I'm still full from dinner." He watched as she lifted up the pie with the crisscross crust across the top, and then a couple of real plates, a pie knife, and even cloth napkins. "Wow, you really came prepared."

"I did, didn't I? I thought the pie would lighten your spirits after the nasty dream."

"Just having you here has lightened my spirits. A guy likes to have company, and you were so nice to agree to come over. Let me get the wine open while you cut the pie. Did you bring those wine glasses?"

"Yep, here they are."

Soon they finished the pie and were on their second glass of wine.

Randy couldn't believe how lucky he was to have Karen here now, to help smooth over the thought that he might have murdered Ingrid. If that was true, he'd have to live with it, but it was going to be a tough hurtle to get over because he didn't think he would ever be a killer. Would it happen again if he got upset?

He thought of Trisha and how she had dumped him for Adam. If he got her alone, could he kill again?

"Earth to Randy? Are you okay? You had this strange look on your face."

"I'm sorry. I was just thinking about the dream and how happy I am that you're here to help me try and forget."

"Do you want to talk about it? I'm a pretty good listener."

"Another time. Then I'll tell you all about it."

"You'll have to tell me all about it. It sounds serious when you say it that way."

"Let's talk about something else. Something happy. Can we do that?" he asked. "Tell me about yourself and your parents."

"Sure. Both parents were teachers, so they had the summers off. Dad was the principal at a middle school and taught a few classes besides. Mom taught third grade. They found a little home on the island just for the summers. As they got closer to retirement, they started making it their own special place. I liked their lifestyle so much, I decided to become a teacher too. My parents retired and had five good years together up here before mom got ALS and died two years later. Dad took care of her twenty-four-seven. She died at home with him at her side. I was there too, luckily, but for him it wasn't the same without Mom. That's when I decided I needed to come up and be with him. About all he does now is read and goes fishing by the ferry docks. It gives him a chance to talk to the tourists."

"I can understand that. I really don't know Washington Island well at all. Maybe you can show me around sometime." He watched her smile.

"I'm off late Sunday afternoon, Monday, and Tuesday. If you're still here, I can give you the tour. There's enough to see here, and we can ride bikes around the island. It's pretty flat."

"I'd like that. I'll just stay Monday, maybe Tuesday. I'm not putting you out or interrupting time with your dad, am I?"

"No. You can meet him later if you'd like. He'd probably enjoy that."

"Okay, then it's a date." They clinked their glasses. After that, it was easy conversation.

Soon it was late. The sunset had come and gone. Karen took her basket and loaded the pie and dirty dishes and glasses. Randy helped her off the boat, and the two walked to her bike.

"I had a nice time tonight," she said. "It was something I don't usually do, and it was fun sitting on a boat watching the sunset.

See you at the hotel tomorrow?"

"Looking forward to it. I'll be there for lunch again. I'm full enough from lunch and dinner plus the two desserts to last me for a while. Would you like me to walk you home?"

"No, it's not far. Besides, the island is safe. Most people here don't even lock their homes or cars." She stepped toward him and gave him a peck on the cheek. "Thanks for the good time this evening, Randy. See you tomorrow."

"I'm looking forward to it." And as she walked away, he was left with a feeling maybe things were finally turning for the better, despite today's unsettling dream.

CHAPTER TWENTY-FOUR

He woke before sunrise, with the boat rocking in its slip. He could hear the rain and wind coming from the squall as it raced across the harbor. When it hit the boat, it sounded like when he was in a carwash.

As fast as it hit, it was over in a few minutes, as most squalls were. Then he heard the soft sound of raindrops on the cabin's fiberglass roof. It was a soothing sound, and he rolled over and closed his eyes. There would be time later to check the weather radio for the marine forecast. He knew he wasn't sailing today. In fact, he wanted to stay here for a couple of days, at least until Tuesday morning, so he could spend the day exploring Washington Island with Karen.

The rain stopped about 9:00 a.m. He was surprised he was hungry, so he walked to the crossroads area on the island and the Red Cup Coffee House for breakfast. He was not disappointed. Two eggs over easy, toast, and a sausage patty with three cups of wonderful black coffee filled him up. What more could a sailor want except maybe a pretty crewmember to share it with? He was hoping that might be Karen.

Was he trying too hard to find love? She had just watched the sunset with him. He shouldn't make more out of it than a simple act of kindness on her part. But he wanted that kindness to continue. Didn't she give him a kiss on his cheek without him making any move? She must like him, if only a little bit.

After breakfast, he walked north to Jackson Harbor on the island's northeast corner. From there he saw Rock Island, with its impressive rock boathouse. Someday he'd boat the short distance separating the two islands. He read the walk around the smaller island was worth the journey.

An hour later he was back at his boat, doing maintenance on his teak. It was a never-ending job that he enjoyed. Today he was lightly sanding the teak handrails and toe rails before touching them up with teak oil. Many boaters varnished, but Randy preferred teak oil, which gave him a better grip when he needed to grab the wooden handholds. Plus, he liked the smell.

Next it was time for a shower. He had worked up a pretty good sweat bending over the deck in the sun, sanding and touching up the teak. He wanted to look his best when he saw Karen at lunch.

It was quiet when he got to the hotel. He heard what sounded like spa music and knew the yoga workshops would soon be over. He didn't have long to wait as twenty ladies in a mixed array of outfits, body shapes, and ages entered the dining area for lunch, excitedly chatting.

His heart skipped a beat when he saw Karen. "Relax," he said out loud.

Saw him in his usual spot, waved, and headed his way with a small tray of flowers for the tables.

"After I get set up, I'll come by. Is that okay, or are you really hungry? I can bring you some bread right away."

"No, take your time. I had a big breakfast at the Red Cup, so I'm fine."

"Since you are full, I'll take care of the women and get their salad orders. We have some good goat cheese from one of the island farms that everyone loves. You might want to try a bit on a side salad."

"I'll think about that. I'll probably stick with the fish."

"Fresh salmon from Captain Jack's. We also have the local favorite, lawyers, which is a unique fish from the area if you're interested."

"Could be. I had a bad taste from a lawyer ten years ago. Someday I'll have to tell you about it. Maybe I'll try it. Something different. It's a fish, right?"

"Yes, it is. See you later."

He watched her walk away, laughing at the thought he was going to eat a lawyer for lunch.

Michael Pritzkow

As it turned out, the lawyer fish was good. The only thing negative about lunch was Karen being very busy. She didn't have a chance to socialize with him. She said she was sorry about it but thought dinner would be better.

Then there was the prospect of another date tonight after she was done with work. That is, if her time with her dad didn't interfere. She was pretty committed to her dad, and rightly so.

He was asking a lot. Randy had just met her. He knew she liked him because she often swung by his table to ask if everything was all right. And then there was the peck on the cheek last night. He looked at his watch. Four hours until dinner and Karen.

"What's the special tonight?" he asked, though he really could care less. He just wanted to talk to Karen and find out if they'd meet tonight after she was done with work, or he'd have to wait until tomorrow to spend time with her.

"Free range chicken, new potatoes, and asparagus, plus Door County cherry or apple pie for dessert. It looks wonderful and of course healthy."

"Sounds good. I'll have a Coke." He watched as she lifted her eyebrows.

"That different. It's nice."

"I'm trying not to drink too much after yesterday."

"That's good. My old flame and eventual husband drank too much, and it was the main reason we divorced, so I like that you're showing restraint. I'll be back with your Coke and some bread."

Good to know about him, he thought. *Interesting.*

His drinking yesterday had been a little more than usual, but that was because of Trisha dumping him for Adam and the dream about Ingrid. From now on, he'd take a cue from Karen.

Dinner was like lunch. Very good, but soon it was time to ask the question about going out tonight.

"Here you go. Not as high as yesterday, but then you didn't have as much wine and beer today. And then there wasn't the bottle for the boat either."

"Well, I didn't spend as much as yesterday, but I'd gladly order another bottle of wine if you'd like to watch the sunset again on the boat. I enjoyed being with you last night. I was hoping we could do it again tonight."

She smiled at him, moving both her hands to her hips. He noticed a slight blush to her cheeks.

"That's so sweet of you to say. I enjoy being with you too, but tonight is Sunday. Dad and I usually go to Nelson's Grill and Pub and have a few drinks. He always loves going there and having one of their old-fashioneds. They're famous for their bitters. It was something he and my mom did every Sunday, so I'm kind of keeping the memory and tradition alive for him. I hope you understand."

"I do. That's great you do that. I know my parents used to go to townie bars like that." His parents liked to go to the AC Tap for burgers and beer, until his dad got too sick.

"How about this?" she asked. "You could join us. It's not too far of a walk to our place. I know Dad would welcome some new blood to talk to, instead of the same people every Sunday. For him, nothing really changes since Mom died. It might not be as much fun for you as being on the boat, but you'll get to learn about the local history and the legend of the 'bitter shot' here on the island. If you want to be together tonight, that's about the best I can do for you."

"That's fine. When? Where is your place?" She gave him her address.

"Give me about an hour so I can clean up and change," she said. "Come to our house about seven o'clock."

He looked at his watch. "Okay. See you then.

The walk from the marina to their house took him about twenty minutes. On a tree-lined street, it was ranch style with a well-kept yard and flowers, with homes on each side. It did not have a view of the water, but it was in a nice neighborhood. Outside on the front yard an older man sat on an aluminum lawn chair, waiting.

As Randy walked up the driveway, the man said, "You must be Randy. Karen is just finishing getting ready. She must like you because on Sunday when she gets done with work, we usually just go directly to Nelson's, but tonight she said she had to change. My name is Ed."

"My last name is Daggett, just so you know. It nice of you, letting me join you for dinner and be part of your family time."

"Karen says you sailed over to the island for lunch and have been stuck here because of the weather."

"Yes. That's how I met your daughter. Karen is special, as you know, and very nice."

"That she is. She's a lot like her mother—looks like her when she was younger, God rest her soul. I told her she didn't need to live up here. She had a nice life teaching and living in Green Bay, but she said she likes the island and didn't want me to be alone. It's nice to see her every day."

The screen door opened, and she came out.

"I see you met Dad," she said, beaming. "I'm ready. Let's go."

As the three walked to dinner, Ed filled Randy in on his daily activities. Mostly, he said, he went to the car ferry dock and saw his three fishing and golfing buddies. "The fishing is surprisingly good there," he said, "with the deeper water because of the ferries. The fish stay near the bottom, next to the pier. So, when the ferries leave, we drop our lines. We really don't care if we catch anything, but sometimes we surprise ourselves with a nice bass or trout. None of the guys keep the fish because they prefer whitefish or the specialty of the island, lawyers."

Randy laughed. "I had some for lunch today, and I have to say I enjoyed having a lawyer for lunch, and it didn't cost me like another lawyer I had in the past."

Ed looked confused, but Karen explained that Randy was making a joke.

The three continued the short walk to Nelsen Hall. It wasn't too crowded for seven thirty, but on Sunday evening, it was easy to get a table.

The three ordered the specialty of the house: the brandy old-fashioned, a Wisconsin favorite, with Nelsen's bitters of course. After being served the drink, Karen and Ed ordered broasted chicken. Randy munched on bread, still full of dinner at the hotel.

Dinner was pleasant. He was thankful to be included in their Sunday tradition.

"What do you do again?" asked Ed. "Karen didn't tell me."

"That's because I don't know either, Dad," said Karen. "Randy and I met because he was stranded on the island. You know he lives on an island most of the time like us?"

"Really? Which island? There aren't too many that you can live on around here."

"Chambers Island, just across from Fish Creek, and in the middle of Green Bay. I have a house in Fish Creek too. I write novels for a profession. I've published six crime novels. They take place primarily in a prison."

"Like *Shawshank Redemption*?" Ed asked.

"The prison setting is similar, but the stories are different. They have a strong following from people that like that sort of thing. They've done well, at least enough to pay the bills and put a little money in the bank. When you write, you really spend most of your time alone. So you don't spend much money. The only big purchase I've made lately was my sailboat, *Island Girl*, and the island house. The house wasn't too expensive because of how remote it is and having no power. I live off the grid. That means no TV."

Ed started laughing. "I don't know what I'd do if I didn't have the TV. Besides fishing and seeing my cronies at the ferry dock, I wouldn't have anything to keep my mind occupied. Even so, most of the shows on the local stations up here are not that great."

"Oh, Dad, you read and write poetry too," said Karen.

"Oh, that stuff. I don't know how good it is. Only you and your mother read it. Someday I'll go to one of those writers' conferences at your hotel and find out. I'll probably get my feelings hurt, but I do enjoy writing poetry. I'm really writing for myself, no one else, so who cares how bad it is?"

"That's what they say a writer should do," Randy said, nodding.

They chatted for another hour about island life, comparing the pros and cons of their semi-isolated lives. For Ed, it was important being in the house that he and Karen's mom had shared. Island life was simple and stress free. Traffic was nonexistent except at the ferry dock. Karen liked being with her father and enjoyed the simple things the island and the hotel offered. She liked how the islanders all supported each other.

"If I want creature comforts," Randy said, "I have to leave Chambers Island and go to my house in Fish Creek. I live there from fall to late spring, but the summers on the island are great, and that's where I like to write."

"That makes sense," said Karen.

He smiled at her. "Maybe you can come visit and tell me what you think."

"Maybe I can," she said with a smile.

After the short walk back to the house, Ed shook Randy's hand.

"Thanks for joining us. Since you are a professional writer, maybe you can read some of my poetry and tell me what you think."

"I'd be happy to."

"I'll let you two say goodbye." Ed turned and walked inside.

"Dad must like you. He's never offered to let anyone else read his poetry besides Mom and me. He's a pretty good judge of character, so if he likes you, so do I." Karen moved closer and gave him more than a peck on the cheek. He returned the kiss.

A few minutes later, they separated.

"Are we still getting together tomorrow or was that a goodbye kiss?" he asked.

She laughed. "Do you really think I would kiss you like that if I *wasn't* going to be with you tomorrow? I'm looking forward to spending the whole day with you, learning all about Randy Daggett."

"Why don't I stop by here tomorrow morning?" he said. "We can find someplace to have breakfast near here. I love a big breakfast to start the day."

"Okay. Say nine o'clock?"

"Great."

The nasty winds abated, and Washington Island offered a sunny, bluebird morning to Randy as he woke up on his boat. He'd slept well to the gentle rocking of *Island Girl* behind the marina's breakwater.

He made a small pot of coffee on his boat's propane stove and waited until it was time to go to Karen's.

Once he finally arrived there, he saw her old Schwinn big-balloon-tire bike parked on the driveway along with another bike he assumed was her father's. The bike with a single wheel and sprocket was probably perfect for Washington Island, since it didn't have many hills.

He smiled as she stepped out of the house. She was dressed casual in shorts, a fleece vest, long sleeve T-shirt, and a Green Bay Packers hat with the sunglasses pushed up, covering the big G logo.

"Hi. How was your night on the boat? It seemed like the winds died down after we got back from dinner."

"It was a nice night. I slept well. Are you hungry?"

"I could eat something. I'll probably need the energy later if I take you to all the places I plan on showing you today. It's not like there's a lot to see and do here on the island, but what we have is scattered around. Yeah, let's have a big breakfast."

"Good. I'm starved," he said, and they peddled the short distance to a café in the middle of the island.

"I'll have two eggs over easy, toast, and bacon," she told the waitress after they'd settled into a booth.

"Sounds good to me. I'll have the same," Randy added. "If you have American potatoes with cheese and onions, I'll have that also."

The waitress nodded and walked away.

"So, what do you want to do today on the island?" Karen asked.

"Well, it's a great day for bike riding," he said. "I need the exercise. I'm not used to sitting, eating, and drinking like I have these last few days."

Michael Pritzkow

As they slowly peddled the island roads, he was surprised how many homes were nestled between the road and the water. Soon enough they passed a fudge shop, the popcorn store, and Nelsen's, where they'd had dinner the night before. They rode north along the main drag, passing the school and the health center where Karen told him her father went for minor issues. Then there was the Lavender Farm and the island's golf course, with its upside-down saucer greens.

They'd peddled for about an hour when they got to Schoolhouse Beach, a beach of beautiful smooth limestone stones of varying sizes.

"There's no sand here, and the water is crystal clear," said Randy.

"It's cold even in August, but it's the favorite beach on Washington Island. See the raft? It's usually packed with kids in the afternoon. The stones are perfect for skipping."

The two walked to the water's edge and tossed the smooth flat-sided stones, making them skip. Karen was good at it, skipping them more times than Randy.

"Why are stones stacked up making a sort of small stone tower? They look like a trail marker if you were a hiker."

"There is no reason that I know of, except it's fun and looks nice." She pointed to the beach and counted eight small stone towers. "This beach is unique. There are only five beaches like this in the United States. It's illegal to take the stones from the beach…

but I'm sure little kids do it. Just don't get caught."

"Ha ha. Well, it's very nice, and I'm not taking any of the stones, although they'd make good paperweights. Where to next?" he asked.

"Mountain Park and Lookout Tower will give you a nice view of the island and the lake. After that, we can circle around. Wish there was more to do here, but it's really about getting away to a simple life."

"Simple is nice. That's why I like my Chambers Island, except this island is like a city with its businesses and restaurants, hotel, and motels, compared to my island. Nothing on Chambers."

"It sounds like camping." Karen's eyes twinkled as she said it.

"Sometimes I think so. I like it. You have a lot more conveniences here."

"Okay, let's get going," she said and hopped on her bike.

It was a pleasant ride, and they stopped at several places along the way, including the Fragrant Isle Lavender Farm Shop and Le Café. The fields were in full bloom, and Randy and Karen sampled some beer. After that, they stopped at Island Popcorn Barn.

"I love this stuff," she said. "It's not fattening either—ha ha."

At Mann's Mercantile, Randy saw the main grocery, hardware, and tourist items all rolled into one store. "Nice store. Lots of stuff packed in here."

They tooled around on the bikes and stopped for ice cream at the car ferry area. After that they rested at a park near the marina, just a short distance from The Hotel Washington. They sat on a bench and watched boats cross the bay.

Under sunny skies, there was a slight wind ruffling the water. He looked at her profile, thinking how much he wanted to kiss her when she turned to look at him. Slowly, she moved closer, touching his cheek lightly and then moving to his lips.

Her arms wrapped around his back and shoulders.

Their lips explored each other's. Small moans came from her as their tongues intertwined. He moved his kisses to her neck, then back to her lips. After about five minutes, they parted, and she leaned her head onto his chest.

"It's been a while since I kissed anyone," said Karen, "especially like that. Was I too forward?"

"Not at all. I wanted to kiss you too, but you beat me to it."

She laughed. "I'm glad we got that straightened out. Would you like to come to the house and have some burgers? It's a simple meal usually on my day off. Dad likes to grill out as often as he can."

"Okay. You're off tomorrow too? Would you like to go sailing? It looks like another nice day."

"I'd love to, but don't you have to get home?"

"I'll leave on Wednesday. You have to go back to work that day anyway. Giving you a sail around the island is the least I can do since you've been showing me such a good time on the island."

"In that case, I accept your invitation."

"Great." He squeezed her hand and gave her another kiss. They headed to her house for dinner.

CHAPTER TWENTY-FIVE

The next morning was classic Door County: a bright-blue sky, sparkling water, and winds that were just strong enough to move *Island Girl* at a nice pace. From the deck, he watched Karen approach the marina on her bike.

His heart raced just at the sight of her. He wasn't sure what to make of this heady feeling because they'd met just a few days ago, but he didn't care.

Randy could only hope she was feeling the same, though last night's kisses indicated there was something there.

"Good morning, Captain," she said with a grin. "It looks like a perfect day to go sailing. I brought chicken salad sandwiches, soda, fruit, and a bottle of wine. The wine's for later when we dock. I could hardly sleep last night, thinking about sailing today."

He reached out his hand to help her aboard. "I was looking forward to today too."

"That's nice. I like spending time with you." She gave him a kiss on the cheek. "Let's go."

Island Girl moved out of the slip and motored across Washington Island's Detroit Harbor and then started sailing north out the Detroit Island Passage into Green Bay, avoiding Death's Door Passage.

Randy started the motor and raised the sails. Every time he looked at Karen, she was smiling. He thought how beautiful she was when a smile lit up her face.

"I can't believe how good this is, being out on the water," she said. "Relaxing and exciting all at the same time."

"That's how I feel when I go out," said Randy, "except for the occasional time it storms or the wind gets too strong. But then again, sometimes those conditions have benefits. After all, they caused me to stay on your island a few extra days and gave us a chance to meet."

They both were quiet, enjoying the sail for about ten minutes when Karen broke the silence. "Tell me about yourself. I really don't know you."

Randy's heart sank. Here it was. Should he tell her? Should he hide the truth? He decided he'd just talk about himself and see what happens. Eventually he'd have to tell her the sad story, but not right now.

"Randy?"

"Yes. Just trying to think where to start."

"Maybe I'll start first," she said. "Would you like a soda or water before I start?

"A water would be good."

"I told you some of this before." And then she went on about her mom and dad and her life. "I went to high school in Green

Bay and later the University of Wisconsin-Madison, majoring in art and art history. Turns out there are a lot of artists here in Door County."

He smiled. "I went there too. Loved it there."

"Fun place and good school. After graduating, I taught at Green Bay West until my mother died, as you know, and I came up to be with dad. Here's what you didn't know. After I graduated from the university and started teaching, I married one of the teachers at the school. It didn't work out. We didn't even make it a year. He was controlling and physically abusive. It only took one time when he hit me after he went out drinking with the boys. I knew right away: I wasn't staying in that relationship. Guys like him never change. I kicked him out, threatening to tell the school principal about him. He couldn't have that on his record, so he left. I cut my losses early and got a divorce. That was five years ago."

"Are you dating someone else now, up here?"

She laughed. "No. After the divorce, I really didn't feel like dating, plus the pickings are kind of slim on the island. Besides, I like spending time with Dad. I cherish my time with him. Life is fleeting."

"Yes, I know. Not too long ago, I lost both parents in a car accident, so I understand wanting to spend time with your father."

"Oh, that's so sad."

"Anyway, I wish I had spent more time with them."

"Again, I'm sorry for your loss. I was happy when you asked me to have wine on the boat that first night. You seem like a nice guy, someone I can trust. I know we just met, but I think I'm a pretty good judge of people, except maybe in my ex-husband's case. Never saw the abusive side of him when we were dating. Not sure I could be with anyone that's violent, you know what I mean?"

"I can understand that."

I hope I can convince her I'm not violent, my dream notwithstanding.

"When we kissed last night, it felt wonderful to be in your arms," she said. "It's been a long time since I let myself go like that. When you get hurt emotionally, it's hard to think you'll ever find that special feeling again. Last night felt really good." She moved next to Randy, took his hand in hers, and squeezed. With her other hand, she caressed his face and kissed him on the lips: a gentle, tender kiss that lasted a while.

When she pulled back, Randy could see her eyes were moist.

"I hope this works between us. I like you." She patted the boat gently. "And I like sailing and being with you on your boat." She slid back and rested her head and shoulders on his chest. "This is heaven."

Randy turned on the boat's autopilot, and they sailed further out into Green Bay. Sooner or later he was going to have to tell her about Ingrid, but for now he was going to enjoy what he had with her, however long it lasted.

———

Karen fell asleep. She sank against his chest, and her breathing slowed. Finally, she stirred. "Oh no! I fell asleep. Did I snore? I hope I didn't." She laughed and looked at her watch. "And it's still morning. That says something."

"Does it mean I'm boring?"

"It means I'm comfortable and relaxed with you." She poked him in the chest to emphasize the point. "It's close enough to noon to eat. Do you want a sandwich and a soda?"

"Sure."

After eating, Randy changed course, turning the boat northward, and eventually they sailed past Schoolhouse Beach, then toward the tip of the island's Boyer Bluff. Randy steered *Island Girl* east across the top of the island, then headed south and down its eastern side, tacking and completing the circumnavigation through Death's Door Passage. He swung past Plum Island and Detroit Island to the ferry docks.

As *Island Girl* sailed down the channel between the smaller islands, he called on the radio and got a new slip at Kap's marina, saving time for tomorrow's departure, as it was at the entrance of Washington Island and near the ferry docks.

Once the boat was tied up, they sat back and had the cheese, sausage, and the wine Karen had brought. Randy ran to the store and grabbed a bag of ice, a few snacks, and another bottle of white wine, just in case.

"It was a wonderful day," Karen said as she grabbed pretzels from a bag. "I can't believe we circumnavigated the whole island. It was wonderful." She smiled at him. "I could use a glass of wine. We need to celebrate the day."

"Sure, I'll open the bottle I just got. It's still cold from the store. Let me just put the ice and stuff away and the bottle in the ice chest." A few minutes later, he handed her a glass and poured himself one too. "I noticed they had a pizza place close by. Island Pizza. Catchy name." She laughed at his small joke. "Let's order the pizza soon because I'm really hungry like you, and we can watch the sun go down."

"Sounds great. Pepperoni and sausage, black olives, and onions. Is that okay?"

"Yep." He got his cell phone out and phoned in the order and then had some wine.

Karen sipped and smiled at him. She patted the seat next to her and said, "Move over here next to me. I want to thank you for today."

When he did, she wrapped her arms around his neck, and all was right with the world.

He tossed and turned all night. While he and Karen did not make love, they had kissed and caressed each other long into the night. Later, he walked her home; it was closer since he got the slip at Kap's Marina.

After they arrived at her house, Randy was surprised to see her father sitting in his chair in the front yard.

"I'm tired," Ed said. "Now that you're here, I'm going to bed. Good night." He walked into the house.

"That's nice that he waits up for you to make sure you got

home safely. My mom did the same thing."

"Once a parent, always a parent, I guess. One question," She said.

"Sure. What?"

"Am I ever going to see you again, or are you going to sail away tomorrow morning and vanish from my life?"

"I hope to see you a lot more, but just to make it easier, maybe I'll just take the ferry here, like most people do—or we can meet on the peninsula. Any town is fine. If you come to Fish Creek, I can show you my house in town and the island cabin too."

"We can do that. I like you, Randy. It's time for me to get on with my life, and I'd like to make you part of it. Does that sound okay?"

He wrapped his arms around her and kissed her, their tongues swirling. He pressed his body against her. When he pulled back, he didn't have to say anything except, "Call me, and we can meet in Ellison Bay at Mink River Basin next Sunday or Monday."

"It's a date," she said.

CHAPTER TWENTY-SIX

The next morning, he had a big breakfast at Ship's Wheel Restaurant before taking off for home and Chambers Island.

Sailing back gave him a chance to think. He knew he had to tell Karen everything about his past before she found out by looking him up on the internet. He wanted her in his life. He hoped she'd feel the same, even after learning about him.

———

Six hours later he was back on Chambers Island. Returning home after being gone for a while meant everything seemed new to him, fresh. The grass was a little longer, but the house was still there, and everything was in its place, just as he'd left it.

After stowing his clothing and the few food items and water bottles from the boat, he got out his computer and started writing. The day passed as he delved into his next gang story. It was hard going. He was struggling to find a unique angle on prison violence. He had started the story with rival gangs outside prison, but when their members got convicted and sent away, they kept on fighting and killing, just like before. Prison was its own world.

Evening arrived, and he went down to Sand Bay with his lawn chair to watch the last of the sunset, a way to decompress after a long day of writing. He liked sitting there alone, letting his mind wander. Then he heard a familiar voice in the darkness.

"Randy, I missed you. It's nice to see you again. Where have you been for the last few days?"

"Simon, what are you doing out this late? Does Marvin know you're out here?"

"No. He and Jessica have been fighting. I mean, really fighting—like hitting. She got really upset and locked herself in my bedroom. Then she went to Trisha's and asked Trisha if she would give her a ride into Fish Creek tomorrow. All I know is she's not at the cabin, and Marvin is yelling and throwing her stuff around, so I decided to get away from all the anger in the house. At least for a while, until Marvin calms down."

The next day after breakfast, Simon showed up. Randy said, "Let's go back to your house, and you can get your paints. I'll walk with you, but I'll stay in the trees. You get your paints, and we'll walk back here."

"I'm not sure that's a good idea. I don't think Marvin wants you around me. He thinks you did a bad thing a while ago. Remember, he told you not to visit me."

"Yes, I know, but he won't see me, I promise."

Simon retrieved his paints, and later that morning he painted an unusual painting, unlike his others. It depicted a woman underwater with a man. His hands were under the water near her shoulders.

"What's this, Simon? You've never done anything like this."

"I saw this man and woman swimming today. I liked the way she looked under the water when he pushed her. Do you like the painting?"

"I always like your paintings. This one is different. I'm not sure if I like it. It's unsettling to me, but it's all right. You're expressing your feelings."

Earlier when he and Simon had gone to his cabin to get the paints, Randy had hidden behind a large tree. He saw Marvin doing some stuff in the shed and noticed his red swimsuit. It looked just like the suit Randy had spotted on the beach the night Ingrid died. You'd think he would have gotten rid of it. Holy shit. If that was the suit, Marvin was there that night.

Just then Simon came out of the house with his paints and paper.

When he got to Randy, he said. "Jessica was there, getting her things. She said she was leaving Marvin and never coming back. Now you and Trisha are my only friends on the island—but she's got Adam, who doesn't like me, so it's really just you."

Actually, it felt good to have Simon with him at Sand Bay. Randy watched him paint some sea gulls and anchored boats in the bay. After spending four days with Karen, he didn't feel like being alone.

Randy liked Jessica. She was always friendly and very pretty. It was upsetting that Marvin had done what he did but maybe not a surprise. After all, Ingrid had taken out a restraining order against him. He had a violent side, and Randy would be wary.

Marvin Jacobs was the only one of Randy's remaining suspects that could have been on the island the night Ingrid was killed. And what about the swimsuit?

Over the next few days, the island was pretty quiet. Randy stopped at Trisha's cabin, but she and Adam were gone. He guessed they were back in Green Bay, working. Even Simon and Marvin were off the island. Maybe Marvin was trying to patch things up with Jessica.

He tried calling Karen a few times, but for whatever reason, she didn't answer. He hoped she had not checked up on him and decided she didn't want to see him again. She had told him she didn't want to be in a violent relationship. Manslaughter was pretty violent.

On Friday, he reached her on the phone at eight thirty in the morning, hoping to catch her before she headed off to work at the hotel.

"Hello?"

"Hi, it's Randy. How are you?"

"I'm great, but I was a little worried you weren't going to call me. So I'm glad to hear your voice."

"I called you, but you didn't answer."

"I thought you were a robocaller. I guess I should have entered you in my contact list. Anyway, I'm glad were talking now."

"Would you like to get together on the peninsula Sunday night or Monday? I miss you."

"Sure. I'll take the ferry over after work. How about meeting for supper in Ellison Bay at the Mink River Basin like you suggested? The food's good, and it's close for both of us. It will have to be quick because the last ferry back to the island is at 6:45. I can leave a little early, say three o'clock, so it will give us a little time before. We don't have any weddings or big groups this weekend at the hotel."

"Okay. I'll see you there at four. That will give you time to get over and drive to Ellison Bay. If you want me to take the ferry over, it will save you some time."

"No, that's okay. I have a pass for the ferry because I'm a resident. To be honest, I enjoy getting off the island now and then. This is one of those times." She paused. "You made my day, Randy. I was hoping we could get together again. See you Sunday. Bye. Running late. Got to go and get ready for work."

"Bye." Randy let out a big sigh. She had not found out about him yet.

That Sunday, sitting at the bar in Ellison Bay, Randy looked at his watch for the fifth time in ten minutes. It reminded him of being in grade school watching the minute hand slowly move across the face of the clock on the wall as it approached the end of the school day.

He fingered the Coke in front of him. He wanted to have a clear head when he told Karen about his past. Just when he was ready to look at his watch again, she walked through the door, saw him, smiled, and walked over.

Before he could say anything, she wrapped her arms around him and gave him a long welcoming kiss. When she pulled back, he heard her say, "I really missed you. I've thought about you all week." Then she sat down and said to the bartender, "I want a cold, cold beer and a big one. It's been a long day."

When the beer arrived, she had a long drink, then wiped her lips. "It seemed like the ferry took forever to get across and unload. I was lucky I didn't get a speeding ticket driving the winding road here."

"Well, you're here now, and I'm glad. I've thought about you all week too. Are you hungry?"

"Not really. I had some food after the kitchen closed at lunch. We don't serve dinner on Sundays, unless we have lots of guests or a function. Tonight they're making brats and burgers on a grill with corn on the cob, and watermelon for dessert. Only need one employee for that, so I was able to get home, clean up a little, and make the ferry. You eat something if you want."

"No, I'm just going to drink this Coke before I have something stronger. You asked me last week to tell you about myself, and somehow the conversation never got to me, and certain things I need to tell you about. Important things. I have a lot to tell. I want to be clear-headed when I explain to you about my life."

"Really? It can't be that bad. Like I said, I'm a pretty good judge of character, and so is my dad. Go ahead and tell me your story so we can enjoy our short time tonight. I told Dad I'd be home on the last ferry tonight so we could go out to Nelson's for dinner. Remember, Sunday's a tradition."

"Yes, I remember." And so, he told her about his early life again. Growing up in Fish Creek and dating Ingrid in high school and during the summer while in college.

"Sounds pretty normal to me. So you dated the same girl in high school and college. Interesting. You both must have liked each other a lot, at least for a while. You aren't dating anymore, I guess."

"No. And she was seeing many men and women behind my back the whole time we were dating."

"Really? What happened when you found out? I'd be mad if that happened to me." She finished her beer, and the bartender brought her another.

"I didn't find out about the others until recently. I was clueless and trusting."

"That seems a little strange. Why are you telling me about something that happened ten years ago?"

"I want you to hear the whole story before you make a judgment about me. I just want you to listen before you speak."

"Okay, I can do that, but it seems like a strange request. Go ahead, I'm listening."

He told her about Ingrid Karlsen's death, about being convicted for manslaughter and serving eight years in prison. He watched her eyes widen in disbelief. She moved her barstool further away as he told his story. When he finished, she said nothing.

"Karen, I have to tell you, I know I got convicted of killing her, but I didn't do it. It was all based on circumstantial evidence. I'm not that type of person. I have never been violent to anyone. I'm like a golden retriever: I like everyone. I want you to believe me because I want to be with you. I'm tired of being alone. I know it's only been a week since we met, but I think you feel the same way. At least I hope you do. I can only ask you to believe me, give me a chance. I'm not a killer!"

Her eyes darted around. He knew she didn't like violent people. She had broken up with her husband because he hit her, was abusive, and now here she was sitting across from someone she had feelings for, and he was a convicted killer.

"I don't feel very good," she said and pushed her stool away. Her hand went to her mouth, and she darted toward the women's washroom.

Well, that's the end of this relationship.

"Bartender, I'll have a beer now," Randy said.

Five minutes later Karen emerged from the washroom. "I'm sorry, Randy. I have to go. As you can imagine, I'm upset by all of this. I need to get home for dinner with Dad. I need to think about everything you said, weigh how I feel about you and if I feel comfortable going forward. You seem like a kind person. I'm sorry. I can see why you waited to talk about yourself. I appreciate you telling me early on. I'm glad I didn't find out some other way. Please don't call me. I'll call you. I need to process all this." She turned and walked out, probably never to be seen again.

There was nothing for him to do but go back to his island and keep on living.

Ten days passed, and, honoring Karen's wish, Randy didn't try calling her. He couldn't fault her. It was hard for anyone to believe he wasn't really guilty, but then he thought of Trisha. She'd believed in him. Too bad she went back to Adam. Randy had really cared about her.

His phone rang. His heart skipped a beat when he saw it was Karen.

"Hello? Karen?"

"Yes. Are you surprised?"

"Yes, very, but really glad you called."

"I thought about us long and hard, and I'm going by my gut. I believe you, Randy. I'm calling because I want to cautiously go forward with our relationship. Let's see what happens."

"Thank you so much," he said.

"I know it's Wednesday, but I can't wait until Sunday or Monday to see you. I took some time off—a whole week! Not much happening at the hotel right now, so it's okay to be gone. I have this week to be with you. I miss you."

"I'm in heaven. What do you want to do? Do you want me

to come to the island?"

"No, I want to come tomorrow and see you and where you live—if that's okay. I've never been to Chambers Island. I want to see it, and we can do things around the peninsula. I spend so much time here on the island. I talked to Dad about everything, and he's fine with it. I just need to call him every day just to let him know everything is okay. You said you have a house in Fish Creek. I assume it has an extra bedroom, so I can stay there." She took a breath. "I need to keep some distance. I need to verify that my instincts are correct. I need to sleep alone, not let sex cloud my perspective of you and what happened with Ingrid. You understand. We'll see how it goes. This is a big leap of faith just to trust who you say are and believe in you. Does this all sound okay with you?"

"Yes. I just want to see you and be with you."

CHAPTER TWENTY-SEVEN

The house was always clean because that's the way he was, but he still dusted and mopped the floors and changed the sheets in her room, even though he knew no one had slept in the bed since Trisha. The house was ready for Karen. The only question now was, Was Randy ready for her?

It seemed like eternity to him before she showed up at his house in Fish Creek. When she stepped out of her car, she was carrying a small duffel bag and a couple of bottles of white wine. He walked out to greet her and was pleasantly surprised when she showed no hesitation, setting down her bag and wine and giving him an emotional kiss.

"I missed you, and I trust you," she said.

He couldn't believe what he was hearing. Karen was willing to move forward unless something caused her to change her mind. He was going to do whatever it took to never cross that line.

"Let me take your stuff and put it into your room." She followed him into the house and into the guest bedroom, his old room upstairs. Once that was done, they went into the living room and sat on the sofa. Once again, he was surprised when she sat close beside him.

"Can I ask you a question that might seem strange?" he asked.

"Okay."

"What made you believe my story?"

"I could see it in your eyes that you didn't do what you were convicted off. Not the restraining orders against Ingrid's other lovers. Sure, that helped my decision, but it was really you."

"Thank you." He leaned close to her. "Can I kiss you?"

When she nodded sheepishly yes, he took her in his arms. It was not a hard, bone-jarring kiss but a gentle kiss that conveyed trust, caring, and love. Maybe his life was finally moving in a positive direction after all. His story was a big hurdle to get past with Karen.

Later that day, they walked around Fish Creek, eating, having Bloody Marys at the Bayside, laughing.

They shopped at Hide Side Corner Store, where Karen bought a tan soft-leather jacket, a leather purse, a couple of silk blouses, and scarves. Besides helping with the clothing, Kathy, the owner's wife, helped her pick out a few pieces of jewelry to go with the outfits.

"I always wanted to buy something like this jacket," said Karen. "I love the feel of the soft leather and matching purse. Kathy helped focus on stuff that was more my style. The silver jewelry helps the look." She held up her wrist so he could see the bracelet. "I'll wear it tonight when we go out. Are we going out?"

"Yes, we're going out. I love the outfit. You'll look great in it."

"You just aren't saying that to make me feel good, are you?"

"No. You look amazing with it on."

"Ahh, I'm glad you think so, because I really bought it for you. I want to look good for you. And a real date."

"How about going to the Coyote Roadhouse in Bailey's Harbor or Alexander's between Fish Creek and Ephraim? Great ribs at the Roadhouse. Great everything at Alexander's. Both places have good food and atmosphere. We can sit outside at the Roadhouse. It's supposed to be nice out tonight."

"Sounds like a plan."

They headed back to the Fish Creek house for a rest.

"Do you want anything to drink?" he asked.

"No. I'm pooped. I know you'd prefer for us to nap together, but I'm still a little apprehensive. Can I just take a nap alone? I still want to take it slow."

"Sure. I'm just glad you're here."

Karen gave him a kiss on the cheek and headed to the guest bedroom. "How about we nap until five o'clock?"

Randy went to his room and lay down, but he couldn't sleep. He just lay there with his hands behind his head. He was hoping things were getting better, but he didn't want to push it along any faster than Karen was comfortable with.

It was a short ride over to the Coyote Roadhouse, and they soon got a table outside.

"You look great in your new outfit. Very sexy."

"Really? It's been a long time since I felt sexy."

"Not only do I like how you look, but most of the men here do too."

"Really, it's just a simple outfit. Now I'm self-conscious. I shouldn't have worn it. I should have worn jeans and a Door County sweatshirt like everyone else here tonight."

"You're just so beautiful. They're looking at you, not the clothes. Don't worry too much about it. I see all the guys are going back to their beer and food now."

She laughed after that. "It's really pretty here. I can see a bit of Kangaroo Lake. It's also quiet here. Not much traffic noise."

"How was your nap?"

"It was good. I got tired with all the walking, shopping, and just worrying about how you and I were getting along."

"And how are we getting along?"

"So far, okay. The more I'm around you, the more comfortable I am. I know I'm attracted to you, but I needed to be sure about everything else. The more I'm around you, the more I believe your story about Ingrid." Her eyes met his. "But if you didn't kill her, who did?"

"I don't know, but I think I'm getting closer to finding out. One of the people that had one of those restraining orders lives on the island and is known to be violent. He's my main suspect." He paused and looked at the menu. "Let's order. I'm starved. The ribs and shrimp are the special tonight. I've had them before, and they're great."

"Okay. I'll try them. I'll try to be careful and not get the sauce on my new outfit." She took off her new jacket and folded it over the chair. "Not sure if I could get that sauce off the leather without leaving a stain, so it's best if I don't eat the ribs with it on."

They ordered a bottle of wine, the ribs, and shrimp. For dessert they drove to Bailey's Harbor and the ice cream shop in town for a cone before heading back to Fish Creek's waterside park. Families milled about, and music was playing close by. When Randy casually put his arm around Karen as they sat on a bench, she snuggled closer to him and rested her head on his shoulder.

"This is so nice," she said. "I'm not sure if it's just Fish Creek or the marina setting with its boats, water, and sunset. It's probably because you're here." She looked at him, and they kissed. With all the people around, they couldn't be too amorous, but it was still a nice full kiss.

After they hung out for about half an hour more, Karen said, "I think I want to go back to your place and sit on the couch and slip into something more comfortable like my shorts and T-shirt. Is that okay with you?"

"Sure, let's go." It was a short drive back to his house. Fish Creek was still busy as they drove the few blocks. Shops and restaurants were bustling well into the evening. With the large tourist population that descended on Door County every summer, particularly in July and August, the town did well. The Door County Peninsula almost became a Chicago suburb, with so many Illinois people visiting.

Karen landed with a plop on the living room sofa. "Do you want to sit next to me?" she asked Randy.

"Sure. Do you want something to drink?"

"Just sit." She patted the sofa next to her. "I want you to put your arms around me and hold me. Am I being too forward?"

"No, that sounds great." He slipped his arm around her and held her close. When he kissed her, she responded. Her hand fell to his lap, and he responded there too. When she pulled back from the kiss, she grinned and said, "Oh, what do we have here? I guess you're happy to see me."

"Sorry, I can't help myself. You're so beautiful."

"I want you too, but it's still too soon. I'm not a prude, but we've only known each other a short while, and I'm still getting used to you. But I'm close to feeling more trust. Let me go and change into shorts and a T-shirt so I'm more comfortable."

"Okay, I'll get us some wine. I need to get up and walk this off."

"That's okay. It makes a girl feel good when she can do that to a guy." She got up and went to her room while Randy pulled out a bottle of white wine, put it in an ice bucket with two glasses, and waited for her.

"I feel much better now," she said. "More normal for me."

Randy noticed she wasn't wearing a bra. Was that really more normal for her? Oh boy, he thought. He felt himself getting aroused again just seeing and imagining her breasts. He handed her a glass and took one himself.

"When am I going to see your cabin on the island?" she asked.

"Tomorrow would be good. Only one bedroom over there, but there is a sofa I could sleep on and give you the master suite."

"We can sleep in the same bed. Is that okay?"

"No argument from me." He leaned over and kissed her.

She reached for his hands and said, "I want you to touch me. It's been so long."

As he caressed her breast and kissed her, he heard a low moan. *Funny, Trisha said the same thing. I hope Karen isn't like Trisha.*

He felt her hands on his pants and started to rub him. She unbuttoned his jeans, and it was his turn to moan. After a while, they retired to his bedroom.

So much for moving slowly, he thought.

When the morning rose bright and sunny, Randy couldn't take his eyes off Karen's naked body with the sheets tangled around her legs and torso, her breasts peeking out with the morning sunlight streaming across them. Her hair was mussed, but she looked beautiful. Was that a slight smile he saw on her face as she slept? He hoped she was dreaming of their lovemaking, which had carried them well past midnight when they finally fell asleep in each other's arms.

He watched her stir. He leaned over, and their bodies touched as he gently kissed her lips. "Umm," she said. He watched as her eyes flutter open and saw the smile get bigger across her face.

"You took advantage of me last night," she said, giggling.

"What could I do? We had to go to bed."

"You're right. It was a wonderful first time. Thank you for being so gentle. It has been a long while since I've made love—not sex. That was special."

"Yes, it was. Now we have to get up, eat, and get to Chambers Island."

"Sounds good. Just need to shower and wash my hair after what you told me about the island and the water supply there."

"Okay. I'll make coffee and some scrambled eggs and toast while you're showering."

They took Randy's fishing boat over to the island. The water was calm, and it was already eighty degrees—hot for late July. Once they got there, they carried a few items to his cabin, getting the ice chest with ice and food into the cabin's refrigerator. Randy started the generator to charge the batteries that had kept things going while he was gone and subsidized the solar power he had.

Karen walked around the cabin, stopping in front of the refrigerator with all of Simon's watercolor paintings. She looked confused about the quality and number of paintings. Then she looked at Randy with a questioning look.

"They're my friend Simon's artwork. He's mentally challenged and very nice."

"Good to know."

"He's really good natured and harmless. He likes to visit and bring me these paintings. I bought him a watercolor set last year for his birthday, and he loves painting. So I keep every single one and hang it up. I'm sure you'll meet him soon."

"I'll look forward to it. Are you going to give me a tour of the island?"

"Sure. You want to go now?"

"Yes, I could use some different exercise than we had last night, and the island looks beautiful."

"It is. Let's go."

Halfway around the island, Randy heard a familiar voice shouting his name. Then he saw Simon jogging toward him.

"Where have you been? Who's this?"

"Simon, I want you to meet Karen. She is my friend. We were in Fish Creek at my house, so that's why you didn't see me. She's going to be here a lot in the future, I hope, so be nice to her. I know you will be because you're nice to everyone."

"Yes, I will. But I have to go. Marvin and I are going to our house in Green Bay. He's got a new girlfriend. I miss Jessica. Marvin says I can't see her anymore. He got me a new helper, but she's not as pretty or nice as Jessica. Bye."

―――

After Karen left for Washington Island at the end of the week, Randy drove the hour down to Green Bay to meet Jessica. She had told him on the phone that the best time to meet her was during her lunch break. She had a full schedule all day. He got to her school fifteen minutes early so she didn't have to wait for him, and he wanted to run through in his mind the questions he wanted to ask.

They met outside on a bench across the street from the school, where it was quiet. Also, she could answer his questions there without worrying about people overhearing them.

"Jessica, thanks for meeting me."

"It's fine. I assume you wanted to talk about Marvin."

"Simon had told me you two were having issues. I never thought it would lead to you breaking up, but then he filled me in more about what was happening."

"How's my buddy Simon? I really miss him."

"He's good. As you know, Marvin still doesn't want me to see him. I try not to instigate the meetings, but now that you're gone, I'm really his only friend he has on the island. I'll tell you this: he really misses you."

"Unfortunately, I don't think Marvin and I can resolve our differences. When he got physical with me this last time, that was it. I feared for my life. He slapped me around. We might have yelled at each other before when arguing, but he never hit me before. I had to run to Trisha's cabin for shelter and protection. I left the next day. I'm never going back."

"I hope you can help me clear up a few things I need to know about Marvin."

"Okay, I'll try," she said.

"As I told you last year, I was convicted for manslaughter in the death of Ingrid."

"I'm listening, but why does that concern me or Marvin?"

"Trisha did some investigative work and found out Ingrid had three restraining orders against a woman and two men. I checked out the woman and one of the men, and they seem to be okay. The third person could have killed Ingrid because he lives on the island and had a history of violence with her."

"Are you telling me you think it's Marvin?"

"Yes. He was violent to Ingrid in the past. She became afraid of him, like you did. She got a restraining order against him—did you know that? And the night she died, she and Marvin had a big argument in the parking lot at the Bayside Bar. Ingrid claimed she was pregnant with his baby."

"Oh my God. Marvin never talked about Ingrid or the restraining order. Of course that was a long time ago. I actually considered getting a restraining order against him, but now I think everything is done between him and me. He's got a new girlfriend. So if you're asking me, do I think he could have killed Ingrid? Given the right circumstances, he could. I found out firsthand how violent his temper could be. Ninety percent of the time, Marvin is a good guy, a good big brother, and I loved him—but that ten percent is why I'm not with him anymore." She looked at the time on her phone. "I need to get back to my classes. I only get a half an hour for lunch. I hope you find what you're looking for, Randy."

Later that day, Randy decided he was going to confront Marvin. He was hoping that Marvin might say or reveal something that Randy could tell Detective Jenkins and get him arrested for Ingrid's murder.

When Randy walked to his cabin, he saw Marvin wearing what looked like the same red swimsuit from that night. He was raking the dead drifted weeds off the beach.

How appropriate.

It had not been left by some swimmer from the day like Jenkins had conjectured. The suit had been left by Marvin when he killed Ingrid.

"Hi, Marvin. I need to talk to you."

"I don't want to talk to you. I told you that before."

"Either I talk to you now or I go to Detective Jenkins about what I've found out about you and Ingrid. Like the violent argument you had with her in Bayside's parking lot the night she died, or the fights with her, and the guy that worked on your cabin, Jimmy DeLeo. You have a dangerous temper. Jessica told me how you slapped her around, and she feared for her life. And I think you snapped when Ingrid said she was pregnant with your baby. When you saw her naked that night, knowing she was screwing me, you went mad and killed her."

Marvin lunged at Randy. He tried to hit Randy in the face, but Randy blocked the blow with his left forearm and pushed him away.

When Marvin came at him again, ten years of frustration developed in Randy's solid blow delivered to Marvin's chin. The guy crumpled to the ground, out cold.

Randy was surprised by the blow, as he rubbed the knuckles of his right hand. He stood over him and yelled, "You killed Ingrid! I got convicted for it, but it was you, and now you're going to pay."

Randy would contact Jenkins again. The red suit he'd seen that night on the beach belonged to Marvin, not someone else.

Just then, Simon came out of the house. "Randy, why were you fighting with Marvin?"

"Because he deserved it. I found things about him that made us argue. Maybe we shouldn't see each other for a few days. Marvin's going to be mad."

"Okay, but not too long. You're my best friend."

CHAPTER TWENTY-EIGHT

The next few weeks went by in a blur. Randy talked to Detective Jenkins. He said he'd investigate things again.

Randy visited Karen at the hotel often. He drove up and took the ferry rather than sailing up. Her dad enjoyed Randy being there.

Randy read Ed's poetry and liked it.

"It's been a long time since I've seen my little girl this happy," Ed said to both of them one night at their house. "That's because of you. Why don't you just stay here at the house? I was in love, and I know what's going on. I'd rather you both stay here, and then I can enjoy your company instead of being here alone. My hearing isn't so good, so your talking won't keep me up, if you know what I mean." He winked at them.

"Dad, I can't believe you're saying that."

"It's true. Just stay here as often as you want, Randy. Stay at Fish Creek too."

Once in a while, Randy sailed up. A couple of times, he took her dad out on the boat, and they sailed and fished, which he really enjoyed. They were one big happy family.

The summer moved on, and soon it was just after Labor Day.

Even though it had been just a few months, their romance had reached the serious level, as far as Randy was concerned. He was in love with her. Karen was in love with him too, although she had not actually used those words.

Randy and Karen docked the boat after making an all-day sail back to Chambers Island from Washington Island.

It was nice how they had grown from friends to lovers. He smiled as he thought of his mother's engagement ring in his pocket. He would give the ring to Karen when the perfect moment presented itself.

After she visited him in Fish Creek, they had a glorious afternoon sail over to Sister Bay. They docked the boat at the municipal marina and walked up the hill for an ice cream cone.

On the way back, Karen was surprised at all the people at Al Johnson's, the town's famous restaurant known simply as the place with goats on the grass roof. It was late in the day for breakfast.

"People don't care what time of the day it is to eat there," Randy said. "They have the best Swedish pancakes and meatballs. They opened a new area called the Stabbur Beer Garden that serves regular food and beer and wine, with a large outside area for afternoon and evening food. I try to get there when I come to town and do my shopping, but this time I'll settle for the ice cream."

"Maybe this winter when it's not so crowded, we can go and have their breakfast," she said. "It'll be the highlight of our day in winter unless there's snow. Then we can cross-country ski."

After a leisurely two-hour sail back to Chambers Island, Randy got out the grill at the cabin and was readying for dinner. Even though it was a simple meal, he was going to make it special.

"Hi, Randy, where is your girlfriend, Karen?" Simon asked, startling Randy and interrupting his thoughts.

"She's in the cabin, making a salad for dinner tonight," he said to a grinning Simon.

"Oh, she's very pretty. I like her. Does she like me?"

Randy laughed. "Yes. She likes you like I like you. You are a good friend."

"Good. Do you think she'll have sex with me like she does with you?"

"Simon, were you spying on us? Didn't we talk about that? You know you're not supposed to go peeping into other people's windows. The sex you talk about is supposed to be only when you are in love with someone. It's a special act of loving and caring about one person. You don't just have it with anyone. So, no, Karen is not going to have sex with you. Just with me."

"Oh. I really wanted to have sex. Everyone has sex, but not with me. It's not fair."

"Maybe someday you'll meet someone special, and then you can have your own sex with that person. But not now. Not with Karen."

"Okay, Randy, but if she changes her mind, I'd like to have sex with her. She's very pretty."

"I don't want you to talk about sex anymore. It will upset her and me if you do. You don't want to upset us, do you?"

"No! Okay, I won't ask her. I'm hungry. I'm going to go home now. See you tomorrow."

"Bye, Simon."

A few minutes later, Randy turned and saw Karen come out of the cabin, a salad bowl and a plate of chicken in her hands.

"All set for you to start cooking. Who was that person I heard you talking to?"

"It was Simon. He was out cruising the island."

"Really? He seems sweet."

"He is, but just so you know, he wanted to have sex with you."

"You got to be kidding me, right?"

"Like I said, he might be a peeping tom. He might have seen us making love last night."

"Well, that gives me the willies. After that, I think I need another glass of wine."

"I'll put the chicken on."

"Sounds good."

Later that night, Randy said, "Let's go down to the water. I've been saving a bottle of Champagne for a special occasion, and having you here with me on the island tonight makes it special occasion. Let's celebrate."

"Don't you think we've had enough to drink? Two bottles of wine seem like enough."

"Humor me. It's so beautiful on the beach, and everyone is probably gone. We can make love there, and no one will see us. Is that special enough?"

"Is that you talking or the wine? You know I always like to make love to you, Randy, but on the beach? Only if it's really deserted. That stuff with Simon spooked me."

"Don't worry about him. He's probably sneaking around Trisha and Adam's cabin. He knows her better than you. Plus, I told him not to sneak that around here. He usually listens to me."

"If you say so."

He collected a large blanket and the bottle of champagne, ice, and two glasses.

"All set; let's go."

At the beach, it was just as Randy had hoped: no one around. The moon was almost full, and the bay was calm except for boats motoring north and south toward some port of call.

"Oh Randy, it's perfect."

"It is, especially because you're with me." He opened the bottle of champagne, poured her a glass, then one for him. "To us."

"Yes, to us."

They touched glasses, saying nothing more, savoring the moment.

After a second glass, Karen snuggled against his chest and sighed.

"I can't believe how happy I am with you, and to think we just met a couple of months ago, all because of sailing and the weather. Who would have thought?" She turned and kissed him.

"I feel the same way."

It was now or never; he thought the timing was right, and he reached into his pocket.

"I love you, Karen. You haven't told me in actual words, but I think you love me too. I think we're good for each other. I love you, and to prove it, I'd like you to wear this tonight and forever. Will you marry me?" He took her left hand and slipped his mother's engagement ring on her finger.

"Oh my god. Really? You want to marry me? I can't believe it. It's so fast. We've just met a couple of months ago."

"A simple yes or no is okay."

She looked at her ring in the moonlight, sparkling like a star in the northern sky.

"I love you too, Randy. I really do." She looked at the ring, then slipped it off her finger, holding it out to him. "But it's too early. We need to be together for a longer time. I'm sorry."

He reluctantly took the ring from her.

She snuggled closer to him again, reached for the glass of champagne, and drank it down.

"You'll think I'm crazy after I rejected your proposal," she said, "but right now I want you to make love to me. Right here." She pulled off her T-shirt and unsnapped her bra.

He took off his shirt and slipped out of his shorts and underwear. By the time he was done, she was naked and bent over him.

She settled on top of him, guiding him in as his hands found her breasts.

"Karen," he said. Sad feelings that had engulfed him a few

moments ago were replaced with feelings of love. Inappropriately, he thought of Ingrid, eleven years ago, on a night like tonight, as they made love. He erased the thought from his mind. Tonight was different. It was about joy, and two people enjoying being in love.

"Oh, this feels so good," she said. "If it's always like this, I might change my mind and say yes to your proposal tonight. Save that ring."

"If that's the case, I have all night to change your mind." They laughed as they continued to make love while gazing deeply into each other's eyes.

Finally, Karen collapsed on his chest. "Oh Randy, that was so good. Let's rest for a while. It's so nice here."

Twenty minutes later, she said, "I think I'll go in the water. I don't get a chance on Washington Island to walk around like this. This is such a nice sandy beach, especially naked. Do you want to join me?"

"I will in just a few minutes. I might close my eyes for a few minutes. I used up a lot of energy, and then there was the champagne."

"Yes, you did. I appreciate it." She giggled. "Come and walk with me soon, Randy."

"Okay." He watched her get up and descend into the water to her waist before diving in.

"It's nice and warm for Lake Michigan," she shouted.

He smiled and then closed his eyes.

"Randy, Randy, help!"

He opened his eyes and saw a man wrestling with Karen. Randy jumped up and started running.

She was screaming, "No! No!"

The man was pushing Karen underwater. She was fully submerged. His hands were on her shoulders.

As he got closer, Randy recognized Simon, naked and aroused. "Simon, stop!"

"I want to have sex with Karen you like do Randy," Simon shouted. "I want to have sex like you."

"Simon let her go," yelled Randy as he rushed into the water. "Let her go!"

Simon didn't.

Randy, consumed with anger, punched Simon's jaw as hard as he could. Then he tackled Simon, pushing him into the water, away from Karen.

Karen staggered upright.

Hearing her coughing, then crying, Randy gave a sigh of relief.

Simon was crying too. "You punched me, Randy." He sat in shallow water. "I just wanted to have sex with Karen like you did. I wanted to have sex."

"What's going on here?" A voice came out of the trees, and a figure was running toward them. Randy recognized the voice.

"Marvin, we have a problem. Simon just tried to rape and almost drown Karen."

"What? Simon, what were you doing?"

"I want to have sex with Randy's girlfriend. She didn't want to, so I got mad and tried to make her change her mind. I pushed her under the water just like I did a long time ago, to the one Randy was having sex with then. She was mean to me once. Remember, Marvin? You were there. She made fun of me back then at our cabin—remember, Marvin? You hit her for what she did to me when Mommy was sick. She made me cry back then. Remember, Marvin? She made me cry, and you hit her lots after she made fun of me that afternoon."

"Yes, I remember her making fun of you."

"I stopped her making fun of me that night on the beach when Randy was sleeping."

"Oh my god," Marvin said, turning to Randy. "When I found my swimming suit on the beach the next morning, I thought maybe Simon did something that night but not murder. I thought you killed her that night," he said to Randy. "This can't be happening. Simon, tell me you didn't hold Ingrid underwater back then."

"I got back at her for not having sex and making fun of me a long time ago. I didn't like her. I made sure she couldn't hurt me anymore and make me cry."

"It was you, Simon," Randy said in a soft, measured voice.

"He could have killed me like he did Ingrid," said Karen. "I was just walking in the water, enjoying the night when, with my back turned to the shore. Thank God you got here fast enough. I could have ended up just like Ingrid."

Simon was still crying, sitting in the water, rubbing his jaw.

Randy turned to Marvin. "What does he mean about Ingrid having sex with him and laughing at him? Did she have sex with him back then?"

"It's kind of a long story, but I'll try to shorten it."

Karen interrupted him. "Randy, I'm going back to the blanket and get my clothes, but I want to hear Marvin's story about what happened. It almost got me killed tonight."

"Okay, we'll wait."

Karen was soon back with her clothes and Randy's. The group of four sat down on the sand.

Simon was quiet, rubbing his jaw where Randy hit him, whimpering like a child. His eyes were wide as he listened to Marvin talk about him and Ingrid.

"One afternoon, I caught Ingrid over here on the island with Simon when I came back from Fish Creek and Sister Bay getting groceries and other supplies. Ingrid had come to the island with friends earlier to drink and party, like she usually did, but this time she was the odd one out. She liked to party a lot, as you've maybe found out. She would push the envelope on excitement. Since she was a single in a group of paired-off couples, she came looking for me. I had hooked up enough times with her in the past. We'd have beer at my place, and she knew where it was. She helped herself to one that day. I was gone. Mom was here then, but she wasn't doing well with her cancer. She took a lot of medications for it. I can only assume it knocked her out." He paused.

"Ingrid realized I wasn't at home, but Simon was. Even back

then, he had the body of a well-developed eighteen-year-old. After a second or third beer, Ingrid started teasing him. She liked to tease me with her body and hands, and she did the same to arouse Simon. Once she had Simon to that point, she told me later, she let him have sex with her, because she knew he was probably a virgin. She thought it would be fun to help him lose his virginity. I came home about that time and saw she was lying on the picnic table with him between her legs. I foolishly watched them making love until he came. I figured it might be the only time he had sex with anyone. Stupid on my part, I know—all in hindsight now. But then Ingrid got ugly, maliciously teasing him, saying he was dumb and not very good. 'If your penis had a mind like yours, you wouldn't be able to do anything, but you're pretty big and good enough.'"

"She said that?" Randy asked.

"How cruel and sick she was," Karen said, shaking her head.

"When I heard that, I came out of hiding in the trees. She tried to get her clothes on like nothing had happened, and she was saying, 'Just was having a little fun with Simon, like I do with you.'"

"Simon was crying then. He knew she was making fun of him. She made some more discouraging remarks to him that made him cry harder. I lost my temper because she was a bitch to him and slapped her hard across the face a couple of times. I grabbed her arms and shook her too hard. I hated her for what she said and did to my little brother. I shouldn't have done that, but I did. I told her I didn't want to see her around here anymore. I guess she was so upset with me that she filed a restraining order. That was just fine because I never wanted to have anything to do with her again. But then she and I had an argument at the Bayside when she unloaded about being pregnant. Not good."

"I know about the restraining order and her saying she was pregnant," said Randy. "I was very suspicious of you."

"When I went out on the beach the next day, I saw my red swimming suit on the sand. I picked it up, suspecting Simon might have worn it. I just wanted to protect him."

"You both cost me almost nine years of my life. You're both guilty."

"What do we do now, about Simon?" Marvin asks.

Randy looked at Simon. "We need to tell the authorities what happened. Simon needs help and supervision. He has a deadly temper. He killed once, and then almost again tonight with Karen. Smarter people than me will have to figure out what will happen to him next. I know he's your brother—"

"I know, but he's really just a ten-year-old," Marvin pleaded.

"I understand, but it has to be done. I need to clear my name. I lost a lot of years of my life for something I didn't do. I can never get those years back. I need to get the guilt in people's minds erased. I only wish my parents were alive to see justice done."

The three looked down at him while Simon looked up at them.

"I'm sorry Randy," he said. "I'm bad. I'm sorry."

THE END

Made in the USA
Monee, IL
20 July 2024